D1059657

JACK OF SPADES

by DIANE CAPRI

Published by: AugustBooks
http://www.AugustBooks.com

ISBN: 978-1-942633-14-3

Original cover design by: Cory Clubb
Digital formatting by: Author E.M.S.

Jack of Spades is a work of fiction. Names, characters, places, and
incidents either are the product of the author's imagination or are used
fictitiously, and any resemblance to actual persons, living or dead,
business establishments, events, or locales is entirely coincidental.

Published in the United States of America.

Visit the author website:
http://www.DianeCapri.com

ALSO BY DIANE CAPRI

The Hunt for Jack Reacher Series
(in publication order with Lee Child source books in parentheses)

Don't Know Jack (The Killing Floor)

Jack in a Box (*novella*)

Jack and Kill (*novella*)

Get Back Jack (Bad Luck & Trouble)

Jack in the Green (*novella*)

Jack and Joe (The Enemy)

Deep Cover Jack (Persuader)

Jack the Reaper (The Hard Way)

Black Jack (Running Blind/The Visitor)

Ten Two Jack (The Midnight Line)

Jack of Spades (Past Tense)

The Jess Kimball Thrillers Series

Fatal Enemy (*novella*)

Fatal Distraction

Fatal Demand

Fatal Error

Fatal Fall

Fatal Edge (*novella*)

Fatal Game

Fatal Bond

Fatal Past (*novella*)

Fatal Dawn

The Hunt for Justice Series

Due Justice

Twisted Justice

Secret Justice

Wasted Justice

Raw Justice

Mistaken Justice (*novella*)

Cold Justice (*novella*)

False Justice (*novella*)

Fair Justice (*novella*)

True Justice (*novella*)

Night Justice

The Heir Hunter Series

Blood Trails

Trace Evidence

CAST OF PRIMARY CHARACTERS

Kim L. Otto

Reggie Smithers
Charles Cooper
Lamont Finlay
Jake Reacher
Margaret Reacher
Desmond Trevor
Patty Sundstrom
Shorty Fleck
Carlos Gaspar
John Lawton

and
Jack Reacher

Perpetually, for Lee Child, with unrelenting gratitude.

JACK OF SPADES

PAST TENSE

by Lee Child

2018

Reacher stuck out his thumb.

The truck stopped. An old guy with a long white beard leaned across inside and wound down the passenger window.

He said, "I'm going to Laconia."

"Me, too," Reacher said…

"…Why are you going to Laconia?"

"I was passing by," Reacher said. "My father was born there. I want to see it."

"What's your last name?"

"Reacher."

…

"I'm not a father myself. But I can imagine…Parenting tip," Reacher said. "Don't leave him lying in the road. He could get run over."

"I won't forget this."

"That's the difference between us," Reacher said. "I already have."

CHAPTER ONE

Thursday, February 24
5:30 p.m.
Laconia, New Hampshire

JAKE REACHER FOUND HIS mother in the kitchen facing the window over the sink, washing dishes, and staring at the bird feeder his father had installed in the side yard. His mother was an avid bird watcher. His father had been, too. More than two hundred species migrate through New Hampshire, Dad often said. His mother kept a diary, meticulously noting the date and time each spring when she saw her first Common Redpoll and Pine Siskin at the feeder.

Jake didn't see the fascination with staying in the same place. He wanted to experience the world, not stagnate here in Laconia, New Hampshire. A long and lazy road trip sounded perfect. Take his time on the drive, see something of the country, and stay awhile once he reached sunshine and beaches.

The aromas coming from the oven declared his favorite pot

roast was almost ready. His stomach rumbled like a hibernating bear awakened in the spring.

His entire life, his mother had had dinner on the table every day at six o'clock when her husband came home from work. Habit of a lifetime.

For a few days after his father's funeral, she'd seemed foggy and unable to focus on much of anything. But she had set the small kitchen table for two instead of three tonight, which meant she had a good grasp on the reality of her situation. She was strong enough that he felt okay about leaving her alone.

Only the two of them were left now. David Reacher would never come through the back door again after a long day teaching science at the university. Would never place his keys on the counter or hang his jacket on the peg by the door. Would never again hug his wife and say, "It smells amazing in here. What's for dinner?"

Jake shrugged. The situation was what it was. Pretending otherwise would not bring his father back. Cancer had killed him, slowly but effectively, while Jake had watched the process unfold over the past several months. There was no mistake. The only father he'd ever known was gone. Jake had accepted the truth. His mother needed to do the same.

She turned away from the sink at the sound of his footsteps entering the kitchen. She'd been crying again. Tear tracks marked her cheeks and glassy tears settled in her eyes making them appear even more luminous than usual. She reached up with the back of her soapy hand and swiped her nose and offered him a weak smile.

"Just in time." She nodded toward the stove before she returned to the dishes. "Take the roast out of the oven for me, will you?"

He gave her shoulders a quick squeeze and said nothing. She felt as small and fragile as one of the songbirds she loved to watch. His father had encouraged her to take care of herself, but his pleas had made little difference. She'd stayed glued to his bedside day and night those last weeks and she'd eaten barely enough to keep a bird alive.

Jake looked down at her petite body. He had towered over both his parents for almost a decade now. He was twenty-two years old, but he had reached his full six feet, four inches long ago. He'd often wondered why he was so much taller and bigger than his parents. Or why he had blue eyes and fair hair when they were both darker. He'd assumed recessive genes were to blame. He knew now he'd been wrong.

He found the oversized oven mittens, which were too small to fit his huge hands. Holding the mitts like hot pads, he removed the heavy cast iron from the oven and set it on top of the stove. When he lifted the lid and set it aside, his stomach growled as the scent of pot roast, carrots, onions, and potatoes nestled in bubbling rich gravy filled the room.

"Put the rolls in the oven to warm, please. And the salad is in the refrigerator." His mother tilted her head toward the appliance as if he might have forgotten where it was located, like she'd done a thousand times before. "I'll just finish up these few dishes and we'll be ready. You can pour the coffee if you like."

Jake found the tossed green salad and salad dressings in the refrigerator and moved them to the table. He poured strong, black coffee for both of them. She would add cream to hers. When the rolls were hot, he carried the plates to the range and dished out the food as usual. All without comment.

Jake was quiet by nature. He saw no reason to fill the silence with idle chatter. When he had something to say, he said it.

Otherwise, he kept his thoughts to himself and appreciated it when others did the same.

By the time they were seated in their usual places, his mother had managed to compose herself, even if her eyes and nose were still red. He had tried to comfort her by holding her hand on the table, without success. Old Man Reacher had told him she'd heal with time and he hoped that was true. He'd done all he could.

"Are you still leaving in the morning?" she asked as she placed her napkin on her lap.

"It's best to get on the road while the weather holds," he replied between mouthfuls.

Laconia, New Hampshire, was experiencing a winter thaw forecast to last another couple of days. The snow and ice had melted on the major thoroughfares and many of the busier side roads. His SUV had four-wheel-drive, but the travel would be easier if he avoided the heavy snow as long as possible.

"It's more than three thousand miles to the Pacific Ocean. How long do you figure it'll take you to get there?" She was making conversation as if she believed his trip would be the grand adventure he'd claimed and she'd made peace with his decision. She hadn't. But it seemed she had finally accepted that he was going, which was good.

He shrugged. "Driving time on the interstates is forty-four hours, but I'm planning to take the back roads. See a bit of the country along the way. Make a few stops."

His mother nodded, pushing the food around on her plate with her fork. "Have you planned the route?"

"Not exactly. Maybe Boston to Syracuse, Cincinnati, St. Louis, Albuquerque. I'm not sure." He was leaving room for serendipity to strike.

He put another forkful of beef in his mouth and chewed appreciatively. His mother was a damn good cook and he'd always had a hearty appetite. Eating well had produced his intimidating, heavily built body, all bone and muscle, which had always served him well.

She nodded again and focused her gaze on her meal. She had nothing new to offer. She'd already made all of her arguments for hours on end.

She'd said it was a long drive for one person to undertake. He was young. He could easily get into trouble. There was no reason for him to go off looking for a man who didn't know he existed. Couldn't he wait until spring when driving conditions would be better? Didn't he have a friend he could take along? Wouldn't he rather fly?

One by one, he had addressed her objections with replies that made sense to him if not to her.

It was a long drive, but he was looking forward to it. He was young, so he had boundless energy for the trip.

If trouble came his way, he could easily get himself out of it, as she well knew. Jake had been fighting his own battles since middle school, and looking out for his friends, too. Several times, she and his father had been called to the principal's office, and later to the local police station, to bail him out after a fight. He never started trouble, but he was more than willing to finish it, and on his own terms.

There was every reason to go now because he had the break in his school schedule and he wanted to get away. If he was going to find the man, now was the best time. Perhaps the only time he'd have a chance of making it happen.

Sure, driving would be better in the spring, but he felt a sense of urgency and there was no reason not to go now. After college, with his dad sick, Jake had decided to take time off. But all of his good buddies had jobs or went straight to graduate school. None of his friends had the free time to tag along on an open-ended trip like this.

Flying was fine, but he wouldn't get to see much of the country that way. And he didn't want to spend his savings on a rental car in California when he had a perfectly good vehicle.

Their arguments had lasted well into the night for several nights. He hadn't persuaded her, but eventually she'd stopped objecting. He'd packed up his Jeep and pointed its nose toward the street. He would be on the road before dawn tomorrow.

While he ate, his mother pushed her food around on her plate. She cocked her head and looked him in the eye. "After you find him, then what?"

Jake shrugged and said nothing because that was the one question for which he had no answer.

CHAPTER TWO

Friday, February 25
7:30 a.m.
Detroit, Michigan

FBI SPECIAL AGENT KIM Otto rushed to make the plane at
Detroit Metro Airport and took her seat on the aisle in first class.
Flying was never her first choice. Not that the Boss ever gave
her a choice. He'd called long before sunrise and delivered her
orders. Same as always.

She'd roused John Lawton, her favorite Treasury agent, from
a deep sleep.

"Where are you going?" he mumbled when she slipped from
beneath the toasty covers into the cold morning.

"Laconia, New Hampshire. I'll call when I can. Lock the
door on your way out. I'll tell the doorman you'll be leaving so
he doesn't come in and shoot you." She grinned, but he wasn't
looking.

"You could give me a key and all of this would be a lot
easier," he mumbled into his pillow.

She didn't reply. Her relationship with John was too new for exchanging keys. But that wasn't a conversation she wanted to have now.

The trip from her apartment and the flight itself were uneventful. When the pilot announced initial descent, Kim said a quick prayer. Now all the pilot had to do was land safely. She crossed her fingers.

High above Laconia, she looked out of the window to see rolling hills, barren trees, and a lot of snow. Exactly the kind of landscape she'd expected after her internet research. She'd never enjoyed the snow or the cold and she got plenty of that at home in Detroit. She would not have volunteered to travel to New Hampshire in February.

But she got lucky, for once. The northeast was experiencing a brief winter thaw. Snow still covered everything, of course. But yesterday, the temperature in Laconia was forty degrees, barely cold enough to need a coat. She planned to spend as little time as possible and then get the hell out before the frigid weather returned.

The municipal airport came into view. The runway was clear and the plane landed without mishap.

"So far, so good," she muttered under her breath as she pried her fingers from the armrests, popped another antacid to calm her rebellious stomach, collected her bags, and deplaned.

She bundled up and made her way downstairs to the exit. The first thing she noticed was a blast of cold air. The second thing was a familiar black SUV waiting at the curb. The driver, a huge black man she recognized, lowered the window. He smiled at her, revealing an envious mouth full of bright white teeth.

"Right on time, Otto," FBI Special Agent Reggie Smithers said. His deep voice was as smooth as silk, just as she remembered.

Smithers was assigned to the New York field office. They had worked together last month on a case there. He had proved to be reliable and competent and she liked him. He was also intimidating as hell, which could come in handy.

Now that Gaspar had retired, she didn't know when she'd get her new partner or who he would be. If he was auditioning, Smithers would have her vote. She could do a lot worse.

"I'm having déjà vu." She smiled because she was genuinely glad to see him. "Didn't we just do this?"

"Feels like it, doesn't it?" He grinned, waving her toward the right side of the vehicle.

She walked around the front of the SUV, stowed her bags in the back, and climbed into the passenger seat. He waited patiently without comment for her to get settled and then he slipped the transmission into drive and rolled into traffic.

"Thanks for picking me up. I wasn't expecting you," she said. "Did you get transferred to Boston?"

"Temporarily. They needed some extra help. I volunteered for taxi duty when I heard you were coming. Give us a chance to talk."

"Something specific you wanted to talk about?"

Smithers nodded. "Is Reacher somehow involved in this thing?"

When they had worked together in New York, Kim's assignment was to complete a background check on Jack Reacher for the Special Personnel Task Force. Reacher was being considered for a classified assignment.

Recently, her assignment had been modified. Not only was she researching Reacher's background, she was looking for the man himself. The Boss would not have sent her here unless he believed the trip would lead her to Reacher. Eventually.

But she was also working under the radar. Which meant she couldn't share everything with Smithers or anyone else. And Smithers had once worked for Lamont Finlay and Gaspar never liked that connection. Which made her somewhat wary of him, too. So she sidestepped the question.

"I never know for sure why I'm sent anywhere. But I'd say it's a safe bet that Reacher's at the center of something around here," she replied before she changed the subject. "I saw the photos of the motel. What happened?"

Smithers let the Reacher matter drop for now. "We're not exactly sure. We're still working on the crime scene. It looks like multiple explosions followed by a fire. There were several vehicles out there and all of them seemed to have had full gas tanks."

"Must've been quite a sight when all of that went up in flames. Noisy as hell, too."

Otto had read the reports, thin as they were.

Laconia, New Hampshire, was a frigid place. Nighttime temperatures in February were single digits. An average of sixty-four inches of snow fell in the winter. Which was about four times the national average. Later in the winter, the snow might have easily piled five inches above Kim's head.

As it was, the total accumulation had been forty-one inches so far this year, but about twelve inches of snow had melted rapidly during the thaw over the past few days. When the snow melted, it revealed what was left of a motel, outbuildings, and several vehicles. All had burned in what must have been a white-hot fire, leaving nothing but charred remains and ashes.

The aerial photographs she'd seen in the files could have been printed in black and white since they were completely devoid of color. They showed a snow-covered clearing in the dense woods. Presumably there was a road that led to the clearing, but if so, it had not been plowed at the time the photos were shot. She saw no indication that any humans had been near the area recently, either.

She shook her head. "And nobody saw or heard anything at the time all this went down? Nobody found the destruction after all these months? How is that even possible?"

"Only thing we can figure is this place is pretty isolated. No neighbors close by. Hardly any road traffic. The motel had been abandoned years ago, we were told. So who would come out there? If it hadn't been for that kid taking pictures with his drone, might have been years before we discovered any of it." Smithers gave her a meaningful side eye. "Not that finding the place earlier would've made a difference, you know?"

"Yeah. I guess that makes sense," Kim replied. She tugged the seat belt which pulled uncomfortably against her neck. She repositioned her alligator clamp at the retractor to increase the slack in the belt for a while.

Smithers navigated the big SUV easily along the narrow backroads deeper into a forested area. The leafless trees closed in, making it dark for the middle of the day. The SUV's headlights had come on automatically, which helped a bit.

The roads had been plowed since the kid's drone photos were taken, probably by law enforcement agencies seeking access to the crime scene. There were no other signs of human life in the area now that Otto could see.

She looked out of the windows at the landscape beneath the denuded trees. Patches of leaves were visible here and there on the ground where the snow had melted. She saw no homes. No shops. No people. No traffic moving in either direction.

"Where are we going, exactly?" she asked.

"About twenty miles from Laconia, give or take. Almost there." Smithers slowed the big vehicle to a crawl as they approached the mouth of a narrow road up ahead on the left. The snow had been plowed aside to create an even narrower lane barely wide enough for the SUV.

"How did you ever find this place?" Kim asked.

"Bloodhounds," he replied with a grin as he turned carefully into the lane.

Snow was piled high on each side of the lane, almost like a tunnel. The trees were so thick that the roads would be dark even at high noon when the trees were fully leafed in the summer. As it was, Kim found herself straining to distinguish objects from shadows.

He moved the transmission into four-wheel drive and slowed his speed further. His eyes looked straight ahead and both hands grasped the steering wheel.

"Nine bodies, right?" she asked.

"So far. Could be more. We haven't finished yet," Smithers replied.

"Cause of death?"

"Impossible to say right off." He shook his head. "They've been out here awhile. Some of them were pretty chewed up by animals. There's a lot of decomposition. There are some gunshot wounds, but other injuries, too. The coroner hasn't finished the autopsies yet."

Otto closed her eyes and kneaded the ache between her eyebrows. "No positive IDs on any of them?"

Smithers gave her a quick glance. "You're thinking one of the bodies we found might be Reacher?"

Kim shrugged but did not reply.

The truth was she knew Reacher hadn't died here months

ago because she had encountered him several times since then. In New York, D.C., Mexico, and other places. Indeed, Reacher had saved her life in Palm Beach just last month. She was sure of it.

No, Reacher wasn't dead. But he must have been in Laconia at some point. Otherwise, the Boss wouldn't have sent her here, she assumed.

"You saw the photos. Everything at the motel was burned to cinders. No way to find any fingerprints. But there's still a lot of forensics to process and we're fighting the approaching weather." Smithers paused, thinking for a moment. "You got a sample of Reacher's DNA for comparison? We'll get DNA analysis from the bodies soon. If you have a definitive sample, we can rule Reacher in or out."

Kim shook her head. "No DNA, so far. Reacher left the army before DNA was mandatory and we haven't found any other personal effects that we could get his DNA from."

"Okay. What about dental records? Take us a little longer, but we'll have those, too." Smithers said.

"Could work," she replied. "The only dental records we have are old. From Reacher's army days. But they are distinctive."

"What do you mean? Distinctive how?"

They'd traveled the narrow lane for more than two miles. Aside from one small patch where the trees did not block the sky for maybe twenty yards, they'd moved in near darkness. The eerie kind of darkness that made you want to talk to another human.

"Reacher grew up on army bases around the world. He had his teeth fixed wherever he was living. Some of the dental work is American, some of it isn't." She paused for breath as the SUV bounced over a snow-packed pothole. "The point is, we should be able to confirm whether one of the bodies you found is Reacher or not by those dental records."

"I'll get the forensics guys on it." Smithers said as he slowed for the last turn. "What's left of the motel is around this next curve."

When the SUV cleared the trees, the weak daylight revealed the scene Kim had viewed in the aerial photos. Maybe a couple of acres of flat, snow-covered land with protruding blackened objects.

Straight ahead were the remains of three substantial wooden buildings. They had been laid out in a wide right-hand arc, maybe fifty yards from the first to the last. The buildings might have been painted once. Now there was very little left but the foundations, which were charred cinderblock.

The first and largest building must have been the motel. It might have contained a dozen rooms. Certainly no more.

The second building looked like it could have been some kind of barn. It was shorter and deeper than the first building and it had a concrete ramp leading to an open maw, probably a door once upon a time.

The third building looked like the foundation of a regular house. Maybe the motel owner lived there with his family. Or maybe it was another storage building of some kind. Impossible to surmise from the ashes.

As if they had been randomly scattered by a giant's hand, the burned-out husks of several vehicles protruded from the snow. Kim counted the charred frames of six ATVs. Quad bikes. Before they burned, each had four wheels, which probably made them perfect for traveling over the property. They couldn't get too deep in the forest, though. They'd get stuck between the trees.

The other charred remains were cars, SUVs and what had once been a tow truck, which was curious. What had they needed a tow truck for?

Near the entrance to the clearing, four intact official vehicles were parked together. Teams of personnel were painstakingly gathering evidence like archaeologists at a site of ancient ruins. Smithers pulled in beside them.

"Have you identified the owners of any of the burned vehicles yet?" Kim asked.

Smithers shook his head. "The ATVs are all the same make and model and they appear to have been the same age. Working theory is they were purchased all at the same time and from the same place. They have a seventeen digit vehicle identification number etched on the frames. But it looks like they were never registered to the buyer and didn't have plates."

"Can the manufacturer identify who bought them?" she asked.

"Not yet. Like I said, we've got a lot of forensics to sort through once we get everything collected. There doesn't seem to be any urgency here aside from the weather." Smithers paused and swept his arm in a wide arc indicating the entire scene. "This whole thing seems to have happened more than a year ago, according to our analysis so far. Nobody's been around asking any questions. We've got plenty of time. We can afford to do things right. No rush. Come on. I'll show you around."

He shut the engine down and stepped out. Kim followed.

She plunged her gloved hands into her overcoat and stomped her boots to gin up some body heat. It was forty-four degrees outside, which was warmer than normal for February in New Hampshire, but certainly not balmy.

"What about the other vehicles?" She walked toward the main building and he fell into step beside her.

"All rentals. Curiously, all reported stolen at one point or another."

"And the tow truck? That couldn't have been a rental."

"Actually, we traced it back to a local guy. No family. No coworkers. No friends, apparently. Or at least no one friendly enough to report him missing."

"You figure he's one of your bodies?" Kim asked.

Smithers shrugged. "We'll see."

"Who owns this place?"

"An outfit called Northern Holdings. Shell corporation registered in Panama. The registered agent is one of those corporate outfits located in Concord. Says the business was done online and paid for with a company credit card. Never met anyone face-to-face."

Otto nodded, turned her collar up and hunched down into her coat. She pointed to what looked like a metal cage around one of the rooms near the end of the first building. "What's that?"

"We don't know," Smithers replied.

Otto felt the wind cutting through her like an icy knife some crazed maniac stored in the freezer. She didn't want to come back out here tomorrow when the weather could be even worse. The forecast was for temperatures above freezing for a couple of days, but she trusted weather forecasts even less than airline flight schedules. Both could turn in an instant.

She said, "I'd like to take a quick walk around before we lose the daylight."

"Let's start with the easy stuff," Smithers suggested, leading the way along a well-trodden path of packed snow toward what remained of the last building's foundation.

CHAPTER THREE

Friday, February 25
6:07 a.m.
Laconia, New Hampshire

JAKE OPENED ONE EYE and peered at the digital clock. He grinned. Precisely seven minutes past six, as expected. He awakened again at six-twenty-one and the clock confirmed the exact time. He tossed the covers aside and yawned on his way to the shower.

While he was getting dressed, his mother had made breakfast, packed a few sandwiches, and poured a large pot of strong black coffee into a thermos for him. He'd had no choice but to eat the breakfast, which meant he got off to a much later start than he'd planned.

"You won't find a place to get food or good coffee for miles, Jake," she said as she poked Dad's thermos under his arm on his way out the door.

"Thanks, Mom. I'll be okay. I'll be careful. I promise," he said for the zillionth time. He nodded, hugged her, and kissed the top of her head for the very last goodbye. "You stay inside. It's really cold out there."

He hurried out to the SUV, where he hoped she wouldn't follow in her nightgown and slippers. He stowed the provisions on the passenger seat and tossed his parka into the back. The motor was already running with the defrosters blasting warm air into the cabin.

He waved goodbye, slid into the driver's seat, and eased the Jeep out of the driveway.

He didn't know when he'd see her again, and he found himself more sentimental about that than he'd expected. His whole life, she'd been the one who supported him, through good times and bad. He'd probably have ended up in prison long before now, if not for her.

After a fight left two kids with broken bones and outraged parents had filed criminal complaints, his mother had begged unabashedly for his future when his father had lost the will to rescue him one last time. She'd insisted the judge reconsider. Eventually, he was moved by her pleas to offer Jake's weary parents an unusual choice. They could enroll Jake in Junior R.O.T.C. for the rest of his high school career, or he could do two years of prison time. Mom's persistence had made all the difference. Junior R.O.T.C. had taught him how to handle himself and instilled a healthy respect for the U.S. military. Win-win, as people say, although he hadn't felt that way about it at the time.

Jake turned and blew his mother a kiss and then watched in the rearview mirror until she stepped back into the warm house and closed the front door firmly against the wind.

A few blocks later, he pulled onto Main Street. In the end, he left the solid and prosperous red brick buildings and neat old-fashioned streets of his hometown behind without a single twinge of regret.

This journey simply felt like the right thing to do. He would come back home one day, sure. Eventually. After he saw a bit of the country. He was admitted to Harvard Law School next year. He'd be back for a visit before then.

He drove along county roads. He'd planned a detour to drive past Harvard at the start to drop off some papers. So he headed toward Boston and then Syracuse, where he figured he'd stop for the night. The winter thaw had cleared the back roads and kept them dry. Speed limits were lower than the interstate which slowed his progress and a couple of minor accidents had blocked traffic for more than two hours.

He didn't care. He was in no real hurry. And the last thing he needed was to come around a corner too fast and end up in a ditch somewhere. Or worse, hit a deer and screw up his Jeep before he covered the first three hundred miles.

The last weather report he'd heard on the Jeep's radio had changed the forecast. Colder wind and snow was headed down from Canada tonight. He noticed the outside temperature had been dropping for the past couple of hours already. Gusty winds blew snow across the road, making the pavement slick. He'd lived in the northeast all his life. He knew deadly black ice could be waiting under the thin blanket of snow.

As he'd told his mother, the county roads weren't the most direct route to California, but he'd see something of the country doing the drive off the interstates. If the bad weather moved in, he could always stop for a night or two and wait for the roads to be cleared again. After all, he didn't have an appointment with anybody. He didn't need to worry about being late.

What he hadn't counted on was the solitude. Or rather, he'd

welcomed the idea of solitary travel before he found himself stuck with it. He'd listened to his music, flipped past all the static on the radio, and run through two audio books before he got sleepy and bored with being alone.

Which was why, when he saw the hitchhiker slogging along the deep snow on the shoulder about two hours from Syracuse, he made the snap decision to pick up the guy and give him a lift. His mother would have been horrified. But she wasn't with him. And if the hiker didn't try to slash his throat or something, at least he'd have someone to talk to if he felt like it.

The guy was bundled up, as if he was wearing every item of clothing he owned. His big army-green parka hood was pulled up, covering his head and face. He carried a well-used backpack with an external frame, like the ones serious hikers wore on their backs for long overnight treks. Heavy gloves made his hands look like catcher's mitts. Brown work boots created waffle prints in the snow on the shoulder of the road.

Maybe the guy would like to talk a little baseball. Spring training was already under way. The Grapefruit League had started this week. Cactus League, too. The guy would help pass the time and the miles and keep him awake.

Jake heard his mother's voice practically shrieking in his head to *be careful, be careful, be careful*. He grinned.

"I'm always careful, Mom," he said aloud as he turned on his indicator and pulled onto the shoulder just ahead of the hitchhiker.

The guy hustled up to the passenger side of the SUV and Jake lowered the window. The wind had picked up and almost carried the hiker's voice away. "Where ya headed?"

"Syracuse," Jake replied.

"Me, too," the hiker shouted against the wind.

Jake jerked his right thumb over his shoulder. "Put your stuff back there and climb in."

A pair of headlights coming up fast from behind him on the road snagged Jake's attention. He hadn't seen a single vehicle for the past fifty miles. His gut clenched. Maybe this was a setup after all. He'd heard about such things. One guy distracts the driver while the second guy attacks.

He swung his head side to side, looking for the others, if there were any. Jake didn't mind a good fight. But it was too damn cold to hang around out there.

He grabbed the Jeep's wheel with both hands, moved his left foot to the brake and prepared to floor the accelerator with his right to speed away, leaving the hitchhiker in the road.

He kept his eyes on the mirrors, watching the headlights come closer.

When the pickup truck slowed and kept moving safely past him, Jake felt a little foolish. His mother's anxiety was stuck in his head and there was no way to get rid of it. He'd been her son for twenty-two years. Her fears would probably be with him forever.

While he'd been watching the approaching truck, the hitchhiker stashed the heavy backpack as instructed, opened the passenger door, and climbed inside.

The door slammed shut and the hitchhiker pulled off the gloves and threw back the parka's hood.

Which was when Jake saw that the guy was a woman. His eyebrows shot up.

CHAPTER FOUR

Friday, February 25
3:00 p.m.
Atlanta, Georgia

DESMOND TREVOR WAITED AT a table in the back of the dimly lit bar, watching the entrance. He had arrived early and settled with a draft beer. He didn't intend to drink it. He simply didn't want the waitress to come around to take his order later. He had come here for anonymous privacy, not socializing.

He glanced at the clock on the wall and compared it to his watch. The clock was ten minutes fast. The knowledge tamped the heat he'd felt rising in his chest. They weren't late. Yet.

Three minutes later, the brothers arrived together as usual. Trevor watched as they made their way to his table. They were fraternal twins. The family resemblance was striking, but the two were easily distinguishable.

Both were big men with brown eyes, broad shoulders and long arms. Both were dressed in jeans and cowboy boots. They wore plaid shirts, one red and one green. Their black leather flight jackets were of the same vintage. The outfits were clean enough and worn enough not to attract unnecessary attention anywhere.

Owen, the older one, was an inch shorter and twenty pounds lighter. He'd shaved his head once when he'd lost a challenge of some kind and decided he liked it. Oscar had a full head of long brown hair he wore in a ponytail. Owen led the way as he always did. He'd been born a minute and a half before his younger brother and he'd been the front runner their whole lives. They stopped at the bar to get a beer and Owen paid the tab. Neither one took a sip. Trevor nodded approval.

When they reached his table, Owen sat directly opposite Trevor and Oscar slouched into the chair on his left. As always, Owen did the talking.

"We haven't found him yet," Owen said without excuses.

Trevor's grip tightened on the beer glass but he held his temper. Time was running out. He had no desire to spend the rest of his years in a stinking prison. "Then why are we here?"

"He was extraordinarily careful. He used several different names. He traveled on commercial flights from Cape Town to Houston, but he stopped a couple of times to change planes." Owen barely paused for breath. He cleared his throat and plunged ahead. "He booked the tickets in the name of a newly created shell corporation nested by ten others. Nowhere does his real name appear on any document. We checked every single one."

Owen paused when the waitress came over. He nodded to indicate the beers already on the table. She smiled and moved on.

After the waitress was out of earshot, Trevor said, "Continue."

"Looks like he chartered a Gulfstream out of Houston and flew into Syracuse. From there, he chartered an air taxi to a small airfield near Manchester, New Hampshire. At that point he was traveling under the name of Hourihane." Owen paused again as the waitress walked by too closely before once again withdrawing.

Trevor shook his head and frowned. "Hourihane? What kind of name is that?"

Owen shrugged. "No idea. The only identification he used was a California driver's license with a home address in San Diego. The ethnicity could be almost anything."

Owen showed Trevor a photo of the driver's license and two frames from a surveillance camera in the Houston airport. The driver's license photo was Trevor's business partner, Casper Lange. No doubt about it.

But the surveillance camera images showed the man's back. He was the right height and weight to be Lange. He was carrying two black leather duffel bags.

Trevor looked closer. One of the duffel bags had a brown leather insert, three inches wide, around the middle. Trevor recognized the bag because it belonged to him.

"Right," Trevor said, thinking about it. "You're sure it was Lange?"

"More likely than not," Owen replied. "The trail is pretty tight. But not a hundred percent sure. No."

Trevor nodded. Everything Owen said tracked. It was all consistent with Lange's behavior in the past. A past that hadn't included evading trial testimony in Belgium next week. The investigations had been going on for years, but the trial was finally scheduled only after Lange disappeared. Over the past several months, Trevor had tried repeatedly to contact Lange to let him know. No success.

If Lange didn't appear in court, they both stood to lose

almost five billion dollars and be sentenced to spend time in prison. Which was not something Trevor wanted to brush off. He figured Lange wouldn't either. Unless he'd simply decided to extend his vacation for some reason.

Trevor needed that duffel bag and its contents back. And if his plan for the contents went south, he'd need Lange to appear at that hearing in Belgium. They'd already reached the end of every viable excuse Trevor's well-paid lawyers had devised.

After Trevor and Lange had made it big enough to be of interest to reporters on every continent, Trevor had insisted on precautions. Lange didn't agree until he'd had two near misses with a tabloid photographer who'd followed him all the way to a Chinese brothel where an unfortunate pair of prostitutes died in his room. Trevor snatched the guy's camera and then hired a man to silence him permanently.

After that, Lange employed better techniques to conceal his identity when he engaged in high-risk distasteful activities. But he hadn't ceased to engage in them, regardless of Trevor's threats or his own promises.

Trevor had long ago accepted that Lange was an uncontrollable thrill seeker. The kind of thrills he preferred were illegal, immoral, and deadly. He had the trophies to prove it.

Lange would have taken the sort of precautions Owen described. Since the brothel incident, he always had.

Trevor's gut told him that the man Owen had tracked was Casper Lange, more likely than not. He breathed a little easier.

But finding Lange wasn't his only problem.

Sixteen months ago, without Trevor's knowledge and while Trevor was out of the country, Lange had removed the black and tan duffel from the office safe. The duffel was filled with one million dollars in untraceable cash. Lange left Cape Town alone and never returned.

To a man in Trevor's tax bracket, one million dollars was a pittance. But keeping his money close was how he'd made his billions. He'd chopped off the hands of thieves who'd stolen much less. Lange knew how Trevor felt about his money. He'd no doubt intended to repay it.

Except Lange didn't know how dangerous that particular duffel actually was. Trevor had never told him about the flash drive hidden in the lining. The reporter who'd acquired the video from the Chinese brothel was dead. But the video he'd shot was on that flash drive, and Lange wasn't the only man in the room when the prostitutes were killed.

Lange had killed one of the women. A Belgian judge had killed the other. The same Belgian judge who was set to preside over next week's trial. Trevor had kept the video for the day when he'd need it. That day had come. Now it was missing. Along with Lange.

Lange had narrowly escaped death several times before. He always said he was too lucky to die. But he'd never been silent so long. He'd never failed to check in when so much was at stake.

Seemed like Casper Lange's luck had finally run out.

The investors were nervous. Very nervous. The tax collectors were practically rubbing their hands with glee. The criminal prosecutors on four continents were sharpening their claws. Even the Belgian judge relished his chance at their public flagellation, the smug little prick.

Lange could be dead. But Trevor needed to be absolutely certain before he'd admit the situation and shoulder the consequences alone. He wasn't going to prison and he wasn't going to pay Lange's share of the debt. He needed to see Lange's body. He needed that flash drive back. He'd do whatever he needed to do.

"What about cargo?" Trevor asked.

Owen frowned as if he didn't understand the meaning of the word. "Cargo?"

Trevor wanted to reach across the table and punch him. "Did he have any cargo with him when he landed in Manchester?"

Owen's face cleared. "There's no video there, but according to the air taxi pilot, Hourihane stowed two soft bags and two hard cases aboard. The soft bags were both black leather duffels. One was significantly heavier than the other."

That was good news. In Trevor's experiences, a duffel bag full of cash was usually heavier than a bag full of clothes. "What happened when he arrived? Rented a car?"

"Someone picked him up. A man driving a Mercedes, the pilot said," Owen replied. "The pilot recognized the guy. Said he had picked up passengers at the airport before. He didn't know the guy's name or anything else about him."

"A chauffer?" Trevor frowned.

Owen shook his head. "No. More like a local. But he was waiting when Lange arrived. Pilot said the guy wasn't just hanging around, hoping to catch a fare or anything. So we figured he'd been expecting Hourihane in particular."

Trevor's patience had worn thin. His face went hot. His hard glare locked with Owen's gaze.

Without warning, Trevor slammed the palm of his hand down hard enough to make the beer glasses bounce. Amber ale spilled on the table's surface and spread over the edge and dripped onto his expensive suede loafers.

He growled in a subdued voice, "Dammit, man! You're wasting my time! Did you find the driver or not?"

The brothers froze in place.

Oscar's eyes widened and his nostrils flared. His face reddened and his jaw muscles clenched.

But his brother Owen, always the smarter one, placed a calming hand on Oscar's forearm. Owen's steady gaze never wavered.

"We might have found him. Or at least, we might know where he went." Owen reached into his jacket pocket and pulled out another photograph. He slid it across the table toward Trevor, careful to avoid the spilled beer. "This picture was taken by a local kid who got a new drone for Christmas."

Trevor looked down at the shot for a second. At first, he thought the photo was printed in black and white. He saw dense leafless trees, snow-covered ground, and then a clearing where a huge fire must have destroyed at least half an acre and everything on it.

Owen said, "Taken about a week ago, near as we can tell. The fire happened a while back. Figure five to eighteen months ago, according to the local gossip. Which would make the timing right for Lange."

Trevor continued to stare at the photo. "Where is this place?"

"About twenty miles from Laconia, New Hampshire. Easy driving distance from that Manchester air strip where Hourihane flew in." Owen paused for a quick breath before he delivered the bad news. "Kid's parents gave the photo to local law enforcement and they called in the feds."

Trevor's rage began to rise in his gut. Not only local yokels from the rural cop shop to deal with, but the FBI. Great. Just great. The very last thing they needed was to draw the attention of one of the most powerful law enforcement agencies in the world. What the hell was Lange thinking?

Owen said, "We've been watching the place. They hauled some bodies out of there a few days ago."

"*Bodies*? There were multiple fatalities in a fire that huge and nobody noticed it for *months*?" Trevor felt the blood pulsing in his head. Felt his temperature rising with every beat of his heart. What the hell had Lange gotten them all into?

Owen nodded. "From a distance, we watched them bring the body bags out. At least nine that we saw."

"You're saying one of the bodies is Lange? Or are you saying Lange did the killing?" Trevor asked through gritted teeth, barely keeping his rage in check. If Lange was dead, that would be fine with him. But if he'd killed nine people, and the feds could prove it, Trevor might never get away from this, even if Lange died in the process.

"Hey, don't shoot the messenger here." Owen held both hands up, palms out.

Trevor glared.

Owen leaned back in his chair, out of Trevor's reach. "Look, it could go either way. Maybe Lange is dead. Or maybe he was the killer and he's on the run. But one choice or the other seems likely, doesn't it? Locals say cops haven't identified the bodies yet. One of the dead could be Lange. On the other hand, this place is fairly close to the airstrip where the man calling himself Hourihane was picked up by the local guy in the Mercedes. Neither the Mercedes nor the driver seem to be around anymore."

"The timing fits." Trevor held his temper. He nodded slowly and took a closer look at the Houston photographs of Hourihane. The guy could have been Lange. Or not.

He thought about the situation for a long few minutes. Owen and Oscar waited for orders.

It didn't make sense that the killer would have started the fire. Why would he do that? Made no sense at all.

A single assassin would have left quietly after completing the kills. A fire that size had the potential to draw too much attention to the scene, making a clean getaway less likely.

Not only that, but the killer couldn't possibly have known that the fire would go unnoticed and the bodies undiscovered for maybe two years.

Trevor shook his head. No. Deliberately starting a fire like that to conceal a crime, or even several crimes, was too clumsy for Lange. He'd been careful getting to the location. He could easily have slipped away unnoticed afterward.

Other facts Trevor had uncovered suggested Lange had planned to be gone for a week at the most. In addition to the potential trouble beginning to brew in Belgium, they had a lot going on in South Africa, and Lange knew that. And he hadn't taken any of his assets with him. He wouldn't have disappeared taking nothing but Trevor's million dollars. Not when he was entitled to so much more.

Trevor figured Lange took the money because he knew it was untraceable. Which meant he'd planned to use it for something that couldn't blow back on them.

But Owen and Oscar had gone as far as they could with this thing. They were paid muscle. Low level. Which was exactly why he'd chosen them. No way were they good enough to find Lange. Trevor knew that now. Which was a good thing, because it made them both dispensable.

A plan was beginning to take shape in his head. He shrugged casually, as if his anger had dissipated. He slipped the photographs into his pocket.

"Okay. Wait here at least thirty minutes. Meet me tomorrow

morning. I'll send you directions. Make sure you're not followed," Trevor instructed.

"Where are we going?" Owen asked.

Trevor said, "To find my money and find out whether Lange died in this fire. Or if he didn't, where the hell he is."

CHAPTER FIVE

Friday, February 25
3:30 p.m.
Near Syracuse, New York

MOST OF THE HITCHHIKER'S bulk came from the heavy winter gear she wore. But she was tall and sturdy enough to take care of herself, Jake guessed.

She held her hands close to the heat blowing into the cabin from the vents in the dashboard. When her hands warmed, she put her palms on her cheeks.

"Wow, it's turned super cold out there all of a sudden," she said. "I was thinking I'd be sleeping in an igloo tonight before you came along. Thanks for picking me up."

Jake shrugged. "No problem. Where'd you come from?"

"Pittsfield. East of Albany. Headed home to Buffalo. The weather was better when I started out." Her gaze fell on the green stainless steel vacuum bottle his dad had given him for their first hunting trip. "Got any coffee in there?"

He glanced at the bottle. He'd filled it up the last time he bought gas a while back. "Yeah, sure. Help yourself. No cream or sugar, though."

"Perfect. Hot and black. Just the way I like it," she replied with a grin while she screwed off the top and poured the aromatic brew into the cup. Her hands were big enough to handle the heavy thermos easily.

Jake kept his eyes on the road. The wind buffeted the Jeep and pushed it sideways on the snow-slicked pavement. He struggled to keep the vehicle between the ditches. Darkness was coming fast and the last thing he wanted was to spend the night stuck out here in the middle of nowhere, USA.

"I'm Julia Mucha," she said, still holding the coffee and sniffing it appreciatively.

"Jake Reacher," he replied.

"Where are you headed, Jake?"

"California. Looks like I might be stuck in Syracuse for the night, though."

She nodded. "Worse things have happened. They get a lot of snow here. Not as much as Buffalo, but pretty damn close. Around here, Rochester gets the most. We were always pretty proud of that. Proud it wasn't Buffalo, you know?"

Jake glanced at her. "You like baseball?"

She shook her head. "Not a sports fan."

He nodded, "Seen any good movies lately?"

"Nope. Too busy at school."

Jake didn't reply. So much for good conversation.

Maybe she'd read his mind or something because she said, "I'll be graduating in May. What about you?"

"Finished college last month. I needed to speed things up because my dad was sick." It wasn't the sort of thing he'd normally have told a complete stranger, but he didn't want to be stuck talking about fashion or something for the next two hours.

"Where'd you go?"

"Dartmouth. My dad went there and it was close to home."

"Big bucks for tuition, though," she said, as if having the money to pay for school was a luxury she didn't have.

"Don't I know it." He shrugged. "I had some savings. Got a bunch of small scholarships from local organizations. Took some loans and summer jobs for the rest. So it worked out. You?"

"Culinary school outside of Albany that you've never heard of. I want to be a chef. Own my own restaurant one day," she replied, jutting her chin forward as if she dared him to argue. When he didn't, she said, "That's why I'm hitching. Missed the one and only flight I could afford. And I need to get home."

"What's the rush?"

"My best friend's wedding. I'm doing the cooking. Can't possibly miss it, you know?"

Jake nodded. "Yeah, I can see how that would be a problem."

"Even if I'm stuck in Syracuse for the night, I can get home in the morning. If I'd waited until tomorrow to fly, the earliest I could get there was too late for all the work I've got ahead of me." She tipped the cup and drained the last of the coffee. "Mind if I refill this?"

"Help yourself."

Snow was falling at the rate of about an inch an hour now, he guessed. Fast enough to cover the roads soon, and these backroads didn't get plowed right away. He needed to get moving.

He glanced at the odometer. Another hour or so to Syracuse, given the weather conditions. He'd briefly considered pressing on to Buffalo for Julia's sake, but driving that much farther tonight was about as appealing as listening to her talk about food he couldn't eat while his stomach growled louder than a hungry predator.

"Can we change the subject before I feel compelled to gobble the upholstery or something?" Jake teased, like he wasn't starving when he really was. Those sandwiches his mother made were long gone and the chances of finding a diner or a drive-through out here were slim to none.

"Sure." Julia smiled as she poured the last of the coffee from the thermos. "I'm sorry about your dad being sick. How's he doing?"

"He passed. Two weeks ago." Jake cleared his throat. He'd wanted a change of subject and now he was stuck with the one he'd chosen.

She lowered her gaze. "I'm sorry."

"Thanks," Jake replied. He didn't want this to devolve into a real downer so he covered the topic quickly. "Cancer. He'd lost the will to fight a few months back. We knew it was coming."

"Oh," she said awkwardly, without looking up. She probably hadn't had much experience expressing condolences or accepting them, either.

Jake had more than enough experience for the both of them. The way to get through the awkward phase was to talk about something else. "That's kind of why I'm here, actually. At the funeral, Old Man Reacher gave me a letter Dad wrote a few weeks before he died."

"Who is Old Man Reacher?"

"Friend of the family. That's what everybody calls him. He's at least ninety, I guess."

"That's pretty old, all right. What did the letter say?" She was probably thinking it was some sort of handwritten will or something. In a way, Jake supposed it was.

"Basically, it said Dad knew I wasn't really his son, but he'd always be my father no matter what." Now that he'd started talking, he seemed unable to stop. Probably because he'd never see her again after he dropped her off in Syracuse. There was safety in spilling his guts to a total stranger, somehow. Like talking around a campfire in the dark. He'd done plenty of that when he was in Junior R.O.T.C.

Julia gasped. "Not really his son? You mean, like you were adopted or something?"

"He was pretty frail by the time he wrote the letter, so it was short. Only a few lines, really." An oncoming pair of headlights swerved into Jake's lane up ahead. He hit the horn and the headlights swerved back where they belonged.

Once the danger was past, Jake said, "I asked Old Man Reacher what the letter meant. He said he didn't know. But Mom overheard the conversation. She was already a wreck, so I didn't have the heart to ask her about it then and there."

"Did you ask her later?"

"Yeah," Jake nodded. "She told me the whole story. She'd been dating my dad and they were pretty serious. But they'd had a fight and broke up. She went to visit a friend for the weekend and she met my bio dad. On the rebound, I guess. The guy moved on and so did she. A few weeks after she and Dad got back together, she found out she was pregnant."

Julia shook her head, holding onto the coffee with both hands and looking down into the dark liquid like it might be magic or something. She said quietly, "She didn't know which one was the father?"

"She must have had her suspicions. I mean, it's pretty obvious that I didn't look at all like Dad, even back then. And I didn't have Dad's temperament, either. He was easygoing.

Lighthearted. A real homebody, you know? He liked gardening and bird-watching. Stuff like that."

"And you don't?"

"Not at all."

Julia nodded, sipping the coffee. "So when did your mom find out about your real dad?"

"Her curiosity got the best of her by the time I was ten. She sent DNA samples off to one of those free services. Sure enough, David Reacher was not my dad," Jake finished up with a flourish.

"Did she tell the other guy?" Julia asked, as if Jake's life was some sort of movie-of-the-week or something.

The longer he talked about this, the less he liked it. The details started to sound too much like a soap opera. He stated the facts simply, trying to steer the conversation in a different direction. "It was too late. My bio dad had already died by then."

Julia's breath sucked in and caught and Jake thought he might have to do CPR, it took her so long to start breathing again.

"Did she tell you anything about him?"

"She told me everything she knew. She'd started talking to him at the party and found out his last name was the same as her ex," Jake replied.

"His name was Reacher?"

"You sound surprised. It's not that uncommon a name in New Hampshire where I come from. Meeting him was one of those small world things, I guess," Jake shrugged. "You know, 'oh, my ex-boyfriend's last name is Reacher. David Reacher. Are you related?' yada yada yada."

"Yeah, that stuff happens. I meet people who attended my high school in Buffalo all the time. People I've never heard of,"

Julia smiled and he thought she might have exhausted the subject. She hadn't. "Were they? Related I mean? David Reacher and the guy your mom met at the party?"

"He said no at the time. She told him she was from Laconia and he said his father was born there but left when he was seventeen to join the Marines. He'd never been to Laconia, but he'd always meant to check it out." Jake shrugged again. She wasn't going to let this go, he knew that now. "But I figured maybe they shared relatives in the distant past or something. Anyway, once she found out the DNA results when I was ten, she knew he was my bio dad, so she looked him up. He'd been in the Army back when they met, so it was fairly easy to trace him."

"She told him about you and he never came around or anything?" Julia's gaze was full of sympathy now for the poor little abandoned boy. Jake didn't like that, either. Last thing he needed was anybody feeling sorry for him.

"Not exactly. By that time, he'd already died. He was killed in the line of duty, they said." Jake had turned the windshield wipers on full speed and flipped all the heat up to the defrosters, but the snow was falling too fast to keep his view cleared.

He slowed the Jeep further and slipped into four-wheel drive. Syracuse wasn't that much farther, but he'd begun to think they might not reach it tonight. Which meant he'd have to work out what to do with Julia. He couldn't just dump her somewhere on the side of the road. Not in this weather, anyway.

CHAPTER SIX

Friday, February 25
6:30 p.m.
Siesta Beach, California

PATTY SUNDSTROM PRETENDED NOT to worry about her boyfriend. She'd already closed out the cash register of their windsurfing shop and prepared the bank deposit. She'd brought all the equipment inside. Now she was wandering around, straightening here, arranging there, simply to kill time until he returned.

She and Shorty Fleck had been together more than five years now. They'd been through a lot. They'd left his potato farm and her sawmill job in the cold, white north, to follow their dreams of sun and sand and surf. A decision they were both satisfied with, even after all that had happened.

They'd driven as far as they could from Saint Leonard, a small faraway town in New Brunswick, Canada, in Shorty's beat-up old Honda. Until the Honda died. After they acquired another car, they went to New York first and then all the way to California.

Patty never looked back.

Even though the money was tighter than she'd like, she never second-guessed their decision to set up shop near San Diego in California instead of Sarasota, Florida.

She never thought about that horrible time in Laconia, either. It was over and they'd both survived. That was all that mattered to her.

But she knew Shorty thought about Laconia. A lot. He had visible scars and invisible ones, too. Laconia haunted him. He still had nightmares. She knew because after they'd settled into bed in the rooms above the shop, from time to time he'd wake her up with his whimpers and screams.

Sometimes she couldn't get him back to sleep for an hour or more.

He always said he didn't remember the nightmares, but she knew that was a lie. His skin would be drenched with sweat and it took him a good long time to fall asleep again. If he didn't remember the horror, then he'd have gone right back to sleep, now wouldn't he?

The only thing that seemed to calm Shorty these days was windsurfing on the ocean. He was quite good at it now, although it had taken him a while to learn. After his injuries healed well enough and his doctors signed off, he threw himself into the sport with a child's enthusiasm that lightened her heart.

Patty didn't object to his long hours with the wind and the surf and the cold nights. Even as she understood he was chasing exhaustion to avoid the nightmares. But he kept at the windsurfing anyway.

She smiled. Shorty's dogged determination was one of the things that had made him a good potato farmer. It was one of the things she loved most about him. Besides, Shorty needed the windsurfing practice. He couldn't teach classes until he was proficient enough himself.

She already knew how to windsurf before they set up the shop. Patty's grandfather taught her. He was born in Minnesota and had slipped north to beat the draft during the Vietnam war. But like many Minnesotans, he had vacationed in Florida where he'd learned to windsurf.

She taught Shorty everything she knew. She was the one who gave lessons to the tourists, too. She kept the books for the shop. She did the banking. She did just about everything, actually.

Turned out Shorty was not as good a businessman as he had been a potato farmer. Not that Patty cared about his business skills. She hadn't fallen in love with him because he was destined to be a master of the universe. He had qualities that were more important to her, like loyalty and steadfastness. Otherwise, she wouldn't have thrown in with him and left Canada for good.

Shorty loved her, too, of course. They'd been close enough before Laconia. But after all the stuff they'd been through up there, they'd grown even closer. They planned to get married, as soon as they could get a few days off for a honeymoon. The way things were going, she figured the wedding was at least a year away.

Where was he? Patty glanced at the clock again. Sunset was an hour ago. The sun's afterglow was almost gone. Soon it would be pitch black out there on the Pacific. Black and cold. Really cold. San Diego was a lot warmer than back home in Canada, but February was still winter time, even here. When the sun went down, cold came in fast. He didn't need to be out there this late.

"Damn you, Shorty," she whispered, although she wasn't really angry. Concerned was all. Very concerned. "You told me you'd be back before dark. Where the hell are you?"

She heard a knock on the door. She whipped around to peer through the window. Shorty was standing there, lips blue, shivering in his wetsuit. She grinned. The idiot hadn't thought to take a towel.

She grabbed an oversized beach towel from the pile near the door and let him inside. She didn't even care that he was dripping wet. She just wanted him to stop shivering.

"Sorry, Patty," he said between chattering teeth as he peeled off his wet suit and wrapped a dry towel around his naked torso like a skirt. His skin was deeply tanned and his shaggy hair was sun bleached to a golden brown. "The waves were amazing today. Lost track of time."

She handed his dry clothes over and he dressed quickly, but he was still shivering.

"Come on upstairs where it's warmer. I'll heat soup for dinner. We've got that good bread you picked up yesterday," she said as he followed her toward the stairs to their flat while she chatted on about inconsequential things.

He'd come home safely. Maybe he would sleep well tonight after all. That was all she cared about because she was exhausted with work and worry and she could use some rest, too.

Shorty dressed in a sweater and jeans while Patty heated and dished up the food. She ladled the hearty bean soup into large bowls, put the bread on a plate, and set out two bottles of Labatt's beer.

They dug into the hot soup and bread like coal miners after a hard day in the mines. Windsurfing always left them surprisingly ravenous. After a bit, Shorty cocked his head and raised the brown bottle in a toast. They clinked the long-necked bottles together and took satisfying pulls on the beer.

Between mouthfuls of soup, Shorty said, "Something strange happened on the beach tonight."

"Do tell," she replied sardonically just to see him grin. Lots of strange things happened in California, in her experience. Especially on the beach. And Siesta Beach seemed weirder than a lot of the others. The never-ending stream of weird stuff was one of the reasons she liked the place. Never a dull moment.

"A big guy, maybe six-five, maybe two-fifty, came up to me," Shorty said, still shoveling in food as if he hadn't eaten in years. He refilled his bowl from the soup pot Patty had placed in the middle of the table.

The moment he mentioned the guy, the little hairs on the back of Patty's neck stood up and a chill ran through her. She stopped the spoon in mid-air, steadied her hand, and kept her voice neutral. "Oh, yeah? What's so strange about that?"

"Well, it was pretty dark already. Nobody out there except the regulars. And he wasn't a surfer or nothin'. Didn't have any equipment with him. He was wearin' work clothes and work boots. A brown leather jacket. On the beach. Like maybe he'd just come from some sort of construction work or something." Shorty had warmed to his story between bites and swigs and didn't seem to notice that Patty had laid down her spoon and simply waited. "Really strange to see that."

Patty clasped her hands under the table where he couldn't see she was shaking with nerves. "What did he want?"

"Didn't talk much. He asked me a few questions about windsurfing. Like was the equipment expensive and how long did it take me to learn. Stuff like that," Shorty said.

She nodded and tried to relax. Maybe it wasn't him. And

maybe she wasn't as cool about what had happened in Laconia all those months ago as she'd thought.

"What did you say?" Patty asked, but the sinking feeling in her gut told her the answer before he replied.

"I told him my girlfriend is the best teacher around. That she taught me and I've got no native talent whatsoever. And I suggested he stop by here tomorrow. Told him you'd give him a couple of lessons. On the house." He shoveled a few more bites into his mouth, chewed, and swallowed. "Who knows? He might even buy some stuff. He works construction. He's gotta have a little money for lessons and equipment, right?"

Patty's mouth had dried up. She sipped her beer so she'd be able to speak, but it turned out she didn't have to say anything.

Shorty finished up his second bowl of soup and went for his third. Potato farmers have big appetites and he still ate like that, even though he hadn't done any real farming in almost two years. He kept right on talking.

"All the times I've been out there on that beach, nobody's ever asked me stuff like that. Especially not when it's this late and this cold. And tonight? Only the diehards are out there. Serious people who already know what they're doing. Already have their equipment, you know? So this new guy wearing work clothes being right there was strange right off the bat." He looked at her with those big brown eyes she loved and she couldn't say anything at all. She simply nodded.

He rested both forearms on the table and leaned forward, giving her that earnest farm boy look that made her fall in love with him back in St. Leonard. "We might be turning the corner, Patty. Maybe business will pick up. We can rent a little bungalow close by. Won't need to sleep above the store. Wouldn't that be nice?"

She nodded, "Yeah, it would."

"I mean, I sure don't want to move back to Canada. Do you?" Shorty cocked his head as if he didn't understand her lack of enthusiasm. He'd found them a paying customer. Why wasn't she more excited?

"No. No, I don't want to move back," she said, stirring her soup with the spoon. She patted his hand and he seemed satisfied with her answer. He returned his attention to his soup and his beer.

Running back to Canada was the last thing she wanted.

Or maybe the second to the last thing.

The very last thing was what she'd worried about non-stop since they'd left Laconia. That this particular big man would come looking for them. Because if he did that, he'd have a reason. A reason she didn't want to think about.

Patty drew a big breath into her lungs and held it there as long as she could. She exhaled slowly, the way Grandpa taught her to survive when the big waves capsized her board. Patty could hold her breath a good long time. Two to three minutes or more, probably. Long enough to stay alive until she could surface again for great gulps of air.

The big man was here. He'd found Shorty, and he was asking about lessons, which meant he was asking about her.

No way for her to fix that. That horse was already out of the barn, as Shorty used to say when he was farming.

It was only a matter of time before the big man walked into the shop. And not much time, either. Maybe even tonight. Or tomorrow.

She had to figure out why he was here.

She needed to decide what to do about him when he showed up.

Most of all, she had to have a plan for how to handle the trouble that would absolutely come along with him.

CHAPTER SEVEN

Friday, February 25
6:45 p.m.
Laconia, New Hampshire

WHEN SMITHERS TURNED THE last corner on the drive into Laconia, Kim saw it was a larger place than she had expected. The sun had set, bathing the town in a warm red after glow that gave the brick buildings an old-time feel. The electric streetlights were meant to mimic gaslights of yesteryear, enhancing the effect. The ambiance reminded her of a lot of other small towns intent on retaining their historic heritage she'd visited over the years.

"I have a reservation at an Inn within walking distance of downtown. Can you drop me there?" She fished around in her pocket for her phone to get the exact address, which was on a side street near the city offices. "There's a bistro close by. The menu looked good online. I'll buy you dinner and you can fill me in on your investigation so far."

"Works for me." Smithers offered his megawatt smile. "I

don't need the directions. We're all at The Laconia Inn, too. There are no hotels in this town and that's the only place large enough to house our team. One of our guys left yesterday. We saved the room for you."

"Good." She glanced at the phone and saw she'd had a call from Gaspar, her former partner. He'd left a message. She slipped her phone into her pocket. She'd retrieve the message later.

Smithers pulled the big SUV into a narrow driveway beside a red brick building constructed during the Revolutionary War. "You can get out here. The check-in desk is right behind those doors in the front lobby. I'll park in the lot out back. We can walk to the bistro. The parking area over there is nonexistent."

Kim climbed down from the SUV and grappled with her bags until she freed them from the passenger compartment. She stood aside, close against the wall of snow that had been shoveled off the driveway, to let Smithers pull through. Then she slipped along the packed snow to the entrance walk.

A sign proclaiming the features of the house was barely visible above the snowbanks, but Kim was too cold to stop and read it. She continued past the sign toward the nicely shoveled porch.

She set her bags down and twisted the old-fashioned doorknob to open the oversized wooden door, which was probably original construction and had swollen tight against the frame. She leaned all of her ninety-seven pounds into it, but the door didn't budge. She peered through the cut glass windows. The desk clerk was nowhere to be seen.

She pressed the doorbell with the palm of her gloved hand while turning her back to the wind in a futile effort not to freeze to death. The doorbell's melodious ringing sounds chimed inside. The tune sounded like a kid playing "Yankee Doodle" on a kazoo.

She figured that noise could get annoying really fast. She grinned and pressed the button a few more times, hoping the song could be heard in the back room or wherever the clerk might be.

After about a dozen choruses, a short, bald man wearing horn-rimmed glasses, a heavy sweater, and tan corduroy pants hurried to the door. His face was scrunched into a comical, horrified look. He grabbed the doorknob, turned it, and yanked hard enough to lose his footing. He stumbled backward but didn't fall, only because he never let go.

By the time Kim had wrestled her bags into the lobby, the man was steady on his feet once more. He closed the door against the wind and swiped the six remaining strands of hair into place on the top of his head.

"Here, let me help you," he said, rolling her suitcase across the floor to the desk. "I'm afraid we're at full occupancy for tonight, but I can call around to find you a room at one of Laconia's other excellent accommodations."

"I have a reservation," Kim said, not the least amused. She reached into her pocket, pulled out her badge wallet, and flashed it close in front of his myopic gaze.

"Oh. Oh. Well that's good then." He cleared his throat and peered closely at her ID through the bifocals on the horned-rims. After he'd examined everything to his total satisfaction, he said dourly, "Let's get you set up."

He hurried around to the other side of the desk and clacked a few keys on his computer keyboard. His words tumbled out as if they'd been propelled against his will. "Yes, here we are, Agent Kim L. Otto. You have our last available suite. It's also one of our nicest. We already have your deposit on file. If you can just sign here while I get your key, I will show you upstairs."

He led the way up the old-fashioned staircase. Kim gave him

a solid head start before she followed behind, just in case he lost his balance and fell backward again. He struggled with her bag, but eventually made it to the second floor, breathing heavily. He used the weighty brass key to open the door to a room overlooking the street.

He bent slightly at the waist and extended his arm with a flourish. Kim shook her head and walked inside. She held out her hand and he gave her the key.

"I can find my way around. I'm sure you'll be needed downstairs," she said by way of dismissing his futzing.

"Of course." He looked a little bewildered, but he backed out of the room and closed the door. She turned the lock behind him.

Kim moved her bag closer to the floral chintz sofa and dropped her laptop case onto the cushions. The queen-sized bed was covered in floral everything, with more pillows than she'd ever seen gathered on one flat surface before. Fortunately, there was enough floor space on one side to store them all. She shoved them off the bed.

The suite only had one room, but it was spacious. A small desk with a chair was positioned near the large windows. When the inn was remodeled, they must have insulated well because the room was warm enough and not drafty, like some historic buildings can be.

The bathroom was large, too. The huge clawfoot tub was big enough to swallow Kim whole if she was foolish enough to get into it. Which she wasn't. A separate shower stall was nestled behind the door. The towels were heavy and had a luxurious feel to them.

All in all, the place was serviceable enough. It lacked a coffee maker, but she spied a room service menu on the desk. So far, so good.

Kim found her cell phone and listened to Gaspar's brief message. It consisted of two word. "Call me."

She prepared to do precisely that, but before the call connected, Smithers knocked and said, "Ready for dinner?"

Gaspar would have to wait. She disconnected, dropped the phone into her pocket, and opened the door. "Come on in. Let me wash up quickly and we'll go."

Smithers stepped into the room and immediately dwarfed everything in it, including her. His bulk made the space seem small and crowded. He had to be three hundred fifty pounds and six-four, at least. Which made her feel glad he was on her team instead of working against her.

She went into the bathroom, used the toilet, splashed some warm water on her face, washed her hands and tucked in the few stray hairs that had escaped the tight bun she wore at the base of her neck. She'd meant to apply a bit of makeup before dinner, but she'd never unpacked and her makeup bag was in the other room with Smithers. She shrugged.

In less than five minutes, she'd returned.

"Takes my wife an hour to put her lipstick on." He grinned. "You really are fast for a girl, Otto."

"So I've heard," she smiled back, slipping her arms into her parka. "Is the bistro far? I'm starving."

Smithers laughed, opened the door, and stepped into the corridor. "I'm always starving."

She followed him through the doorway, used the big brass key to lock her stuff inside, and they headed down the stairs. When they reached the lobby, Smithers yanked the front door open without fanfare and they went outside.

"Watch that door," he said, turning up his collar and slipping his big hands into black leather gloves. "It sticks."

She smirked. "Good to know."

The wind had picked up and the temperature had dropped in the past hour. She pulled up her hood. She stuffed her hands into her gloves and her gloves into her pockets. But damn, Laconia was one cold place in February. How did people actually survive here?

Smithers chose the north sidewalk, which had been shoveled wide enough for them to walk side-by-side, and set off at a fast clip. He didn't talk. She didn't either. The air was so cold that even opening her mouth practically caused her saliva to freeze.

They hustled about four blocks in the biting wind until Smithers finally stopped in front of a narrow bistro. They went inside where a big fire roared in the fireplace. Behind the long counter was a nice selection of wine and booze, allowing diners to warm up on the inside as well as the outside. The aromas coming from the kitchen in the back were, as Kim's younger sister would say, "to die for."

The place was surprisingly busy. Kim saw only two open tables, which meant her conversation with Smithers could be too easily overheard. A serious exchange of intel would have to wait.

Smithers said, "The wine is great, and the food is excellent. But portions here are tiny. Be aware."

A slender woman wearing a white apron tied around her waist seated them near the fire. She told them the specials and Kim ordered the salad with roast beef in it. Smithers ordered the same thing, but he asked for three servings instead of one, and extra bread.

The woman looked bewildered. "Are others joining you?"

"No. I'm just hungry." He gave her the blinding smile and she relaxed.

They ordered wine and waited for the bread.

Kim looked at the menu again, just in case she needed more food later, and then laid it on the table. Once the server had brought the bread and wine and left them alone, Kim asked, "What's on your agenda for tomorrow?"

"Same as yours, I expect. Nose around. See if we can figure out what happened out there. Find out whether Reacher is involved." He tore into the bread like a man who hadn't eaten in weeks.

She smiled. Gaspar ate like that, too. As if every meal might be his last.

"Have you talked to the local cops?" Kim nibbled on one of the hot dinner rolls, fresh from the oven.

Smithers nodded and lowered the volume on his sonorous voice to avoid casual and purposeful eavesdroppers alike. "The Laconia Chief of Detectives is Jim Shaw. Good guy. Seems to have a solid grasp of local activities. Detective Brenda Amos has been our contact. From the look on your face, I take it the names mean something to you?"

"I'm scheduled to meet with both in the morning," Kim said. "Usually, if I'm tasked with interviewing them, it means they had some contact with Reacher. Otherwise, they wouldn't be on my list."

Smithers nodded again. "I'll come along. If Reacher was involved in this, we might as well work together. Save us both some shoe leather and briefing time."

Kim shrugged, which was Gaspar's all-purpose gesture. It could mean anything, or nothing. But she wouldn't mind having Smithers along. He could do the driving and be the muscle should she need any, since she wasn't totally sure that her Glock would actually fire in this frigid weather. Some handguns fired well in extreme cold and some didn't. She kept the lubricant to a minimum to avoid freezing, but she would prefer not to be forced to find out.

"Tell me what you know about the ruins, the fire, everything," she said after the salads were delivered.

"Not a lot. The place was a motel once upon a time. It hadn't been operating for a couple of decades when some investors took over. They had trouble with their renovations and their permitting, I guess. No one we've talked to so far thinks the place was open for business when it burned to the ground," Smithers said as he ate his salad and sopped the plate with the bread. He refilled the wine glasses from the bottle on the table.

"Why would anyone destroy an abandoned building in the middle of nowhere?" Kim wondered aloud. "Kids? Arson to collect insurance?"

"Motives could have been just about anything." Smithers shook his head. His entire plate was almost as clean as if he'd put it in the dishwasher. A man his size had to have a hearty appetite, sure, but he was an eating machine.

"*If* the place was deliberately destroyed," she said.

He nodded. "Right. Could have been a lightning strike or a gas leak or even spontaneous combustion if they had flammable stuff stored in one of those barns. We just don't know yet."

Kim cocked her head. "Who owned the place?"

"Offshore shell corporations, near as we can tell. We've got the Boston field office working on that angle," Smithers replied. He picked up the menu and studied the dessert offerings.

"So you don't have much to go on at all, do you? No identification on the bodies or the vehicles. No theories about what happened to the buildings. No motives for criminal activity out there," Kim said, frowning. "Am I missing anything else you don't have?"

Smithers grinned. "Nope. We've got a big bunch of nothin' so far. And nothin' on the horizon, either. Except frostbite if we're not careful."

"How much more time do you need for processing the scene?" She asked.

A troubled look marred his features. "More than we have. Bad weather is moving in. We've got to pack up and go by the end of the day tomorrow."

Kim finished her salad and pushed the plate aside, feeling comfortably full and warm and a little bit sleepy. None of what Smithers said made much sense as far as Reacher was concerned.

Everything she knew about Reacher led her to believe that he was a violent man when provoked. She figured he would've burned the place to the ground under the right circumstances. But what were those circumstances? And what was he doing out there in the boondocks in the first place?

Maybe Gaspar had something to contribute on that score. But she couldn't call him back now and he'd be sleeping by the time she returned to her room.

Laconia Detectives Shaw and Amos might fill in the blanks tomorrow morning. Tonight, she relaxed in front of the big fire, ordered another glass of wine, and watched Smithers wolf down two big slices of apple pie a la mode.

CHAPTER EIGHT

Friday, February 25
8:15 p.m.
Syracuse, New York

JAKE'S SHOULDERS WERE TIGHT with the tension of holding the Jeep on the road.

The last fifty miles had been harrowing. Driving the Jeep at a top speed of thirty miles an hour, the wind buffeted the boxy SUV like a kitten with a yarn ball.

His eyes felt hot and dry. He needed a shower, a meal, and about ten hours sleep.

They'd lost cell service for a while, but Julia had looked at the map and located a no-frills hotel with a brew pub across the street just inside the city limits. "The hotel's not a name brand, and the area is a little dodgy, but it should be okay."

Jake had nodded and kept his eyes on the road. "When we get there, we'll stop for the night. Unless you'd like me to drop you somewhere else first?"

"That place is fine with me. There's a campground close by

and the burgers at the pub across the street are pretty good," Julia replied, a little nervously. "Burger and a beer won't cost us an arm and a leg, either."

Half an hour later, he parked in the hotel lot and then turned to face her. "This is a little awkward, but we can cut costs if we share a room with two queen beds."

Her eyes widened.

He rushed on before she could get the wrong idea. "You said you couldn't afford to fly home, so I figure money is tight. And you can't possibly sleep outside tonight, even if you do have a tent in your backpack."

She didn't reply.

"No strings attached. I promise." He raised both hands, palms out. "Look, what's the big deal? We had co-ed dorms at school and you probably did, too, Right?"

Still, she hesitated.

He said, "Come on, Julia. We're only going to be here a few hours. I'm harmless. And even if I wasn't, I promise you, I'm too tired to try anything tonight anyway."

She didn't say no, but she seemed like she wanted to refuse, which made no sense to him at all. The temperature would be well below zero out there tonight. And he'd seen the look of gratitude on her face before she'd squelched it, which made him feel good about nudging her to say yes.

After a bit of silent internal argument, she shrugged and swiped a long lock of blonde hair away from her face. "Seems like a reasonable thing to do."

"Right," he said. "Let's get going. I'm hungry."

They grabbed their bags and mushed through the snow to the hotel entrance to check in. They took the elevator to the third floor, dropped their bags in the room.

Jake abandoned his plans for a shower before food. He was too hungry to wait. They washed up quickly and then trudged outside again and across the parking lot toward the street. The pub was on the opposite side of the road. Maybe a hundred yards from the hotel's entrance. With the blizzard the way it was, those hundred yards would feel more like two hundred by the time they made it all the way.

But they did make it. Snow-covered and cold and shivering, but without damage.

Julia opened the pub's door and the aroma of yeast common to warm and cozy brew pubs everywhere rushed out, along with a cacophony of noise too loud to be contained. She went in first and he followed close behind, stomping the snow off his feet on the way.

The place was jamming, which he hadn't expected, given the miserable weather. She flipped her hood back and looked around until she spied an empty booth on the other side of the bar. She pointed and walked in that direction, unzipping her parka and pulling her gloves off along the way.

When she passed a table of four burly guys about Jake's age, one of them reached out and grabbed her arm.

"Long time no see, hot stuff," he said, with a sloppy sneer.

"Let's keep it that way, Carl." She jerked her arm hard and he lost his grip.

His arm fell back and his elbow nudged a full beer glass off the edge of the table. It dropped to the floor and shattered, sending beer and shards in all directions. Carl's face reddened instantly.

His three buddies laughed, which caused Carl's face to flush a darker red and his nostrils to flare. He placed both hands on the table, preparing to stand. Jake increased his stride and came up behind Julia before the argument could escalate. Carl looked him up and down, but he made no move.

Julia stared Carl down and cast the same withering look of contempt toward his tablemates. When none of the four stood or hurled more insults for a full minute, she tossed her head and continued toward the booth.

Jake nodded at the guys, one at a time, before he followed her. He could feel their eyes on him, but if they said anything more, he didn't hear it. Which was lucky for them. The last thing he wanted tonight was a fight, but he wouldn't run from an asshat like Carl, either.

Julia slid into the booth and Jake sat across from her. They ordered burgers, fries, and mugs of the house-brewed lager. The beer arrived quickly. Julia sipped and then leaned closer across the table.

"Carl is a jerk," she said.

Jake nodded. "I could see that."

"I dated him a couple of times in high school," she said, as if she owed him an explanation but was embarrassed to admit the fact, which Jake absolutely understood. Carl wasn't the kind of guy an accomplished woman like Julia would want.

"Let me guess. He was an athlete. Captain of some team. Football, probably. He looks like he might have had the bulk for it before he developed a thirst for beer," Jake said with a smile. He sipped the lager, which was actually good. He liked brew pubs in general, and he liked the good ones especially.

Julia shrugged. She frowned and her tone was troubled. "I know it's a cliché. But yeah. He was popular. All the girls were jealous of me, which felt good for a while. They didn't know him like I did."

"You dumped him, right?" Jake knew how this story went. Carl's pride was wounded. Julia stayed out of his way. Which was smart. "He never got past it."

She nodded but didn't meet his eyes. "He followed me home one night. And he…wouldn't take no for an answer."

Jake felt his neck flush and the heat moved up. His pulse pounded in his ears. "He raped you?"

"No. But he tried. You noticed his hair is pretty long. That's because he's missing a good chunk of cartilage on his right ear from our last, uh, encounter." Julia grinned briefly before she cleared her throat to finish her story. "I stayed out of his way after that. We graduated and he went off to college to play football. Haven't seen him since."

Jake nodded and said nothing, giving his blood pressure a chance to stabilize. The server brought the food and Julia talked about inconsequential things while they ate. The burgers were big and juicy, the fries were hot and crispy, and the beer was cold. Everything was just the way he liked it.

He swallowed a mouthful of food and washed it down. "This meal is incredible. We got lucky here. How'd you find this place?"

Julia ate with no less enthusiasm. She must have been starving, too. "I told you, I come through here fairly often on my way home to Buffalo. I like great food, and a long-haul trucker I hitched from Albany with once recommended this place. I've stopped here several times since then. Never been disappointed."

Julia kept him entertained with stories of her classmates' kitchen disasters for another half hour. Jake glanced toward Carl's table from time to time. He didn't want any trouble, but he didn't want to be blindsided, either.

Carl and his buddies finally stood to leave. They tossed a

few bills on the table to pay for their beers and headed toward the exit. Jake watched them go through the door and confirmed the clock in his head by checking the time on the big clock over the bar. He'd give them a solid head start. Twenty minutes, at least.

He considered a second burger but opted for a second beer instead. After precisely thirty-two minutes, Jake yawned. "I'm sorry, but I'm exhausted. Are you ready to go?"

"Yeah. Let's do it," she replied. They split the tab, left a generous tip, and bundled up for the trek through the blizzard to the hotel.

At the exit door, Julia flipped her hood up and donned her gloves. She pushed the door open and walked through, lowering her head against the blinding snow. Jake pulled a knit cap low on his ears, turned his collar up, and followed.

The snow had piled about three inches higher while they were inside and the wind gusts had pushed the snow into five-foot drifts alongside the pub building. Vehicles in the parking lot were buried in heavy, wet snow.

The entire area felt deserted. Jake put his hand over his eyes to keep the pelting snow away long enough to check for traffic. The light at the corner was out and no headlights were traveling along the road.

Julia made her way around like a woman from Buffalo who had plenty of experience navigating the perils of winter. Jake stayed cautiously aware of their surroundings. The last thing either of them needed was a sprained ankle or a broken bone. Things like that could happen quickly in this kind of weather.

He wasn't too worried about Carl and his friends. Maybe revenge was a dish best served cold, but that was just a metaphor, not a solid plan for a long life. Only a total idiot would hang around outside on a night like this waiting for a fight over an ancient grudge. Whatever else he was, Carl surely couldn't have been that stupid.

Besides, Carl got what he deserved back then. Maybe he wasn't the sharpest knife in the drawer, but he must have known Julia could have had him arrested. He'd have been charged. Done jail time, probably. That would have been the end of his football career, such as it was.

Carl got off easy back then. Surely he was smart enough to keep going tonight.

But Jake fell back and kept a vigilant watch just in case.

The next time he looked up, Julia had widened the gap between them. She was trudging straight ahead, bent forward against the wind, making steady progress toward the street at a faster clip than he expected. She walked past a barely visible white mini-van almost completely covered by drifting snow.

Jake blinked at the wrong moment. He didn't see exactly what happened. When his eyes popped open, he saw the aftermath.

Julia went down. He saw her falling, like a slow motion film clip. She landed flat on her back, boots out in front of her. Her head smacked the soft snow.

She might have slipped on a patch of black ice.

Maybe.

Jake made the reasonable assumption that Carl was responsible.

He wasn't wrong.

Carl stepped around the mini-van, laughing like a maniacal hyena in the cold wind. His three pals stood close by, enjoying the hilarity.

Then Carl bent over Julia, putting his face close enough to kiss her.

"Carl!" Jake shouted into the wind. He launched fast and increased his pace, gathering momentum on the slippery snow. He made a straight line directly toward Carl. Long strides. Hands at his sides. Shoulders loose. He kept his head up and his eyes hard.

He didn't care about the other three fools. When he took Carl down, the others would scatter. Or not. It didn't matter. Either way, Carl was going down first.

Carl didn't seem to hear Jake coming. The wind carried his warning away before it reached Carl's ears. But something snagged his attention because he lifted his head and glanced toward Jake.

Carl's eyes jumped to life. He seemed confused by Jake's change of pace. He managed to scramble to his feet and throw the first punch, which Jake caught easily in his left palm, like a soft liner to first base.

Carl's fist was big, but Jake's open hand was bigger. He clamped down on the fist and squeezed and continued his forward momentum. Jake added a twist to the squeeze and the push.

The paunchy ex-footballer screamed when his elbow bent at an unnatural angle and he fell awkwardly onto the ground, writhing in pain and holding his elbow. The screams kept coming, but Jake held on for a while to make sure Carl never forgot the point. The wind carried Carl's screams away.

Jake looked around for Carl's posse. They'd scattered into the blinding snow. Just as he'd figured they would. He finally released the pressure on Carl's arm and dropped it.

He turned to help Julia off the ground, but she was already up, dusting herself off. She looked at Carl with no sympathy whatsoever. Her right foot drew back slightly and Jake thought she might kick Carl square in the face. He would have. Hell, he might do it yet if she didn't.

Instead, she glared at Jake. Her tone was as hard as nails. "What the hell is wrong with you? I can fight my own battles. If I need your help, I'll ask for it. Otherwise, keep your Sir Galahad routine to yourself."

She watched Carl's whimpering for a few seconds, like she might still haul off and kick him. But she didn't. She gave the scum more mercy than he deserved. She flipped her hood up.

"Come on. Let's go," she said, heading once again toward the hotel.

Jake was barely breathing hard. He was cold. He wanted to move on, too. But he didn't want Carl following them now or in the morning, either.

He waited until Julia was out of range and then Jake drew back and kicked Carl a couple of times. Carl yelped and moaned.

Jake curled his lip. What a coward. Julia was right. She could have beaten this guy to a pulp. But she didn't. Which meant Jake had to finish the job.

He kicked a third time, hard enough to keep Carl on the ground but not hard enough to do any permanent damage.

So he wouldn't jump up and ambush them from behind.

So his friends would think better of stupid ideas like that, too.

So Carl would remember the fight in the morning when he tried to move and his body revolted.

Carl fell silent. Jake nodded in satisfaction.

Then he followed Julia across the street.

CHAPTER NINE

Saturday, February 26
3:15 a.m. Pacific Time
Siesta Beach, California

PATTY SANDSTROM SLEPT FITFULLY. She awakened at
three fifteen in the morning, like she always did.

Or at least, like she'd been doing since that time in Laconia.
Since then, every morning like clockwork, she'd awaken at three
fifteen with a vague sense of disquiet. Never anything tangible.
Nothing she could specifically identify.

Most times, her eyes simply popped open and she was
instantly awake. She'd lie there, listening to Shorty's steady
breathing. She'd try to identify exactly what had awakened her.
But she never could. After thirty minutes or so, her eyelids grew
heavy and sleep would come again.

Not this night.

Had she heard something? Was someone in the flat? In the
shop?

She lay quietly for five minutes, listening. She heard nothing out of the ordinary. Shorty snored softly, as always. The surf pounded the sand in the distance. Once or twice a car horn blasted from the street.

Nothing else. But she was uneasy.

She got out of bed and grabbed the flashlight she kept on the nightstand. The flashlight was big and heavy. It looked like it had been made out of a solid billet of aluminum. It would make a good weapon, if she needed one.

She slipped out of the bedroom as quietly as possible to avoid waking Shorty. She padded silently to the door and closed it behind her before turning the flashlight on. She walked every inch of the flat. She flashed the beam around the corners and behind the furniture.

Nothing was amiss.

She unlocked the entry door, walked through, closed and locked it behind her. Just in case.

Then she made her way down the stairs, listening for intruders. She heard none.

At the bottom of the stairs, she paused and listened harder. Silence.

She turned the flashlight's beam on again and investigated every inch of the shop. It was a relatively small place, filled to capacity with windsurfing paraphernalia. She spent a full fifteen minutes looking in all of the dark places.

She unlocked the front door and stepped out onto the sand. She inhaled the cool salty air. The moon was full tonight. The brilliant orb illuminated the darkness better than a klieg spotlight at the county fair back home in New Brunswick. She watched the waves crash against the Siesta Beach Pier for a couple of minutes. The moon cast a bright light on the crests of the waves giving them a magical quality that never grew old.

She walked all the way around the small building, shining the light on the sand near the windows. No footprints, big or small. No indication that someone tried to obliterate footprints, either. The windows remained closed and locked.

Patty returned to the front entrance having found no evidence of a break-in or indication that a burglar had tried to enter and failed. She should have felt better. She didn't.

Because she'd heard something that had awakened her at three-fifteen. She was sure of it. So she made the rounds once more, just to calm her nagging worry.

When she'd eventually satisfied herself that no home invasion had happened, and no proof that a burglary was imminent, she reversed her steps, locked the door securely, and trudged up to the flat. She unlocked the door and locked it again when she went inside.

In the corridor, she turned the flashlight off, opened the bedroom door, and slipped into the warm bed next to Shorty.

If Shorty had noticed her absence, he gave no sign of it. He slept as peacefully as any baby Patty had ever seen.

She listened to his gentle snoring, focusing on the rhythm like a metronome, until she fell into an uneasy sleep.

Patty awakened again four hours later. The sun's early rays brightened the bedroom through the closed window blinds.

Before she was fully conscious, she knew Shorty was not there. She reached across the bed and touched the cold sheets to be sure.

He'd gone windsurfing, probably. Nothing to be alarmed about. He went out early most mornings to take advantage of the waves and the mostly deserted beach. He'd be back in a few hours.

She stretched and looked at the clock across the room on

Shorty's dresser. It was seven thirty. Which would be ten thirty on the east coast. Her body clock had finally adjusted to the three-hour time difference, but her brain still did the quick calculation several times a day.

The shop opened at ten o'clock and her windsurfing lesson with a tourist wasn't until noon. She could sleep another hour. So she did.

Strange dreams invaded her sleep this time. The man she'd met that night in Laconia. He was tall and broad. Fair hair and steely blue eyes. Not quite handsome. He'd been dressed in work clothes. Brown work boots. He'd appeared out of nowhere just when she'd needed him most. She might never have found Shorty, let alone saved his life, without him.

He'd helped her get Shorty into the car and the money into the car. Then he'd sent them on their way. Reacher, he'd said his name was.

She'd never seen him again or tried to find him. No reason to. She'd tried to put that entire Laconia experience behind her. And Shorty had been out of his head with pain that night. He didn't remember Reacher at all.

In her dream, he was there. In Siesta Beach. Watching them. Menacing.

She sat bolt upright in bed, her back wet with sweat.

In the weeks and months that followed Laconia, she'd half persuaded herself that she'd imagined him.

Why the hell was she dreaming about Reacher now? After all this time? She'd never done that before.

But she knew the answer.

Because of Shorty's story about meeting a big man on the beach. A big man dressed in work clothes and work boots. A man who could have been Reacher.

Which was crazy, wasn't it? Why would Reacher approach Shorty here and now? She'd told him they were going to Florida, not San Diego. What could he possibly want?

Whatever it was, she'd give it to him. He'd saved her life, and Shorty's too. She owed him. Where she came from, people paid their debts. Simple as that.

CHAPTER TEN

Saturday, February 26
6:30 a.m.
Laconia, New Hampshire

A HARD KNOCK ON her door followed by a male voice proclaiming, "Room Service!" loud enough to be heard on the street jarred Kim awake. She jumped out of the warm bed onto the icy floor and belted the inn's plush fleece robe around her on the way to the door.

The peep hole was positioned above her head, but she grabbed her gun, stuffed it into her pocket and took a chance. She opened the door, secure in the knowledge that the Boss would eventually see the whole scene on video if anything went awry here.

A tall young man stood holding a heavy tray.

She waved him inside, let him set up, signed the check, and he left. The whole business didn't take more than sixty seconds, which was long enough to start her teeth chattering. Apparently the inn tried to save fuel costs by lowering the heat at night. The room didn't have a separate heating system, so she couldn't turn up the thermostat. She glanced longingly toward the still warm bed, resisting its magnetic field only with superhuman effort.

Kim poured a cup of hot black coffee and took it to the sofa out of range of the bed's field of attraction. She folded her legs under her body, opened her laptop, checked her encrypted messages, and located her phone to return Gaspar's call from yesterday.

Gaspar had taken a job working for a hotshot private investigator based in Houston that paid about five times his FBI salary. But that didn't mean he'd changed his sleeping habits. Or rather, his nonsleeping habits. Gaspar slept whenever he could, but never for very long. He'd probably been awake at least a couple of hours already.

He answered on the first ring. "Good morning, Sunshine."

"You sound tired, Chico," she replied, falling back on the easy banter they'd enjoyed when they were teamed on the Reacher case. Truth was, she missed him. They hadn't been partners for long, but they'd been through some tough times. She trusted Gaspar, and that was a rare thing for her.

She heard the weary grin in his voice when he replied, "Yeah, well, I'm always tired. You know that, Suzie Wong."

Gaspar had been wounded in the line of duty, more than once. He was collecting disability pay before she'd met him. But he never gave up or gave in to the pain, and he'd never left her without backup, either. As he'd put it, he had five kids and twenty years to go before he could rest.

But all of that was before he'd retired and left her without a partner.

"So what's up?" Kim pulled the heavy robe closer, took a big swig of the coffee, and waited.

"I heard you got called out to New Hampshire," he said quietly.

Kim frowned and her tone notched over into annoyance. "How the hell?"

Did she have a leak to worry about now? Since her Reacher assignment was so far off the books even the FBI's black ops people couldn't find it, the only person who might have told him where she was and why was the Boss. Which was not the least bit likely. She felt her resting heart rate kick up about twenty beats a minute.

"Climb down off the ledge, Otto. Smithers called me from the Laconia airport yesterday. Said he'd be picking you up and wanted to know whether he should wait for me," Gaspar replied patiently. He paused to let his explanation sink in. "I called to offer my help. Long distance. Such as it is."

Kim's pulse slowed and after a couple of steadying breaths, she said, "Thanks. I may need to take you up on that. You have all that pricey tech at your fingertips now. Could come in handy."

"Exactly. And I'm not constrained by FBI rules or unbridled ambition or any sort of neurotic need to please the Boss," he said, suggesting she was laced tightly into a straitjacket by all three.

Which she was. No way around it. Not until she found Reacher and could claw her way out. And maybe not even then.

She did have a driving ambition and she wouldn't apologize for that. Even though she'd need a miracle to make it to the FBI Director's job after everything that had happened. She'd bent a lot of FBI rules and broken a few more since this assignment started, all of which would hound her indefinitely.

But she'd have a snowball's chance in hell of making

Director if she quit the bureau. Not that she'd quit. Except for her marriage, which was not her fault or her choice, she'd never quit anything in her life. She wouldn't start down the quitter's road now.

"How long are you going to keep me hanging here, Sunshine?" Gaspar asked in that low, lazy way that meant his wife and kids were still sleeping.

Gaspar's fifth child and only son had been born a few weeks ago. The latest arrival proved to be the last straw for his FBI career. He'd said he needed a better paying job and that's why he retired. Which was probably true. Or at least, the desire to take care of his family was a big part of his motivation.

He'd promised to keep helping her until she found Reacher. Neither of them were sure exactly how he could help without being physically by her side, though.

"I can't send you the files now that you're no longer on the team," Kim said, and he picked up the bait just as she'd hoped. Every conversation taking place on this phone was recorded.

"10-4, copy that." He hesitated as if he had more to say, and then she heard a baby crying in the background. Instead, he rang off. "Gotta go. Keep in touch."

The next thing she heard was dead air. Which lasted about five seconds before she got confirmation. A padded envelope on her breakfast tray that she hadn't noticed earlier began vibrating. The envelope was exactly like several she'd received before.

She picked up the envelope, tore it open, dumped the burner cell phone onto the sofa beside her, and stared at its dancing for a while.

"Otto," she said when she answered, whipping her head around. She narrowed her eyes, looking for devices the Boss might have commandeered to spy on her.

There were several options. The television, the phones, and her laptop could all have been remotely programmed to do the job. Hell, about a zillion flowers on the ridiculous wallpaper could hide almost anything.

"You've become exceedingly paranoid lately," the Boss said, confirming her suspicions. He could see her. Otherwise, why say something like that?

She said nothing.

"You're interviewing Shaw and Amos this morning," he said.

"Yes."

"And after that?"

"Nothing in the files you sent me would have attracted Reacher to Laconia." She picked up a well-worn flimsy booklet, not many pages, maybe about the size of an L.L. Bean summer catalogue but not nearly as sophisticated. It wasn't dated, but the yellowed pages suggested it was a few years old, at least. It looked like someone had created it on a home computer for locals to use and passed a few copies around. She flipped it open to the correct page. "But I found four Reachers living in this general area. If Jack came anywhere near Laconia, he probably had a good reason to look them up."

"Such as?"

"You tell me."

The silence lasted awhile. She waited.

"Give me the names. I'll get whatever intel we have," he said, finally.

"David Reacher, Mark Reacher, William Reacher," she said, reading the addresses and phone numbers from the page slowly enough for him to jot them down.

"I thought you said four?"

She smirked. "So I did. The fourth is listed as Old Man Reacher."

"And you think there's some significance in that?"

"You tell me," she said again.

He sighed, as if he'd long ago resigned himself to her insubordination. "Call me back after you interview Shaw and Amos."

Once again, she was holding nothing but dead air. She'd have called him a few choice names, but she knew he could see her and hear her and she wouldn't give him the satisfaction.

She dropped the burner phone onto the sofa, grabbed her toiletries, and walked into the bathroom. He might have listening devices planted there, too, but even the Boss wasn't crude enough to put cameras inside her bathroom.

She hoped.

She brushed her teeth, flushed the toilet, and turned on the shower. Before she stepped into the hot water, she sent a text to Gaspar. He'd know what to do.

It was already after seven o'clock. Smithers would be here in forty-five minutes.

She took a brief hot shower, toweled off, and dressed quickly in black jeans and a black turtleneck sweater. Heavy socks and boots on her feet and a wool blazer completed her outfit, which was pretty much the same as yesterday's. She swept her hair back into a tight bun and pinned it to the base of her neck.

Kim rummaged in her laptop bag until she found what she wanted, snagged her parka, and moved into the corridor. She'd bought three burners from three different locations at the Detroit airport, just in case. She'd also sent three burners to Gaspar by overnight delivery service. She'd labeled them to be sure she called the correct numbers.

Seven-thirty. She barely had time to leave the building, place the call, and get back before Smithers showed up asking too many questions. She slid her laptop into the bag, tossed the strap over her shoulder, and hurried down the front stairs to the lobby, prepared to do battle with the sticky front door.

A couple of agents on Smithers's team were on their way out. Kim wasn't a particularly religious person, but she gave a little prayer of thanks when she saw they'd opened the front door. She hurried up behind them and slipped through before they closed the door behind them.

On the porch, she pulled out the first burner and dialed the number she'd memorized. Gaspar picked up immediately.

"I don't have much time," she said, as she hurried to the sidewalk, trusting him to understand the situation.

"Tell me what you need."

"I'll text you four names, addresses, and phone numbers on burner number two. I need everything you can get as soon as you can get it," she replied.

"Is this going to get me killed, Suzie Wong?" he teased, with a hint of seriousness.

She squeezed her eyes shut and crossed her fingers and forced a lighthearted tone into her voice. "After all the times I've saved your ass, Chico, you think I'd want your corpse on my conscience now?"

He rewarded her effort with a genuine laugh before he hung up. She pulled the second burner from her pocket and texted the data she had available on the four Reachers as she made her way back to The Laconia Inn.

CHAPTER ELEVEN

Saturday, February 26
7:05 a.m.

Syracuse, New York

LAST NIGHT WHEN JAKE returned to the room, Julia was already in her bed. She hadn't spoken to him, which probably meant she was really pissed off. Not that he'd expected her to be grateful or anything. Especially after she'd called him Sir Galahad in that sneering tone.

He'd ignored her.

She might have lain awake for a while, but Jake had been blissfully unaware. The tension of driving through the blizzard, beer drinking, and fighting Carl, had compounded his exhaustion. He had slept eight hours and twelve minutes without interruption.

When he opened his eyes lazily he heard a noise. He turned his head toward the closed door. Maybe maids outside his room.

He stretched and yawned loudly enough to be sure Julia heard, just in case she awakened disoriented or something. He needn't have bothered. She was already gone. Her backpack was gone, too.

Which suited him just fine.

He was in no rush to leave. But his stomach growled and he realized he was hungry. Coffee would be good, too. This wasn't the kind of hotel that provided room service, but there was a do-it-yourself breakfast set out downstairs, he recalled the desk clerk telling him last night.

Jake threw back the covers and pulled on his jeans. He slipped his torso into yesterday's sweatshirt, stuffed his feet into his boots, and grabbed his coat off the desk chair near the door. Which was when he noticed Julia had written something on the notepad by the phone.

Thanks for the lift. Sorry about Carl. Drive safely. And almost as an afterthought, she'd dashed off *Don't pick up hitchikers! Julia.*

The note made him grin. He crushed the paper in his big paw and tossed it into the trash can on his way out in search of breakfast. He'd come back to shower and then get on the road. He was going to Cleveland by way of Buffalo, which was where Julia was headed. If he saw her on the road, maybe he'd pass her and wave before he backed up to offer her a ride.

He tired of waiting for the elevator and hoofed it downstairs in search of the advertised free breakfast in the lobby. The best thing about the setup was a two-gallon urn of hot coffee. The rest was pastries and bite-sized muffins. No eggs or toast or bacon. He filled two large cups with the coffee and grabbed a paw full of muffins to quiet his rumbling stomach, wondering how far he'd need to travel to find a good diner.

Jake went back to his room for the shower, dressed in clean jeans and a clean sweater, stuffed the dirty clothes into a plastic bag and made a mental note to find a laundry at some point. He donned his coat again, collected his backpack, and glanced around the small room to be sure he hadn't left anything.

He'd paid the bill last night, but he stopped at the registration desk to drop off the keys and formally check out. These roadside hotels had been known to add a few extra charges to the credit card. He wanted a receipt to prove the extras weren't his. Just in case. He didn't have money to burn. Briefly, he wondered what that would be like.

"Okay if I fill my thermos before I hit the road?" he asked the young woman behind the counter.

"Sure thing," she smiled and waved toward the small breakfast nook.

She seemed friendly enough, so he asked her another question. "Any place near here where a guy with a big appetite can get some reasonably priced eggs and bacon?"

"Not really." She shook her head and waved her hand in the right direction. "But if you get on the interstate going toward Buffalo, you'll find some breakfast places the long-haul truckers like not too far down the road. Shouldn't be too expensive."

He nodded. "Got it. Thanks."

When he stepped outside he noticed the blizzard had ended. The sun was already up and rising in one of the bluest skies he'd seen for days. But the temperature was still below freezing so he didn't stand around to admire the weather.

He hurried toward the Jeep, stowed his gear, found his thermos, and returned to fill it before he got going again. He had plenty of gas for now. While the Jeep was warming up, he took a quick look at the map on his phone. Five hours to Cleveland if he took the interstate and seven hours if he didn't. He had plenty of time, but he was hungry. Food first. Then he could enjoy the scenery.

He pulled out of the hotel parking lot and followed the signs to I-90 west. Two and a half hours to Buffalo. He glanced at the clock. Yep, it was almost eight o'clock. Surely, he'd find a truck stop with a decent diner before he reached Buffalo.

CHAPTER TWELVE

Saturday, February 26
7:59 a.m.
Laconia, New Hampshire

KIM HAD FINISHED HER texts to Gaspar and was almost back to the inn when Smithers called. The sun had finally peeked over the horizon, bathing the snow with pink as if a child had spilled her watercolors everywhere.

"Are you running late?" she asked and picked up the pace as much as possible, given the snowy sidewalk.

"I came down a few minutes early to start the SUV and get some heat going in here. I'll pick you up at the front door in three minutes," he replied.

"Perfect." She disconnected and trotted the remaining distance to The Laconia Inn where she stood reading the historic marker out front.

The marker touted the inn as one of the finest early Federal period houses in the state. Originally built by Thomas Finch, the town's most prominent citizen, the inn was both modernized and virtually unchanged. The description said it was a two-story structure, with a hip roof, large central chimney, clapboard siding, and a rubblestone foundation capped by dressed fieldstones. The Laconia Inn had remained in the Finch family and was now owned and operated by Theron Finch.

By the time she'd finished reading, her toes were numb, her nose was red, and Smithers had pulled the SUV to a stop at the curb. Kim hustled around the front of the vehicle, placed her laptop case on the floor, and climbed inside. He handed her a cup of hot coffee before he rolled the big vehicle into the travel lane.

She grinned. "You're a good partner, you know that?"

He nodded and turned the wheel to make a right. "That's what they all say."

She held the cup in both hands for warmth and sipped. "Tell me about Laconia P.D. Detectives Shaw and Amos. How much cooperation will we get?"

He shot her a quizzical look. "Whaddaya mean? They're cops. We're cops. Of course they'll cooperate. We're all on the same team. Good guys against the bad guys, right?"

Kim hesitated and gave a quick nod. "Yeah. Sure. Why not."

Normally, he'd be right. But nothing about the Reacher assignment had ever been normal. She'd been tasked to interview local cops in several jurisdictions while she was collecting background data on Reacher. So far, none of the cops she'd approached had been anything close to cooperative. Not if they knew anything about Reacher, anyway.

Smithers was different. He'd never met Reacher. He had nothing to hide. He'd done the job the right way from the beginning. Which was one of the reasons she was willing to pair up with him now.

But Smithers wasn't her partner. He hadn't been read in on

the Reacher file. And he wasn't likely to be. So she changed her approach.

"Any clue how or when Shaw and Amos had dealings with Reacher?"

Smithers shook his head. "I didn't even know Reacher was a question to ask until I heard you were coming. I haven't spoken to either Shaw or Amos since I found out. How about you clue me in."

"I would if I could."

Smithers scowled. "You want my help, don't you think you owe me some honesty?"

"I don't make the rules," she shrugged.

"No, you just pick and choose which rules you're going to follow," he said angrily. "I'm volunteering here, Otto. My assignment is not Reacher. I've got plenty to do out at the motel. You want my help, you owe me the intel I need to do the job."

She cocked her head as if she was thinking about it. He wasn't wrong. But she wasn't, either. If she told him any intel at all, the Boss wouldn't like it. Not even a little. "You've got a valid point. I'll ask. For now, just tell me about Shaw and Amos."

He breathed heavily for a bit before he relented. "Both seem pretty solid. Exactly the kind of locals the FBI wants these days. They called us in because the motel scene was way over their heads."

Kim said, "It's a good sign that they recognized they lacked the right stuff to do the job."

"They didn't have the manpower or the budget or the expertise." Smithers stopped for a traffic light and rolled through when it turned green. "Helped us set up. Answered questions. Gave us some desk space and a secure internet connection."

"That's it?" Kim asked.

"That's all we needed." Smithers parked the SUV out in front of another historic building not too far from the hotel. The sign out front said *Laconia Police Department.*

Kim unfastened her seat belt and reached for the door latch. "Since I have the appointment, let me take the lead."

"Works for me," Smithers replied curtly.

She pulled up the hood on her parka and walked quickly. Smithers followed behind her along the sidewalk and inside the building.

The public lobby was tall, tiled, and formal. The mahogany reception desk was manned by a civilian. Kim pulled her badge wallet from her inside pocket and showed it to the woman. "We have an appointment with Detectives Shaw and Amos," she said politely.

The woman picked up the phone and waved them toward a couple of chairs. They didn't wait long. The two detectives pushed through the double doors to the right of the desk. Both looked like the profiles of solid professionals she'd studied from the Boss's file.

The man nodded toward Smithers and extended his hand toward Kim. "I'm Laconia P.D. Chief of Detectives Jim Shaw, this is Detective Brenda Amos."

Shaw was mid-fifties, red hair, and heavier than he should have been for his five-ten height. His Irish face was pleasant enough. He looked like exactly what he was. A cop, through and through.

Amos wore her experience well enough. The Boss's file placed her mid-forties, which looked about right. She was blonde, slender, and seven inches taller than Kim. Most people were taller than Kim, so she didn't hold that against the detective.

What struck Kim immediately, and not in a good way, was how Amos was Reacher's type. Early on, Gaspar had noticed that Reacher's women were always about the same height, same build. Often blonde, but a few she'd met were dark-haired. And always cops of one kind or another. Gaspar said Reacher had a fetish or something.

It was possible that Amos and Reacher had been lovers. If true, the assignment would be a lot more difficult. For some reason, Reacher's women were abnormally suspicious and tight-lipped where Reacher was concerned. Kim chalked the reticence up to a desire to both protect Reacher and to hide Reacher's illegal activity. Which made little sense unless the woman was also involved in that illegal activity. After all, Reacher certainly didn't need anyone else's protection from physical threats.

Shaw said, "Let's get into a conference room where we can talk. This way."

He led them back through an open area staffed with plainclothes people milling around. The desks were paired, back to back, but only half a dozen were being used. It was Saturday and winter, which probably meant a skeleton crew. Like every cop shop everywhere, the desks were cluttered with computers, files, papers, and phones.

Kim followed Shaw into a conference room at the end of a long corridor with offices on either side. An oval table ringed by leather chairs on wheels filled the room. A mahogany cabinet topped with a coffee service and a tray of pastries filled one corner.

Smithers walked in behind Kim and Amos brought up the rear. When she came inside, she closed the door.

"Coffee?" Shaw said, as he moved toward the aromatic corner.

Kim said, "Sure."

He offered her two cups, one of which she gave to Smithers.
They took seats across the table. When everyone was comfortable,
Shaw folded his hands in his lap, leaned back in the chair, looked
at Smithers and asked, "What kind of progress are you making out
there at the motel?"

"Not much, I'm afraid. We're still processing the scene.
We've expedited the autopsies and we hope to have some of our
forensic results next week," Smithers replied.

"Still nine bodies?" Amos asked. Her accent was slightly
southern, but the rounded tones were well sanded. Probably by
her military service.

Her file said U.S. Army, Military Police, like Reacher.
Which meant she'd have even more loyalty to him, Kim figured.

Smithers said, "Yep. Nine bodies so far. Are you expecting
us to find more?"

"Hard to say." Amos took a deep breath and shook her head.
"We've looked at our missing persons reports. We have three
still unaccounted for. All males. We sent the files to you guys
yesterday."

"That'll help," Smithers said.

Kim waited to talk until after the chatter died. "Speaking of
missing persons, we're looking for one. We're hoping you can
help."

Shaw raised his eyebrows along with his coffee cup. "Happy
to do it. What's the name?"

"Reacher," Kim said.

Amos replied, "There are a few Reachers around here.
Which one are you trying to find?"

Kim cocked her head. "Jack Reacher."

"You think he's involved in that business out at the motel?"
Shaw asked.

"We don't have any evidence to support that idea. Right now, we need to find him. Then we can ask. First things first," Kim replied.

Shaw did what most people did when Kim asked about Reacher the first time. He stalled.

He rolled his chair toward the coffee, picked up the pot and rolled back to the table. He held the coffee out invitingly. Kim offered her empty cup and so did the others. Shaw rolled his chair back to the server, replaced the almost empty pot, and returned to his spot across the table.

During the stalling process, Shaw had made a decision. He turned to Amos. "A guy by that name came through the year before last looking for his family, didn't he?"

Amos nodded. "He said his father had been born here. But we didn't find any record of the birth. We did find an old police report suggesting that his father had been a witness to an assault and battery here in Laconia. But no arrests were made and there was no follow up in the files."

Her delivery was straightforward. No facial tics or obvious efforts to obfuscate the truth. If Amos was lying, she was damn good at it. Kim figured she'd told the truth, or most of it, anyway. It was curious that Amos and Shaw remembered Reacher after all this time.

Interrogating cops was a tricky business under the best of circumstances. Cops had good training so they knew all the interrogation tricks. And they were good at avoiding the questions they didn't want to answer truthfully.

Kim would have bet fifty dollars that Amos knew a lot more than she was saying. But Shaw was her boss. Whatever Amos and Reacher had been involved in, she might not want Shaw to know about it. Especially if a few laws had been twisted or broken.

Kim had been through the same dance with Reacher's contacts several times before. Reacher did whatever the hell he wanted, regardless of the law. The local cops joined in for unknown reasons. But cops couldn't join up with Reacher's illegal activities and expect to keep their jobs. At least, in theory.

"What did Reacher do with that intel?" Kim asked.

"Hard to do something with nothing," Amos replied.

Uh huh. Kim cocked her head. "So after you came up empty searching the old files for his family, Reacher just quit and walked away?"

"I didn't have him followed or anything. How would I know?" Amos said, a little too sharply.

"He comes all the way out here, looking for something, and then he just gives up? Because you told him there was nothing in the files? And you never saw Reacher again?" Kim paused to let the absurdity settle. "I have to tell you, that doesn't sound like Reacher at all. I'd say that's downright unlikely."

"Unlikely in what way?" Amos raised her chin and lowered her voice, as if she might be offended by the implications. Offended enough to fight about it.

Kim ignored the question and directed her gaze to Shaw. "Reacher get into any kind of trouble while he was here?"

Shaw said, "Why do you ask?"

"Wherever he goes, trouble finds him. And usually local law enforcement knows about it," Kim replied.

Shaw refused to meet her steady gaze when he said, "It was a year and a half ago. We've had a lot of people through here since then. But as far as I know, we didn't get any complaints about him and he wasn't arrested. He must have solved his problems on his own."

Kim said, "I'd appreciate it if you'd check your files. I'd like to know whether any complaints were made about Reacher while he was here."

Shaw nodded. "We can do that. But I think one of us would remember complaints if we'd had any."

Kim paused for a bit, as if she was thinking things over. Then she glanced at Smithers. "Anything you'd like to know?"

He shook his head and grinned. "Nope. I'm good to go."

They thanked Shaw and Amos and stood to leave.

Shaw said, "Come back again if you need anything else."

Amos said, "I'll walk you out."

They headed through the corridor and back to the open area where the skeleton crew was still working. Things were quiet in the room and probably in the town, given how freaking cold it was outside. Cold was a deterrent to crime everywhere, according to FBI statistics.

At the door before she walked through, Kim turned and said, "You were an Army MP. Reacher was an Army MP. You're not protecting him out of some sort of misplaced bothers-in-arms loyalty, are you?"

Amos replied, "No."

"Did you find him attractive?" Kim asked to shake her up.

Amos's eyes widened and her nostrils flared. "You mean were we dating or something? Absolutely not."

If true, that was far from Reacher's usual MO, but Amos played it so straight that Kim actually believed her in the moment.

"Okay," Kim said, offering her hand. "We'll call you if we need anything else."

"You do that," Amos said curtly. The clear implication was that it would be a hot day in Laconia in February before Amos would help Kim Otto with anything.

Smithers stepped in to smooth the ruffled feathers. "I'll get those autopsy reports to you as soon as we have them, Detective Amos."

She nodded and turned her back and stomped away without another word.

"That went well. You make friends wherever you go, don't you? Always a good idea to piss off the local cops," Smithers said, a heavy load of irony in his tone.

Kim said nothing as she bundled up and marched toward the SUV. Smithers followed.

At the vehicle, Smithers climbed in and started the engine and the heat while Kim checked her phones. On Gaspar's burner she found a text message: "Data located. Find it in the usual place."

When she was settled in the passenger seat, Smithers pulled away from the curb as he asked, "Now what?"

She briefly considered telling him the truth. She might have done so on the spot if they hadn't been sitting in a bureau vehicle that was fully wired. Instead, she said, "I'm starving. Is there any place in this town to get a decent breakfast?"

CHAPTER THIRTEEN

Saturday, February 26
11:15 a.m.
Manchester, New Hampshire

TREVOR HAD SPENT YESTERDAY afternoon and evening arranging the mission. They boarded his private jet in Atlanta and landed at the executive airport in Boston, where Owen had rented a battered SUV. Less than an hour's drive put them in the back parking lot at a Day's Inn in Manchester, where a second rental awaited.

The five-year-old Chevy Suburban with the dirty New Hampshire license plate looked like it had battled an eighteen-wheeler in a road rally and barely survived. Most witnesses wouldn't even notice the filthy white giant on the snow-covered roads, which suited Trevor's needs perfectly.

"Okay. Let's hit the road," he said as he moved into the passenger seat.

Owen took the wheel while Oscar lifted the hatch and stowed the bags, and then sat behind Trevor in the back seat.

Owen and Oscar had previously examined the air field where Trevor's partner, Lange, was last seen before he disappeared months ago. Trevor wanted to see it for himself. He didn't explain his reasons. They worked for him. He owed them no explanations.

He had made some calls last night before he finalized his plans. The air field wasn't on any kind of map. Which meant that Lange had to have known about it in advance. Otherwise, he'd never have found the place.

The field was too remote and private to qualify for executive aviation. It was a hobby field at best. No tower, no log, no reporting requirements of any kind. The sort of landing strip where pilots might set down and passengers deplane and no one would see it happen.

Trevor had organized an air taxi from Syracuse because he wanted to observe the process Lange had used. The last time anyone had seen Lange alive was deplaning in Manchester almost two years ago. The air field was the perfect place to start the hunt.

"Park inside the fence. Level with the runway," Trevor said. Owen performed as instructed. Trevor checked his watch and lowered his window.

Ten minutes later, he heard the distant roar of a propeller plane. He raised binoculars to his eyes and waited. In the distance, he saw what he knew to be a twin engine Cessna bouncing in the wind.

"Flash your headlights twice," Trevor said. It was the pre-arranged signal.

Owen reached for the switch, flipped it off and on.

The plane came in low and landed. It rolled toward the Suburban and stopped. The pilot didn't shut down the engines.

No reason to. He had no passengers embarking and the grassy air strip had no amenities to visit. Nowhere to get coffee or wash up.

The pilot turned the plane around in a half circle, the engine noise loud enough to wake the dead, and then revved up and sped down the runway in the opposite direction.

Trevor watched until the plane lifted into the air and checked his watch again. From the time Trevor had seen the Cessna in the distance until it was airborne on its way home, thirty-four minutes had elapsed.

He figured ten minutes, max, for Lange to collect and store his gear in the Mercedes that had arrived to meet him. Meaning a total of forty-four minutes.

"Stay here," he instructed. He got out of the Suburban and used the binoculars to search the area around the open field. He saw no homes or businesses, no vehicles of any kind, and no evidence that anyone might have been close enough to see Lange's arrival back then, either.

Of course, that was almost two years ago. And from what Trevor had been able to piece together, Lange had arrived in the early dawn when even fewer people were likely to be in the area. But Trevor was willing to bet no one had seen Lange or the plane he rode in on.

He had a good grasp of the situation now. He nodded approval of Lange's likely successful efforts to be discreet. The situation might be salvageable still.

He checked his watch again, made a mental note of the time, and returned to the Suburban. "Let's go."

Owen slid the transmission into gear and pulled out of the gate. He turned left and then right navigating the back roads toward Laconia. The interstate would have been faster, but

Trevor was calling the shots. He'd said Lange would have taken the back roads, leaving no room for discussion.

They'd traveled about twenty miles when Trevor directed Owen to stop at a decrepit mail box store near Concord. It was privately owned and not at all prosperous. The place had been selected by Trevor's associates in South Africa.

"Park around back and leave the motor running," he said. Again, Owen did as he was told without comment.

Trevor handed Oscar three packing slips. "Collect these three packages inside. Don't talk to anyone."

Oscar took the packing slips, trudged through the snow to the entrance and disappeared inside. He returned a few minutes later, breathing heavily, arms laden with three large boxes, and stored them in the back of the Suburban.

Once Oscar was settled inside the cabin again, Trevor said, "Drive another ten miles north, toward Laconia. There's a rest stop. Pull over there."

Owen nodded and followed directions.

The rest stop was deserted, but the parking lot had been cleared of snow recently enough. Trevor pointed toward the far end of the lot. "Park there and turn the ignition off."

Owen complied. He glanced in the rearview mirror. Oscar relaxed in the seat behind him. If Oscar was feeling tense, he'd have shown it. One thing Oscar couldn't do was mask his emotions.

"Let's get those packages opened," Trevor said as he got out of the SUV.

He looked for surveillance cameras and, as expected, didn't see any. His intel had been perfect so far. No reason to suspect otherwise.

He closed the door and walked around to the back of the SUV. Owen and Oscar joined him there.

Trevor gestured toward the three boxes. Owen and Oscar pulled them closer. Trevor pulled a knife from his pocket and slit the tape seals on all three. He tapped one box and nodded toward Oscar, the second one was for Owen. Trevor kept the third box for himself.

Oscar's box contained a steel briefcase. Inside the briefcase were expensive handguns and extra ammunition.

Owen's box was longer and narrower and heavier. It held a long gun case. He unzipped the case to admire the two rifles, two scopes, and enough ammunition to take out an entire village.

All of the weapons and assorted paraphernalia were untraceable. They had been acquired and shipped overnight. Trevor's networking operation was illegal but effective and never failed. He had set it up himself long ago specifically to handle such things.

Trevor's box was the shape of a large cube and had arrived via the same route. He slid the knife blade along the tape seal slowly, careful to avoid any damage to the contents. He opened the cardboard flaps and lifted a black, long range quadcopter drone from the box. He set it down carefully before he unpacked two chargers and three fully charged batteries. The serial numbers and all identifying marks had been removed from each item, as he'd instructed.

Trevor had significant experience with drones and cameras. He'd used this particular drone before. It was good enough to suit his needs, and not so rare or specialized or expensive that it would encourage too many questions from bystanders. The drone boasted seven kilometers of operating range. Which was about four and a half miles, give or take. Each fully charged battery would last twenty-seven minutes. He didn't expect to need anything more powerful.

"Break those shipping boxes down and get rid of them. I'm going to test this." Trevor flew the drone around the parking lot for twenty minutes, getting the feel for its idiosyncrasies. It handled well enough. The images captured by the camera weren't good enough for a feature film at the multiplex, but would suffice for his purposes.

Owen and Oscar made quick work of the boxes. They stuffed three batches of the now flat cardboard into three different trash barrels at the opposite side of the parking lot. Owen used a disposable lighter to start the fires and they watched the cardboard burn to ashes.

Oscar lifted two of the barrels and dumped the ashes into the third barrel. He carried the third barrel to the top of a hill behind the comfort station and scattered the ashes in the wind. He watched until the swirling gray and black ash dissipated into the trees and then he put the barrel back where he'd found it.

When Owen and Oscar returned to the Suburban, Trevor had placed the drone on the carpet in the back of the vehicle. He opened the silver briefcase and removed three handguns. All three were loaded. He handed one to Owen and one to Oscar, along with extra ammunition.

Trevor collected the third pistol and extra ammunition for himself. "Let's go"

Owen closed the hatch on the Suburban and all three men settled again into the same places in the vehicle's cabin, like school children with assigned seats.

When they were on the road again, Trevor glanced at his watch. The stop cost them half an hour. But the weapons and the drone would prove to be worth the delay.

CHAPTER FOURTEEN

Saturday, February 26
12:00 p.m.
Laconia, New Hampshire

SMITHERS PARKED OUTSIDE A busy family restaurant
bustling with kids. He said, "This place is a madhouse, but the
food is great."

"Sounds perfect to me," Kim replied. Not because she was
particularly hungry. She wasn't. But a busy place full of
screaming kids and probably half the patrons using their phones
and the internet presented greater problems for the Boss and
anyone else who wanted to spy on her. Simply put, she might
get away with briefing Smithers in a place like this. It was a
damn sight more likely than discussing things with him in the
vehicle.

She slung the strap of her laptop case across her body and
climbed out onto the sidewalk. She put her head down and
trudged through the driving wind and bitter cold toward the
entrance, moving as fast as the snow-covered sidewalks allowed.

Smithers soon caught up with her. He reached the front door before she did and pulled it open, waiting for her to pass through first. Some women might have objected to the courtesy, but Mrs. Otto's daughter wasn't one of them.

"Thanks," she said, once she was inside and managed to stop her teeth from chattering. She stood behind a sign that said *Please Wait to be Seated.*

"You're welcome," Smithers replied. He unzipped his coat and pulled off his gloves. "We have more than our share of cold weather in New York. But I can honestly say I've never been colder than I've been here on this case."

She simply nodded because there was no way he'd be able to hear her reply. She could barely think over the cacophony of kids in various stages of shouting, screaming, laughing, pounding silverware, and just generally being kids. Combined with the parents making futile efforts to quiet them and the restaurant staff raising their own voices above the din to take food orders and the like, the noise was a palpable force.

Kim glanced around the place. She'd been right about patrons using phones and tablets, too. This must have been the busiest place in Laconia right at the moment. Which suited Kim's needs perfectly. She needed to download and read Gaspar's files on the four Reachers. The longer she could keep that information from both casual and determined spies, the better.

A harried woman dressed in a blue uniform with a checked apron noticed them from across the room and hustled over. She grabbed menus and placemats and waved them to follow her along the aisle between crowded booths.

The combination of spilled syrup and juices, slushy snow tracked in, and whatever else the diners had dropped, adhered Kim's boots to the tile floor with every step.

They fought the crowds deep into the restaurant and around a corner to a table where it was marginally quieter. The harried hostess laid paper placemats, flatware rolled in a napkin, and menus on the table.

"Someone will be here to take your order shortly," she promised before she hustled away.

Kim worked quickly and efficiently. She set up her laptop and a new encrypted hot spot with an untraceable internet protocol address. While she downloaded the encrypted files Gaspar had placed in her secure server, Smithers walked over to a serving station nearby. He poured coffee into two brown plastic mugs and brought them back to the table.

"Thanks." She nodded, sipped, and kept her eyes on the screen. The files downloaded swiftly and she disconnected.

Kim trusted no one except Gaspar. She'd developed and honed her healthy sense of skepticism over the course of the Reacher assignment and it had kept her alive. Her work was under the radar. She'd learned the hard way that she was better off keeping her secrets buried.

The Boss could easily trace her laptop, of course. She was betting that he was too busy doing other things at the moment. She'd delete the files as soon as she read them, along with all traces of the download. Which would be enough to keep the intel away from the Boss as long as he had no reason to suspect they ever existed.

"Are you going to clue me in here, Otto?" Smithers asked after a few minutes. The grumpy tone had returned to his voice. She didn't really blame him. She hated being kept in the dark and it made sense that Smithers wouldn't love it, either. But it wasn't her call. Never had been.

"Yeah. Just hang on until I read through this."

Gaspar had included maps to the homes and offices of all four of the Reachers listed in the ragged local phone book pamphlet she'd found in her room at the Laconia Inn. The first thing he'd noted was that the pamphlet was at least five years old. Maybe more.

He'd done more digging to update the data. And he'd sent short dossiers on each subject. Gaspar had always been her secret weapon on this assignment because he understood the way Reacher thought. Both men were army vets with similar backgrounds and training. She'd relied on him for Reacher's perspective when much of what Reacher did seemed unfathomable.

Since Gaspar retired from the FBI, she missed his constant presence. The loss was mitigated by the new job he'd transitioned to because he had full access to all sorts of intel that she simply couldn't access any other way. He'd promised to help her see this assignment through, and she'd promised to hold him to it.

Kim read through Gaspar's reports quickly. There were five names on his list, one more than the four listed in the pamphlet.

Only one was a viable subject for a personal interview today. The others were out of range.

Gaspar hadn't been able to identify the first, "Old Man Reacher," on short notice. The phone number was out of service. Without a first name, available databases were unable to locate him. Gaspar promised to keep looking.

The second, William Reacher, had retired to Arizona four or five years back. His biographical data was neither interesting nor relevant to Jack Reacher.

Things started to get interesting with the third name, Mark Reacher. He grew up near Laconia but no longer lived at the pamphlet's listed address. He'd moved to Boston from here.

After that, he worked as a hedge fund manager in Europe. Exact location currently unknown.

Fourth was David Reacher, Mark Reacher's older brother. David's dossier was slightly longer than the others. Kim scanned it for highlights. A local college professor until declining health made working impossible, he'd recently lost his battle with pancreatic cancer. He was cremated earlier this month.

Which meant she'd struck out. The pamphlet had seemed like a solid lead, but four out of the four potential interview subjects were not available.

But Gaspar's files contained a fifth name. One that seemed promising.

David Reacher's wife, Margaret. She still lived in Laconia with their son, Jake, who had recently graduated from Dartmouth. Margaret was a professor at the local college, too. And Jake had been accepted into law school starting in the fall. Harvard, no less.

The waitress finally showed up at their table, looking harried and exhausted. Smithers ordered the breakfast special by pointing to the sticky picture on the menu, and added a pot of coffee.

Kim glanced up from the laptop. She hadn't opened the menu, so she said, "Make it two, please."

The waitress made a couple of check marks on a notepad before she moved off toward the kitchen.

After a few minutes of silence, Smithers asked, "You gonna tell me what's so interesting in those files?"

Kim cocked her head and studied Smithers's annoyed expression. "Turns out there's a woman to interview for the background check I'm doing on Reacher. Her name is Margaret Reacher. Do you know her?"

Could she trust him? Should she? He wasn't her partner. He had no idea what her real assignment was or how it had changed since they'd worked together last. She wasn't authorized to read him in on the file or on her work.

Smithers had proved reliable when she and Gaspar worked on the Green Paint Killer case on his home turf. She'd relied on him then and he hadn't let her down. But she'd had Gaspar then, too.

Before she had to make a final decision, the waitress returned with their food. She plopped the plates down in front of them and dashed over to the serving station to fill up a plastic coffee pot and collect a small basket containing a variety of jams and butters. After she dropped those off at the table, she rushed away again without another word.

"That poor woman must be dead on her feet at the end of her shift every day," Kim said.

Smithers nodded as he tucked into the hot food.

The breakfast special turned out to be more fried food than she normally ate in a year. Fried eggs, fried ham, and fried potatoes. A slice of toast was the only thing that hadn't been fried. The rest was swimming in grease.

Kim picked up her fork and moved the eggs aside carefully to avoid breaking the yolks. Eggs prepared over easy were the worst. All that yellow stuff on the plate, congealing around everything else, was revolting. She lifted a bite of ham to her mouth and chewed while she waited.

Smithers seemed to understand she'd tell him nothing more in response to his inquiry about Gaspar's files. He didn't push her, but the scowl on his face meant he didn't like it, either. She wondered what he was holding back from her and whether his intel was something she needed to know.

His phone vibrated in his pocket a few minutes later. He answered, "Yeah…I see…okay. Send me what you've got so far. I'll follow up."

"Something turn up on the motel fire?" She asked by way of changing the subject when he hung up.

His case wasn't classified. Dozens of people were working on the motel fire. No one was making an effort to contain the results of that investigation. He had no reason to keep information from her. Which didn't mean he was being transparent, either.

Kim's case was different. He wasn't supposed to know anything about it beyond her cover story. She should keep it that way. At least for now. Controlling the flow of intel was the smart thing to do, even though she didn't feel good about it.

He nodded. "Yeah. The lab isolated the identification number on one of the torched vehicles. The Honda. The forensics guys chased it down."

"And?"

He shoveled a few more bites into his mouth, making her wait before he relented. "Turns out it came from Canada."

"You think the owner might be one of those nine bodies you found out there?" Kim asked.

"Maybe. You know how this goes. There are several possibilities and we just have to run each one down until we get a hit. The car could have been stolen. Or sold. Or a dozen other alternatives. First we've got to find out who owned the vehicle. We're looking at that now. But identifying the Honda is more than we had before. Progress." Smithers finished eating as he talked. He pushed his plate away and refilled his coffee.

"Do you need to get back to your team, then?" Kim pushed her barely touched food aside, too.

"They don't need me out there at the moment. I can drive you to your interview first. Unless you want me to drive you somewhere else," he replied.

Kim hesitated briefly, considering the alternatives, before she said, "That would be great. Thanks."

CHAPTER FIFTEEN

Saturday, February 26
2:00 p.m.
Laconia, New Hampshire

THE GPS SYSTEM AND the satellite radio system was easily
trackable for any hacker. Nothing she could do about that. Some
hackers put tracers in place on a GPS that were voice activated,
turning on only when they heard human voices requesting
driving directions using certain words such as *find* or *go to*. In an
attempt to buy a little time from those, she turned off the GPS
and put her finger across her lips to signal Smithers not to ask
about their destination.

He frowned.

Kim entered Margaret Reacher's address into one of the
burner phones and pointed toward the display as she gestured
straight ahead. Smithers arched his eyebrows but he didn't ask
questions.

Once he was on the road, she said, "How was your
breakfast?"

Smithers frowned. "Fine. I noticed you didn't eat much."

She smiled, pointing to the phone's screen to indicate a right turn up ahead. "The ham was okay. I'm not a fan of eggs."

Smithers shrugged.

Smithers followed the directions along Main Street and turned into a residential neighborhood near the river. Three more turns and he slowed to read the house numbers on the historic old homes.

The street was unnaturally quiet. Houses were widely spaced, but close enough that residents could be neighborly during the warmer months. Kim imagined barbeques and kids playing on the sidewalks. The area felt like that kind of place. Nice way for a kid to grow up.

Kim held up her palm and gestured toward a green two-story bungalow that had been constructed at least a hundred years earlier. The snow-covered lawn was probably well tended in the summer. Kim imagined flower gardens surrounding the house and flowing into the back yard. But today, snow drifted and piled and packed everywhere.

There was a detached two-car garage in the back and, running along the left side of the house, a narrow, snow-covered driveway.

They climbed out of the SUV and stomped across the snowpack to the front steps. The wide porch had been cleaned off recently, which made movement a little easier. Kim knocked the snow off her boots and rang the doorbell. She stepped away from the door to wait.

Smithers stood stiffly beside her, gloved hands clasped in front of his flat belly. "Are we expected?"

"You mean, do we have an appointment? No," Kim replied. "But this seems like the kind of town where we don't need one, doesn't it?"

He nodded. "Indeed, it does. But cops are not usually as welcome as the neighbors."

A light flipped on inside and the heavy door opened on the other side of the glass storm door. Kim recognized the woman from the driver's license photo Gaspar had included in her file. Margaret Reacher née Preston was a slender brunette. Brown eyes. Average height, meaning about five-four. Her date of birth placed her squarely in the fifth decade of life.

Kim pulled her badge wallet out of her pocket and displayed it. Smithers did the same. Then she pulled open the storm door. "Mrs. Reacher? I'm FBI Special Agent Kim Otto. This is my colleague, Special Agent Reggie Smithers. May we come in?"

Mrs. Reacher blanched. She looked as if her knees might give way and she tightened her grip on the doorknob.

"Are you not feeling well, Mrs. Reacher?" Smithers stepped forward to offer a steadying hand to guide her into a chair in the living room. "Let's sit here."

"Can we get you something?" Kim asked as she closed the front doors against the wind. In all her life, she'd never met a woman with a tendency to swoon. She didn't know exactly what to do now that she'd met one. "How about a cup of hot tea?"

Mrs. Reacher nodded weakly and waved Kim toward the back of the house.

Kim followed along the corridor until she found the pleasant kitchen. She filled the electric tea kettle and plugged it into the outlet. She searched the cabinets nearby for tea, sugar, and milk. Kim liked her tea black, like her coffee, but not everyone did.

A woman who swoons would most likely want milk and sugar. She found a box of shortbread cookies and a plate to put them on, but she drew the line at paper doilies for the cookies. Kim wasn't domestic.

While she waited for the water to heat, she stepped into the hallway to look at the photos hanging on the wall. Most of them were decades old.

She pulled out her phone and took quick snaps of the pictures before she studied a few of them more closely.

A formal wedding photo, maybe twenty years old or so. Margaret Reacher was the bride and, Kim assumed, the groom was David Reacher.

He might have been related to Jack Reacher, but if so, recessive genes in the pool had asserted themselves. David was a slight man. Dark hair and dark eyes. He looked gentle and kind. If he'd ever been in trouble of any sort, he bore no scars to prove it in any of the photos.

There were also several framed pictures of the boy Kim assumed was Jake Reacher. Gaspar's file had not included any photos of him.

These chronicled his growth from infancy through various sports, proms, and the like. The high school and college graduation photos of the boy flanked by both parents drew Kim's focus like a magnet attracts steel.

Jake was fair haired and his eyes were an icy blue. Even in high school, he was big. Six-four, Kim guessed. And heavy. Maybe two-fifty. His hands were huge. So were his feet. Jake towered over both parents and he looked like neither of them.

He was spawned by Reacher. Had to be. He looked like Jack Reacher. He had the same body type. His coloring was the same.

Could Jake Reacher have been adopted by these two people? Is this why the Boss had sent her here? What was she supposed to do with this intel?

Kim started again with the infant photos and walked along the corridor, pausing a moment before each picture. Viewing the images in sequence was like watching Jack Reacher grow up, if he'd been born into a kinder, gentler family and raised inside the continental U.S.

She leaned closer to the most recent photo of Jake with an old guy in a wheelchair and studied it intently, as if it might answer all of her questions.

The whistling kettle startled her and she jumped. Her heart rate elevated for a couple of seconds until she realized what the noise was about. She rushed to turn off the kettle before Smithers came looking for the cause of her distraction.

By the time she returned to the living room with the tray, Mrs. Reacher seemed to have gathered some composure. Smithers was seated across from her, soothing her with his resonant tones as he might have settled a terrified wild animal.

Mrs. Reacher poured tea, added cream and sugar, and sipped, all deliberately, as if she wasn't quite ready to face conversation.

"Has something happened?" she finally asked, in a breathless voice.

Kim cocked her head. It was a curious question to open with, but it made the woman's behavior understandable. She must have assumed they'd arrived with bad news. Since her husband had already passed away, she was probably worried about her son.

That made sense, but did nothing to explain her reasons.

"You're asking about Jake?" Kim said. With the mention of his name, Margaret Reacher tensed. Her eyes widened and her face blanched again, as if she might faint. Kim would never learn anything from her if she didn't relax the woman first. "Nothing's happened to Jake, Mrs. Reacher. We're here to ask you some questions for a background check. That's all."

"A background check? What kind of background check?"
She seemed more bewildered than afraid now.

"I'm sorry we frightened you. We didn't intend to," Smithers
said. He gave her shoulder a pat and poured tea for himself and
for Kim. Perhaps an effort to normalize the situation. He sat back
in his chair.

Kim took the cup and then set it down on the table next to
her chair. "I'm assigned to the FBI's Special Personnel Task
Force, ma'am. We're doing a background check for a man who
is being considered for a classified assignment. His last name is
the same as yours. That's how we found you. We need to learn
what you know about his fitness for the work."

"Please call me Margaret," she said absently as she shook
her head. "You mean, like a military assignment or spying or
something? I don't have anyone in my family who would be
applying for anything like that. None of the Prestons are working
for the government at all, unless you include the teachers. And I
can't imagine what elementary school teachers would have to
offer the FBI."

"The man we're interested in might have been your
husband's relative, Margaret," Kim replied.

"Oh. Well, David came from a very small family. His
parents are deceased and he only has one brother." She paused
and her eyes widened as if she'd experienced an epiphany. "Is it
Mark Reacher you're asking about? Because I don't know much
about him. Mark was a lot younger than David. They were never
close. I've never even met him. And I haven't heard anything
about him in years."

Smithers asked, "Do you know where Mark Reacher is?"

Margaret shook her head. "Last I heard, and it was a long
time ago, he was working somewhere in Europe. Like I said, he

and David were estranged. Mark didn't even come to David's funeral."

Kim nodded. "Why were they estranged?"

"It bewilders me, too. I never had a brother and always wanted one. I can't imagine anything that would make me stop communicating with a brother." Margaret shook her head again. "All I know is that Mark left home right after high school and he never came back. He wasn't at our wedding. He's never met my son."

She'd offered a solid opening by mentioning Jake again, giving Kim a logical reason to follow up. "I saw the photos of Jake on the wall when I went to the kitchen. How old is he now?"

Like every loving mother everywhere, Margaret seemed happy to talk about her only child. She smiled and her eyes almost twinkled. "Jake's twenty-two. Graduated from Dartmouth early so his dad could be there."

Smithers chimed in as if he was glad to have a safe topic, finally. "Dartmouth's a great school. I'd love my kids to go there. But I've heard it's pricey…"

"Very expensive," Margaret nodded. "We were thrilled when Jake got admitted. It was a stretch for us, but he received some smaller scholarships from a few local groups. He worked summers. We borrowed the rest because David thought it was important."

"Jake's a good student, then?" Kim asked.

For the first time since she first mentioned her son, Margaret frowned. "Good enough to get admitted to Dartmouth. But mainly they wanted him to play football."

"The Big Green." Smithers said with the appreciation of a man who'd played football in college himself. He flashed a wide grin of approval. "Very competitive. He must have shown significant talent in high school, too. Good for him."

Margaret smiled weakly and with a lot less enthusiasm. "He survived college football long enough to graduate. I'm grateful for that."

"Jake looks like a big guy in those photos. Along with the talent, he certainly has the bulk for the game," Kim replied.

Margaret nodded. "He was a star on the Laconia High School team."

"My brothers played college football, but they weren't good enough for the pros. What about Jake? Is he planning to play professionally?" Kim asked, attempting to build rapport for the more difficult questions to follow.

"He's going to law school." The proud mama smile returned. "Harvard. Starting next fall."

"Harvard's a great school and studying law will serve him well in life. I went to Georgetown law school, myself. Double major along with my MBA. But that was a long time ago," Kim said. "I'd love to meet Jake. Sounds like we'd have a few things in common. Is he here?"

Margaret's frown seemed to darken her entire body. She shook her head. "He's on vacation."

"Good man. I'm sure he needs a break. Sunshine and beaches would probably be welcome to him right about now," Smithers shivered like it was cold inside as well as out. As if he and Jake were besties or something. "Where'd he go?"

"He's driving. He said he wanted to see the country." Margaret closed down completely. Her lips formed a hard line and she folded her hands together in her lap, gripping tightly as if she might be holding a valuable treasure she was determined to keep to herself.

Kim moved through the roadblock. "Margaret, as I mentioned, we're completing a background check. We're after information about a former Army officer. Actually, Jake looks a bit like him in those photos."

As soon as the words were out of Kim's mouth, Margaret's spine seemed to lose its stability. She crumpled in a heap on the sofa, dissolving into tears.

Kim glanced quizzically toward Smithers who shrugged and gave her a "beats me" look. She found a box of tissues on a table near the door and handed them to Margaret. She could think of nothing soothing to say, so she simply waited.

After a few minutes, the woman seemed to gather enough composure and Kim tried again. "Margaret, I'm sorry, but we do need to know the answers to our questions. If we can finish up now, we won't need to come back to bother you again to complete the background check."

Margaret sniffled, blew her nose a couple of times, and nodded. Her eyes still leaking tears and her breathing uneven, she said, "You came here to ask me about Jack Reacher, didn't you? Well, I can save you some time. I never met the man and I don't know anything about him."

Kim had consoled a lot of witnesses over the years, but this was a first. She'd never had a witness sob like that over a man she'd never met. What the hell was up with her? And how did she jump right to Jack Reacher, anyway?

Kim cocked her head and her brain connected the dots at lightning speed.

Jake looked like a young Jack Reacher. Right size, right coloring, right facial features. Not to mention those icy blue eyes.

Although if she'd never met Jack Reacher, Margaret wouldn't know it.

Jake also looked like Joe Reacher.

Joe and Jack resembled each other more than brothers sometimes did. Joe was slightly shorter and a bit smaller. Otherwise, the two brothers might have been twins.

Yet, Margaret hadn't guessed Joe Reacher was the subject of Kim's investigation. Why not?

Kim had mentioned a classified assignment, which meant the man who filled it would need to be alive to do the job.

Joe Reacher wasn't alive.

He'd died fifteen years ago in Margrave, Georgia.

And if Margaret had never met Jack Reacher, as she'd claimed, she might have guessed the background check was for Joe Reacher.

But she hadn't. She'd guessed Jack.

Why?

Only one answer made sense of the known facts, including why the Boss sent her to Laconia in the first place. He must have known about Jake Reacher.

Kim took a deep breath. "That's not exactly true, though, is it?"

"Are you calling me a liar?" she replied huffily.

Kim replied, "Maybe you never met Jack Reacher, but you do know some things about him, don't you?"

Margaret blinked and dabbed her eyes with a clean tissue but didn't respond.

"You know that Jack is Joe Reacher's brother, for example."

Margaret's face paled, but she said nothing.

"You also know that Joe Reacher is dead, don't you? That's why you guessed we were here about Jack instead of Joe."

Margaret's eyes widened.

"One more thing." Kim lowered her voice. "You know that

Joe Reacher was your son's biological father. Who else knows? Your husband? Jake?"

"My son is none of your business," Margaret replied sharply. She rose off the sofa and stood ramrod straight. "You can show yourselves out."

She stalked through a door on the other side of the room and slammed it closed behind her. Kim heard a deadbolt slide into place.

Smithers said dryly, "Well, I guess this interview's over."

"I guess it is. Let's go," Kim replied. Once she was outside, she stepped away from Smithers, found Gaspar's phone and pressed redial. He picked up immediately. "I need a search of all DNA databases, public and private, for Margaret Preston Reacher, David Reacher, and Jake Reacher. Pronto. Can you help?"

"Why?" Gaspar asked.

"Because I think she had an affair with Joe Reacher and Jake Reacher is his son."

"Ah," Gaspar replied. She visualized the grin on his lips.

"And while you're at it, search for Joe Reacher's DNA, too," she said.

"Why?" Gaspar asked again.

"We've never looked for Joe's DNA because it wasn't relevant. Now it could be. And with your new resources, we could actually find it. We know when and where Joe Reacher died. You should find sufficient tissue samples from his autopsy," Kim said, thinking aloud. "And if there was no DNA run on the samples at the time, you can run them now. Once you find Margaret and Jake's DNA in the systems, that is."

"You're a genius," Gaspar deadpanned.

"So you've said, Cheech," Kim replied just as sardonically, but she was feeling better already. Finally, some kind of break in this maddening hunt for Jack Reacher. And it was about damned time. Solid intel, even if the intel was about his brother, could prove helpful. "Oh, and get whatever intel you can find on Margaret Reacher's son, Jake while you're lounging around by the pool down there."

"Ten-four, Suzie Wong. I'm on it," Gaspar replied with a laugh before he gave her another address and hung up.

She made her way through the snow to the SUV.

"Where to?" Smithers asked when they were settled in again.

"I've only got one more subject to interview and you're welcome to come along," she replied and supplied the address for Old Man Reacher.

CHAPTER SIXTEEN

Saturday, February 26
2:45 p.m.
Laconia, New Hampshire

OWEN SLOWED HIS SPEED seeking an unmarked turnoff to a location two miles away from the motel. He'd been here twice before, but fresh snow had swept over the road like a broom since then.

When he found the tracks marking the drive, he swung wide and pulled into the ruts. A bumpy mile further along and his destination materialized.

A square two-story farmhouse and two outbuildings occupied the space at the end of the drive. The buildings were painted white once upon a time. There was enough of the white paint left to make the house hard to spot from a distance.

Functional shutters closed over dirty windows, keeping what little light existed inside away from prying eyes. There weren't likely to be many eyes looking for the place. The farm had stopped producing decades ago and had been abandoned.

Owen drove in the tracks along the side of the house and parked in a flat spot around back. He put the transmission into park and looked at his brother in the rearview mirror. "Oscar, sit here. Keep the engine running. We won't be long."

Owen left the warm cabin and circled to the back of the SUV to open the hatch and retrieve the drone. By the time he'd closed the hatch, Oscar had moved from the back seat to the front, as instructed.

Trevor stepped out of the cabin. He felt the cold wind on his face and neck and turned his collar up. The temperature was dropping and another blizzard was headed this way from Canada. Weather reports said the blizzard had dropped four inches on Buffalo already. Today would be his only chance to gather data before the motel was blanketed in snow once more.

He followed Owen toward the ramshackle farmhouse.

"How solid is this guy? Will he keep his mouth shut?" Trevor asked as he mounted the steps to the back porch.

"I paid him enough." Owen replied, "Besides, he's a little paranoid. Not that chatty by nature. I doubt he knows anyone well enough to brag to."

Trevor nodded because it didn't matter much. The guy would be dead in an hour or less, either way.

At the top of the steps, Owen turned the handle and pushed the door open, calling out as he trespassed. "McCoy! It's Owen! Are you in there?"

Whether McCoy replied or not, Trevor heard nothing but the whistling wind and the noisy generator in the yard near the porch. He followed Owen into the kitchen and closed the door behind him.

"McCoy! Are you here?" Owen continued to shout as he moved from room to room. "It's Owen! Where are you?"

Trevor looked around the place while Owen attempted to flush McCoy out. The kitchen was furnished with a heavy farm table that was probably constructed on site back in the day. The top was gouged in some places and worn smooth in others.

Owen had left the drone and the extra battery on the table on his way through.

A tea kettle's electric plug lay next to an extension cord. Next to that was a hot plate. There were no other appliances. Not surprising since the decrepit generator could only supply limited electricity. If McCoy needed refrigeration, all he had to do was walk outside and store cold items in the snow.

The next room was an open space, cold and drafty and unoccupied. Trevor went no further into the house. He had no reason to flush McCoy from his hiding place. Owen could keep trying, but the light was fading fast. Trevor had more important work to do.

He returned to the kitchen, picked up the drone and the remote, and took them outside. What remained of the scorched motel and its contents was two miles northeast from here. Trevor set up and launched the drone in that direction.

The drone fought the wind blowing in from Canada, but Trevor managed to keep it on course. The drone could have covered the distance easily in better wind conditions. Considering today's wind gusts, Trevor reduced the flight speed to conserve power and allow the drone to stay airborne for at least thirty minutes.

The quadcopter was replaceable, but it would take too long to locate and ship in a second one. He wasn't willing to crash it on the first flight. If the drone went down in these woods, it would likely be destroyed. He calculated eight minutes travel time to and from the motel site, and ten minutes for video, with a reasonable margin of error.

This farmhouse was suitable for a single flight. Once McCoy was dead, Trevor wouldn't return unless there were no alternative locations from which to launch the drone next time. He watched the camera's video display on his phone as the quadcopter covered the distance, looking for a second location.

As the drone approached the motel site, Trevor's first impression was that the place had been used as some sort of military target in a training exercise. Equally plausible that it had been destroyed by a film crew making a disaster movie.

The charred remains of the motel and outbuildings were nothing but black on white images. He engaged the zoom lens on the camera to keep the drone a safe distance from the FBI technicians on the ground where it was less likely to be noticed.

Using the zoom, the video captured everything effectively. Trevor would study it on larger screens later. For now, he moved the quadcopter in a wide circle around the site to capture images from alternative viewpoints. The drone's battery life was waning. The return flight would be somewhat easier because the drone would be pushed by tail winds. Still, Trevor refused to engage unnecessary risks.

He'd maneuvered the quadcopter around to complete its wide circle when he noticed movement in the trees and saw the two heavy lumps on the ground nearby. The movement was a black bear, making steady progress toward the lumps, at least a mile from the motel and deep into the woods from the two lane back road.

He figured today's hard winds had blown the last of the snow cover aside, leaving both lumps visible and carrion-aromatic enough to catch the bear's attention. If the bear was moving around instead of hibernating, it was likely because he'd had sufficient food this winter. Trevor shuddered.

Given the size and shape of each black lump, they had to be human bodies. They were far enough from the motel site to have avoided damage from the fires. They'd been exposed to the elements and hungry wildlife for at least eighteen months and perhaps longer. They were no doubt gruesome from a closer viewpoint.

Had either of those bodies once been his partner, Casper Lange? If Lange had died here, was his body identifiable? How much longer would Lange's status, quick or dead, remain unknown? How much time did Trevor have to get what he came for and get out?

His questions couldn't be answered from the drone's video feed. He maneuvered the quadcopter to return to the farmhouse as he considered what to do next.

CHAPTER SEVENTEEN

Saturday, February 26
3:15 p.m.
Laconia, New Hampshire

LACONIA WASN'T SUCH A big place. The GPS system led
Smithers directly to Old Man Reacher's home in record time.
They parked and walked through a decorative gate into an
interior courtyard with neat three-story town homes around it.
Old Man Reacher lived in the house on the left.

Kim walked up and rang the doorbell. She looked through a
pebbled glass pane set into the door. Inside the long, narrow
space was a distorted view of calm cream colors and pictures on
the walls.

A woman came into view. She was stooped and gray and
somewhat unsteady on her feet, even with her gnarled hands
gripping the walker.

She came slowly closer and closer, pushing the walker in front
of her. It was bright orange with four aluminum wheels, and a
fabric seat built into the design so she could sit when she got tired.

"Just a minute," she called in a frail voice. She fiddled with the deadbolt and then rolled the walker aside. Finally, she opened the door and a blast of warm air spilled out.

Kim showed her badge wallet and said, "Good afternoon, ma'am. We're looking for Mr. Reacher. Does he still live here?"

The woman moved her walker backward slowly as she said, "Please come inside. It's too cold to talk here."

While they waited for her to move away from the door, Smithers's phone vibrated. He turned his back and picked up the call.

"Yeah...Okay...Canada?...Right...Got it...Okay. Keep me posted. I'll get there as soon as I can." He ended the call and dropped the phone into his pocket just as Kim walked inside. She shot him an inquisitive look over her shoulder and he shook his head as he followed close behind and closed the door.

The woman pushed the walker deeper into the foyer until she reached a bench placed along the north wall. She turned herself carefully and sat in the walker's seat. She gestured toward the bench. "Please sit down. It's not comfortable for me to peer up at you."

The bench wasn't large or sturdy enough to hold Smithers, but Kim perched as requested. "We're with the FBI, ma'am. We need to ask Mr. Reacher a few questions."

She pulled her badge wallet out again and held it open while the woman's rheumy brown eyes, magnified by her glasses, studied Kim's ID thoroughly.

"He's had a few TIAs recently. You know what those are?" Before they had a chance to answer the question, she said, "Mini-strokes, some call them. But the doctors say they're a warning he might have a major stroke. He's ninety-four, you know. He needs to take it easy, they said. He can't talk long."

Smithers knelt down to her eye level. "Are you his wife, ma'am?"

"Just a friend. I'm Myrna Fredericks. Before you ask, he's got no family, either. Never married, as far as I know. No kids. Nobody but me." She smiled and shook her head.

"How do you and Mr. Reacher know each other?" Kim asked.

"Known him since our birdwatching days. A person gets to be our age, we don't have a lot of contemporaries to share our experiences with any more." She paused to catch her breath. "When he started having the TIAs a few months ago, he asked me to leave the assisted living place and move in here. I told him if anything happened, the only thing I could do to help was call the ambulance. But he said that would be enough."

"I'm sure it will." Smithers gave her a warm smile. He was good with witnesses, Kim noticed.

"We just have a few questions. We won't take too much of his time," Kim said.

Myrna grinned, showing a gold tooth in front. "Oh, he'd love to talk to you all day long. He's very chatty. Always has been. So it'll be up to you to keep it brief. Can I trust you to do that?"

"Of course." Kim nodded. "Can we see him now?"

"My rooms are upstairs. We moved his bed down here to the first floor when the elevator became too much for him to manage." Myrna pointed a gnarled finger, oversized knuckles swollen by arthritis, toward a closed wood panel door across the narrow hallway. "I'll wait here. It's easier for him if there aren't so many people to entertain all at once, you know?"

Myrna pulled a tattered paperback from the side pouch on her walker. "I'll just read until you come back so I can lock the door after you leave."

"We won't be long," Kim replied.

The door to Old Man Reacher's room was four feet away. Smithers followed behind her, heavy footfalls marking his progress on the hardwood floor. She approached, knocked, and turned the knob. The old hinges creaked as she pushed the door open.

Reacher was seated in a green leather armchair staring into a pleasant fire with a blanket over his legs. His feet were propped up on a matching ottoman. Only his head and hands were exposed. Translucent skin covered his bones like parchment showing his veins and abundant brown age spots. Wispy gray hairs danced across his skull.

"Mr. Reacher?" Kim said on her way into the cozy room.

"Yes," he said, his voice stronger than she'd expected in the quiet space. He cleared his phlegmy throat and took a sip of water from a glass on his side table.

"Myrna said it was okay to come in for a quick chat," Kim said.

He nodded and waved her closer to the armchair across from his. She shook his icy cold hand before she perched on the seat.

The walls featured framed photographs and lithographs of common and exotic birds. He might have spent his entire lifetime accumulating those birdwatching experiences.

"You came to talk about the birds?" he asked, hope in his voice, as if too few people came to talk about the birds these days.

"I'm afraid I don't know much about birds, sir," Kim replied, sorry to see his eagerness fade at her reply.

"People are too busy for bird watching nowadays, I guess. There's other ways to watch from a bird's eye view." He'd warmed to his subject and needed little encouragement to continue. "A young man came by last week to show me video captured by a drone flying high over Laconia and Ryantown, where I grew up. It was a chance for me to see what the birds were watching all those years when I was watching them, you know?"

Smithers replied, "Indeed. We don't need to imagine ourselves as birds. Eyes in the sky come in all different forms now, don't they?"

Reacher smiled as if he'd found a kindred spirit. "We always had binoculars. But they weren't as good as watching with the naked eye. You get the whole picture. With binoculars, you're focused too close. All you see is the closeup beauty."

Smithers nodded. "That's kind of how life is, too, isn't it? We live it up close, but we don't often get the panoramic wide shots, you know?"

"Exactly. You should try bird watching, Smithers. You'd like it." Reacher paused, smiled broadly, and turned his gaze to Kim. "Now, how can I help you? If you're looking for something important, we'd best get to it. A guy like me, doctors say I could go any time now and you'd lose your chance."

Kim wanted to protest his gallows humor, which would have been the polite thing to do. But he seemed to be enjoying himself, so she didn't argue.

"Mr. Reacher, I'm trying to locate two men who might be related to you. Do you know Mark Reacher? He grew up in this area," Kim said.

"Sorry," he replied, shaking his head. "I don't know him. Never met him as far as I recall."

"He was David Reacher's brother," Kim said to jog his memory, which had seemed perfectly fine until now.

"I knew David. Sad thing when a man that young dies while an old man like me hangs on and on, way past the day when I should have kicked the bucket. Really tough on his boy, too," Reacher said sorrowfully.

"Jake?" Smithers said.

"Yeah. Good kid in his own way."

"What do you mean?" Smithers asked.

"Jake's had more than his share of trouble over the years. Nice kid, but he has a strong sense of right and wrong that not everybody agrees with. He thinks you've done something wrong, he makes it his business to make sure you never do it again."

"Kids like that usually end up spending some time in jail," Smithers said.

Reacher shrugged, "He's got himself under control now. But underneath, he's a bomb waiting to go off. You do the wrong thing and Jake's going to hunt you down and make you sorry. And he's a good fighter. Kid shows no fear. I'm not sure he feels any."

"Which means he's done some damage to others," Smithers said.

Reacher nodded. "Some. But he's the one I told you about. He showed me the drone video."

"Why did he bring it to you?"

"His mother has an interest in birdwatching, and he'd come around here from time to time to talk with me about it when he was a kid, before he went off to college. I had plenty of time on my hands and his folks were both working." He shrugged. "You know how it goes."

"We'd like to meet Jake. Do you know where he is?" Kim asked.

Reacher shook his head. "He's driving across the country. Headed to San Diego."

"Do you know why?"

"Yeah. I'm afraid I'm to blame. He's looking for a guy," Reacher explained. "Thinks he might be in that area somewhere."

She knew who he meant. Kim's gut clenched. The hair on the back of her neck stood up sending tremors along her spine. She'd developed a sixth sense when it came to Jack Reacher.

"Mark Reacher? We were told he is working in Europe somewhere and his family hasn't heard from him in a while," Smithers replied.

"Not Mark. Told you I'd never met him and don't know anything about the guy. He and his brother hadn't been in touch for years." Reacher shook his head. "The guy Jake's looking for is Jack Reacher. He came through here a while back. He said he was headed to San Diego for the winter. Jake thinks it might be a regular thing. Like he spends winters there or something."

Smithers opened his mouth to follow up and Kim cleared her throat as a signal to remind Smithers to let her take the lead. "Why was Jack Reacher here? Did he say?"

"Told me he was looking for his father's birthplace."

"Did he find it?"

Reacher shook his head. "No record that he was born in or around Laconia or any of the other little burgs in this area back then."

"Why is Jake looking for Jack Reacher?" Kim asked.

Reacher shrugged. "He's got it in his head that the guy might be related to him somehow. I'm not sure why exactly. I mean, Jake and I have the same last name and we're not related, unless it's way back."

"How do you think that happened?" Kim asked.

"I always heard about a distant cousin who got rich back around the end of the first world war. He had a bunch of kids and grandkids and cousins and such. So maybe we're all related, in a sense." He paused as if he'd given this idea quite a bit of thought at some point. Then he shrugged again. "One of those small world things, you know?"

Kim opened her mouth to ask about the distant cousin. Maybe she could track down some actual relatives of Jack Reacher if she had the right starting place. Reacher could be living with them. Maybe that's how he'd stayed off the grid all these years.

But before she got the words out, Old Man Reacher's face went slack on the left side. His eyes widened and he turned his head in an odd way, as if he suddenly had trouble seeing her.

"Mr. Reacher? Are you okay?" she asked.

He opened his mouth but the sounds that came out were garbled noises, not words.

"Can you raise your arms?" she asked. He tried, but nothing happened.

Smithers lifted the phone on his chairside table from the receiver and dialed 9-1-1. "We need an ambulance. Quickly. Mr. Reacher is having a stroke."

He stayed on the phone until the dispatcher's questions were answered while Kim checked Reacher's pulse and tried to calm him, but the throbbing pace she felt in his jugular was much too rapid.

"You stay here with him. Paramedics are on the way. I'll go to the door to meet the ambulance and let Myrna know what's happened," Smithers said while striding across the room.

"Help is on the way, Mr. Reacher," Kim said quietly.

Whether he heard her or not, she couldn't tell.

He closed his eyes and rested his head against the chair but his heartbeat never slowed.

CHAPTER EIGHTEEN

Saturday, February 26
3:55 p.m.
Laconia, New Hampshire

OWEN CAME OUT OF the farmhouse as Trevor landed and retrieved the drone. The wind had picked up and navigating the drone back had proved more difficult than expected. The battery's charge was almost gone. There would be enough juice left to download the video, but no more.

Trevor tilted his head toward the house. "Took you a while in there. Did you find McCoy?"

"Yeah. He must've spent every penny I gave him on booze. He's passed out in one of the back rooms. I thought he was dead at first, but he's just sleeping it off." Owen said, buttoning his jacket against the cold. "I searched the house, just in case he'd had a friend over to party or something. Didn't find anything. Guy's a real hermit."

Trevor nodded. "Get my laptop bag out of the SUV. I want to look at this video on a bigger screen than my phone."

He carried the drone inside while Owen did as he was told. Trevor was set up on the kitchen table by the time Owen brought the bag. Trevor connected the cables and transferred the video first. Then he played it.

The whole video was too long to study carefully on the laptop screen sitting in the cold in this shithole. So he adjusted the video to the section where he'd seen the bear. He zoomed in on the images. The video wasn't as sharp as he'd like at this magnification, but the black moving thing was definitely a black bear on the prowl.

The two lumps on the ground that had been uncovered by the wind were less clear. As the bear came closer to them, the proportions definitely suggested they were big enough to be humans. But they could have been two bears or even a couple of moose.

Whatever the two lumps were, they were definitely dead. Predators had probably been feeding on them for a while. The footage of the bear's dinner was particularly gruesome.

Trevor hit the pause button and pointed to the lumps. "Does that look like humans to you?"

Owen squinted, as if that would make the images clearer. "Can't tell. But given where they are located and the other bodies the FBI found at the motel site, I'd say it's more likely more human victims than a couple more dead bears. Wouldn't you?"

"Maybe."

Owen said, "Could be Lange. We'll probably need DNA to be sure, after all this time. That bear is not likely to be the only kleptoparasite using those two as a smorgasbord."

"Right." Trevor had a strong stomach for violence. And he was mad as hell at his business partner. But his gut twisted when he thought about Lange out there exposed for almost two years to scavenging animals. Whatever was left of him wouldn't be recognizable, even to his own mother.

"It's not likely the bears killed them," Owen said. "Black bears don't usually attack humans and the bodies are too close together. Bears might have killed both, but these two were probably killed at the same time, the way the bodies are positioned. Only one apex predator kills like that. Humans."

"Right." Trevor nodded. "We need a closer view. The only way to get in there is on snowmobiles, which we don't have. The FBI will be packing up soon. It'll be too dark to work out there and the weather is coming in faster than expected."

Owen replied, "We can try to get closer. Take another look with the drone. Then go out there after the FBI leaves."

Trevor considered the logistics. Flying the drone directly overhead at the motel from the farmhouse again was a big risk. If luck was against him, as it often was, FBI personnel might see it and investigate. Much safer if he flew this particular drone over the area after the FBI was already gone.

But the blizzard would cover those two lumps in the snow long before midnight. Later might literally be too late for the drone to capture anything helpful on video. And he wanted to get a lot closer to those two bodies anyway. He couldn't get DNA from photos. Which meant he'd need to rent a couple of snowmobiles and get them towed out there.

"When is the FBI packing up?" Trevor asked.

"My contacts at the local cop shop say they'll leave tonight. Like you said, the blizzard is getting worse and they won't be able to get back out there tomorrow," Owen said. He stuffed his hands in his pockets for warmth. "They've collected a lot of forensics already. There's no rush to sweep up the rest because all the evidence is already old. Chances are they'll be coming back at some point regardless of how much they can get done."

"Okay. Let me think about logistics," Trevor said. "Take the drone out to the SUV and put a new battery in it. I'm right behind you. I want to look at this footage one more time."

Owen grabbed up the drone and left by the back door.

When he was safely out of range, Trevor closed the laptop and slipped it into the bag. He reached into his pocket and located his gun and silencer. He walked deeper into the house, following a stench strong enough to gag a maggot until he found McCoy, still sawing logs on the floor in one of the back rooms like Owen said.

The man was a mess. Long, stringy gray hair. A gray beard as unkempt as the rest of him. Looked like he hadn't eaten a solid meal in weeks. He reeked of body odor and a dozen other noxious stinks.

McCoy had outlived his usefulness. Both to Trevor and to society.

Trevor stood at an angle where the least amount of body parts would spatter back. He shot four rounds into McCoy's head and watched it burst apart like a melon thrown against a brick wall.

Trevor nodded, satisfied with the result. He didn't need to dispose of McCoy. He broke the windows to release the scent and left the door open on his way out.

Bears had a notoriously keen sense of smell. They could locate food from several miles away. The odors emitting from McCoy's bloody body would attract predators of all sorts.

Problem solved.

When Trevor emerged from the house, Owen sat behind the wheel and Oscar was in the back seat of the SUV. If they had heard the gun shots inside, they gave no indication. Trevor put his laptop case in the back and returned to the front passenger seat.

"We're done here for now," he said. "Head back to Manchester. I need to make some calls."

CHAPTER NINETEEN

Saturday, February 26
4:05 p.m.
Laconia, New Hampshire

SMITHERS LEFT THE DOOR to the study open. Kim saw Myrna wheel her walker away from the front door when Smithers admitted the paramedics into the house. Smithers said, "He's in his room. First door on the right."

They loaded Reacher onto a stretcher and placed him in the ambulance quickly while Myrna watched from the doorway. Kim stood near her to be sure she didn't faint or something. Smithers followed behind the stretcher and closed the front door after the paramedics left.

"Would you like us to drive you to the hospital, Myrna?" Kim followed along with the old woman as she wheeled herself into the foyer once again.

"No, dear. That's not necessary. I'd only be in the way right now," she replied. "If it's like the last time, he'll be back in a few hours anyway."

Kim's limited medical experience suggested Reacher's stroke seemed more serious than a minor TIA. Strokes were unpredictable, but he would probably require more than a few hours at the hospital. Maybe more than a few days, even. Actually, he might never make it home this time, but there was no reason to say any of that to Myrna.

"Do you have someone who can come to stay with you while he's gone?" Kim asked.

"I'll call a couple of the neighbors. Don't worry. We were taking care of ourselves long before you got here, dear," Myrna smiled kindly to take the sting out of her words.

"Of course," Kim replied, although she was uneasy about leaving the frail woman alone in the house. When Old Man Reacher was there with her, at least one of them could call nine-one-one if the need arose. Now Myrna didn't have that backup. "Are you sure one of the neighbors will get here soon?"

"Lonnie next door always brings our dinner anyway. Like meals on wheels, but the neighbors take turns cooking for us and the food's a lot better. Lonnie delivers. She'll be here by five o'clock. Every day. Never fails." Myrna explained in her breathy voice. She smiled, but not wide enough to show her gold tooth. "Really, there's no need to worry. You go ahead. I'm sure you've got better things to do than watch me rest until he gets back."

"All right. If you're sure. But here's my card. You call me if you need anything at all," Kim said, placing her card in the old woman's hands. "We'll let ourselves out. Can you lock up behind us?"

Myrna gave her a fierce look.

Smithers laughed, which lightened the tension. He gave Myrna's shoulder a final gentle squeeze. "I'm sure Myrna is capable of locking the door, Agent Otto. Come on. Let's leave her in peace."

"You take good care, Myrna." Kim zipped her parka and pulled her gloves on. She turned up her collar and went outside.

"Thank you both. I'll be sure to call you if I need to," Myrna said, just before Smithers closed the front door behind them.

They stood on the porch until they heard the deadbolt slide into place behind them.

They walked down the sidewalk to the SUV and climbed inside. Smithers started the engine to get some heat moving. But he didn't immediately pull away from the curb.

"Are you going to San Diego tonight? Look for Jake?" he asked while he cinched up his seatbelt.

Kim placed the alligator clamp she kept in her pocket at the seatbelt retractor and loosened it enough to rest comfortably across her slight frame. "Most likely."

"How about you wait until tomorrow and I'll come along?"

She arched her eyebrows. "Why?"

"Because I can't go tonight and that call I got earlier was good news. We found the owner of the Honda. The car was bought off a used car lot in Canada a long time ago by a guy named Shorty Fleck. He was a potato farmer in Saint Leonard, New Brunswick. Now he owns a windsurfing shop in San Diego."

"Just because a Canadian bought the Honda, that doesn't mean he drove it to that Laconia motel on the way to San Diego. It could have been stolen. Or resold. Or a thousand other things," she said as Gaspar's phone vibrated in her pocket.

"It's worth following up the connection," Smithers said while she located the vibrating burner phone. "There's at least three people now connected to San Diego who have a connection to Laconia, maybe around the time that motel burned. Which makes it worth my time to go out there instead of handing off the interview to the San Diego field office."

"Hang on," she said as she fished the burner out of her coat and left the SUV to take the call. She walked a few feet away from the Reacher house in an effort to confound electronic eavesdroppers before she answered. "Find anything?"

Gaspar said, "Yeah. I've uploaded several files to your server. But it's just as you thought. Margaret Preston Reacher submitted three DNA samples to one of the consumer ancestry databases twelve years ago. Samples were hers, Jake's, and David's."

"Interesting," Kim replied. She wondered whether David had known about the testing at the time. "And?"

"And David Reacher was not Jake Reacher's biological father," Gaspar said.

"Meaning that there must have been some question about Jake's bio-dad even back then. Otherwise, she wouldn't bother to have the DNA tested. But when Jake was ten, that question was at least partially settled by the test results," Kim said slowly, thinking aloud. "What about Joe Reacher's DNA? Find anything there?"

"Sorry, Suzie Wong," Gaspar said. "Struck out, I'm afraid. No DNA samples to test. When Joe's autopsy was done fifteen years ago, his brother made a positive ID. Along with Joe's unusual dental work and fingerprints, that was enough to confirm the identification at the time."

Kim nodded, although he couldn't see her.

No fault to find with the Margrave P.D.'s procedures during Joe's autopsy back then. Like his brother, Joe had grown up on military bases around the world. Some of his dentistry had been done by American dentists, but the rest was no doubt a hodgepodge of techniques and materials. No one else could have had teeth exactly like his. Dental records would have proved his identity as positively as DNA. Add the fingerprints on file, and every agency in the world would have stopped there.

"Any of Joe's autopsy samples still around? Blood, tissues, clothes, anything? Can we get DNA from those samples now and compare it to Jake's?" Kim asked, stomping her feet trying to stay warm.

The wind slapped her face hard enough to redden her cheeks, cause a redder nose, and watery eyes, too. She looked longingly at the warm SUV and noticed the snow was accumulating faster than she'd expected. She made a mental note to check the weather report.

"I'm working on acquiring samples of Joe's DNA," Gaspar said from his no doubt sunny, warm, Miami office. "Now that I'm no longer with the FBI, some things are easier. Like hacking into private DNA registries. But getting physical evidence from a fifteen-year-old autopsy performed by an official medical examiner following a homicide is trickier. You'd probably have better luck asking The Boss."

She paused briefly before she replied, "You've been retired less than a month and you've already forgotten how impossible that idea is?"

She *could* ask The Boss. But of course, she wouldn't. Gaspar knew that.

Everything she learned about anything related to her assignment now was conveyed to The Boss on a strictly need-to-know basis. To put it bluntly, she didn't trust the bastard and with good reason. He'd hung her out to dry too many times.

How could she get the samples?

Smithers could do it, but it would take a while and he wasn't technically on her team, either. He'd report anything and everything up the chain of command unless she asked him not to—and explained her reasons. Which she hadn't done so far and preferred not to.

But the problem of acquiring the autopsy samples for testing was real. For starters, the samples had been collected back in Margrave, Georgia, where Joe Reacher was killed in the line of duty. The actual samples might have been destroyed or discarded in the past fifteen years. Or they could be stored somewhere under less than optimal conditions, which would make them useless even if she did find them. Or a thousand other possibilities, most of them problematic.

Kim knew only two people besides The Boss who could help acquire what she needed. Gaspar was one, but he'd already hit a brick wall. The other one would be both willing and able. Lamont Finlay, Ph.D. Now Special Assistant to the President.

He'd been selected by the highest-ranking civilian responsible for Homeland Security and Counterterrorism and placed one heartbeat away from the U.S. Commander in Chief. Fifteen years ago, when Joe Reacher was killed, Finlay had been the top cop in Margrave.

"Don't do it," Gaspar said.

"Do what?"

"Don't ask Finlay."

"What do you mean?"

"I know how your mind works, Otto. You could try getting new DNA from Jack Reacher's maybe baby, Jacqueline. But the mother doesn't want that whole thing stirred up again. She's been through enough. Leave her alone."

"I wasn't even thinking along those lines, Chico," Kim said.

"You've lost your mind reading abilities."

"Not quite." Gaspar took a deep breath as if he needed fortification for the second point. "Asking Finlay is a spectacularly bad idea. You've *got* to have figured that out by now."

Kim said nothing. Lamont Finlay was always her ace in the hole. She called on him when she was backed into a no-win situation. So far, he'd always come through for her.

Gaspar believed Finlay's motives were as twisted as whatever motivated the Boss, and he was probably right. They despised each other, for sure. So far, Kim had benefited from their feud, whatever its source.

Not that it mattered.

By the time she asked Finlay for help, she'd already eliminated every other possibility anyway. Finlay was her last resort. When there's only one choice, it's the right choice, as her mother often said.

Kim and Gaspar had argued about Finlay many times already. There was nothing new to say on that score, so she moved on.

"Anything else, Chico? I'm freezing my ass off out here." She'd been walking up and down the sidewalk in an effort to gin up enough body heat, but it was a losing battle. The wind gusts were strong enough to blow her over when coupled with her forward momentum. And when she turned to walk into the wind, it was a slow slog. The rapidly accumulating snow compounded her problems.

"Yeah," Gaspar sighed. Not that he was giving up on his point about Finlay forever. Not a chance. "I'll make it quick. I sent arrest records and court files on Jake Reacher. Three are juvenile arrests for assault. All pled down to lesser charges.

There was some jail time involved, but the records are sealed because of his age. Two of the files are arrests after he became an adult, but the charges were dropped both times."

"Sounds like the kid's got a knack for finding trouble," Kim said thoughtfully. "Also sounds like he's displayed some skill at getting himself out of trouble."

"Like my father used to say, the apple doesn't fall far from the tree," Gaspar replied. "But you be careful around him, Otto. He's twice your size and a lot less patient. Hot-headed, too."

"Okay. Let me know if you find anything else." She paused as a new idea popped into her head. "Can you find out what kind of vehicle Jake is driving? If it's newer, we might be able to hack it's systems and locate him."

"Yeah, I can handle that," Gaspar replied. "Where are you going?"

"I'm not sure. San Diego in the morning, probably. Old Man Reacher says both Jack and Jake were headed that way." She glanced at the SUV and saw the passenger door standing open. The flashers were blinking. Smithers had done everything but blast the horn to get her attention. "I've gotta run. Talk later."

She ended the call, dropped the phone into her pocket, and shuffled as fast as she dared toward the SUV.

"Close the door," Smithers said when she'd climbed aboard and snapped her seatbelt into place. "My team found something. I need to get out there before the storm gets worse. Want me to drop you at the inn?"

"What did they find? More bodies?"

He nodded. "Two more victims."

CHAPTER TWENTY

Saturday, February 26
4:45 p.m.
Laconia, New Hampshire

SMITHERS TOOK THE LAST turn leaving town and toward the motel site, away from the Laconia police station where his team had been headquartered for the past two weeks.

Kim said, "All nine of the previous victims were found within a mile of the motel. Did they do a wider ground search today?"

Smithers shook his head. "A black bear alerted them to the location in the woods, about a mile off the two-track. They saw the bear first and then located the bodies with a drone."

"Lucky break."

"Yeah. Otherwise, what's left of these two victims would probably have been buried tonight and stayed buried until Spring. We might never have found them at all."

Kim nodded, thinking things through. "Only one bear?"

"So far. There's more in the vicinity. Bears don't generally travel in packs, but that doesn't mean they'll show up only one at a time," Smithers said. "Why are you so interested? Still think one of the victims could be Jack Reacher?"

Kim remained silent.

He drove along the county road at a rapid rate of speed too fast for the driving conditions. The blizzard had picked up strength. Wind and snow buffeted the big vehicle on all sides. At least a few inches of new accumulation blanketed the ground. The windshield was covered with icy snowmelt, even with the defroster blasting and the wipers slapping time.

Kim cinched her seatbelt tighter and held onto the armrest as the vehicle bounced and swayed. "How'd they get rid of the bear? We've got black bears in Michigan. They don't hunt humans, but they definitely can be deadly. Especially if humans interfere with their feeding ground."

"They didn't find the bodies until about half an hour ago. They chased the bear off using flare guns before they realized he was feeding or that he was possibly feeding on human remains. But he made it pretty clear he didn't want to go. And they figure he'll be back tonight." Smithers swiped one of his big palms over his face. "My team is working on getting the bodies out of there before he comes back. I called Amos. She and a deputy are on their way with a couple of snowmobiles. That's the only way we're going to get in and out of those woods before Spring."

He didn't say it, but Kim knew the working conditions had to be brutal. Lifting bodies and carrying them more than a mile through the deep snow and the dense woods would be a daunting task under the best of circumstances. There was no way to get electricity back in there without a generator. Battery operated lights and heaters were probably not in the cards tonight, either. All of that would need to wait for daylight.

Tonight, the area would be cold, dark, windy, and with the bear involved, extremely dangerous. Bears were fast. Strong. They could do serious damage to members of the team before anyone could stop them. Collecting evidence safely, or at all, would be close to impossible.

But if they waited until conditions improved, the evidence might well be gone. Only one choice.

"Have you got helos on the way?" she asked. Helicopters would have search and rescue equipment. Better lights. Additional crew. If the ground crew could load the bodies onto the lift systems, the helos could raise them out of the trees and away from hazards.

He shook his head. "I checked. Flight conditions won't permit them to get in there tonight. If we had live victims, I'd make the request anyway. But we can't ask them to risk their lives for evidence retrieval tonight. We're on our own."

He slowed the SUV and turned onto the two-track leading toward the motel, and then slowed even more. He'd been driving with his headlights on the whole way, but now they were essential. The dense forest crowded out the last of the daylight.

Which meant the bear was likely on the prowl.

CHAPTER TWENTY-ONE

Saturday, February 26
5:30 p.m.
Laconia, New Hampshire

SMITHERS NAVIGATED THE SUV around a curve and came
to a stop twenty feet behind a Laconia P.D. Ford 250 diesel truck
pulling a flatbed trailer loaded with two Polaris Titan 800
crossover snowmobiles. The truck's red and blue light bar was
flashing on top of the cab. A big spotlight on the passenger side
was pointed east, shining into the dense trees.

Detective Amos and her deputy, Max Gonzalez, dressed in
high visibility yellow monosuits with full helmets and face
shields, were busy unloading the big machines.

Smithers shuffled in the glove box for his encrypted digital
radio. He tuned the radio to the correct channel and connected to
his two-agent team who were setting up in the two-track on the
other side of the truck.

Amos walked back to the SUV and Smithers buzzed his
window down. "Thanks for coming out on such a nasty night,

Amos. Tell Deputy Gonzalez we appreciate his assistance, too."

She nodded. She raised her voice to be heard over the howling wind. "We're going in to take a look at the bodies. Your agents are going with us. It'll be slow going to maneuver through these trees in the dark on hilly terrain. Hard to hear the radio with the engines running, so we'll call you when we reach the site."

"Visibility is bad out there, especially once you get deep into the trees, too. You know where you're going?" Smithers asked, frowning.

"We've got GPS coordinates from the drone footage," she replied. "If we see bears near the bodies, we'll attempt to flush them away from you. We'll try to give you some warning, but be ready. Black bears are protective of their food supply and their behavior is unpredictable. They're damn fast runners, too. They'll be on you before you know it."

"You've got rifles we can use in the truck?" Smithers asked.

"Couple of them. We'll want to get DNA from the bear's gut or off its claws and teeth. So there's a spring powered tranq gun with darts, too," Amos replied, pulling her big yellow gloves over her hands. "You're not dressed for this weather and we shouldn't need you. We'll report back as we go. We've got helmet and body cams, and you can watch our progress on the screens from inside the cab. Stay inside our truck. Stay warm. Last thing any of us needs is to get frostbite tonight."

"Got it," Smithers said. "Be careful out there. Keep us posted."

Two members of the FBI team also dressed in Laconia P.D. yellow monosuits with gloves and helmets, walked around the big diesel truck from the other side. They were indistinguishable from each other with the weather gear in place. One agent waved toward the SUV and climbed aboard the snow machine behind Deputy Gonzalez, who was already seated, engine running.

Detective Amos put the face shield down on her helmet and returned to the other big snowmobile. She took the driver's position and the second FBI agent settled in behind her. Amos was the team leader, responsible for the lives of all four.

She fired up her engine and took the pole, moving slowly eastward from the two-track into the woods. The deputy followed. Within a couple of seconds, both snowmobiles were no longer visible. Even the big spotlight's beam lost the high visibility yellow-clad cops among the dense trees.

Smithers shut down the SUV's engine. He and Kim slid out and trudged through the knee-deep snow toward the big truck. The diesel's engine noise and the howling wind filled the air.

On a ski vacation or relaxing by a fire with spiked hot chocolate, Kim might have been enthralled by the snow-globe like scene. Snow coming down, blanketing the world around her as far as her eye could see, might have been almost magical.

As it was, everything about the mission felt dangerous and life-threatening instead. She shivered from head to toe and not totally from the cold that enveloped her, burning her nostrils as she inhaled.

While Smithers found the rifles in the back seat of the truck and loaded them, Kim climbed into the cab and got the screens working to receive images from the team's four helmet and body cameras.

Detective Amos left the evidence collection to the FBI agents. She and Deputy Gonzalez stood guard with rifles at the ready, alert for bears or other predators common in the New Hampshire forests.

Kim checked the clock and matched it's time to the video feed. They'd been gone five minutes already. So far, the only images she'd seen were tree trunks and snow and blackness surrounding them.

Kim cracked the back window about two inches for a bit of fresh air and to allow her to hear the engine noise from the snow machines. All she heard was the diesel and the wind.

Smithers readied the rifles and left them within reach on the back seat. He climbed in behind the steering wheel and they watched the screens together.

The video returned by the cameras from the snow machines was as clear as natural visibility. Meaning not very clear at all because the blinding snow reflected the headlamps and collected on the camera lens as it did on the windshields and face protectors.

Leafless trees stood so dense that the snow machines were forced to move slowly and erratically toward the clearing, weaving between the black trunks, straining to climb hills and avoid crashing into trees on the other side.

Removing the bodies strapped to any kind of transport sled might be impossible given these circumstances.

When they reached the clearing, Amos and Gonzalez positioned the two snowmobiles opposite each other to light up the ground and capture broader video images on the cameras. The storm still interfered with the video feed. The images were not clear. She saw no bear tracks in the fresh snow, which she hoped was a good sign.

The two FBI agents climbed off the back of the snow machines and made their way over to two large lumps covered by new snowfall. Each agent held a small broom and used it to sweep the snow aside. The lumps became increasingly visible.

Both victims were wearing black clothing in stark contrast to the white snow. As the snow was swept away, Kim saw the bodies were as gruesome as she'd expected. One was missing most of a leg and an arm. The other was missing both legs and both arms. The heads were uncovered. The remaining tissues and bones were frozen and frosted. The faces were no longer recognizable.

Smithers spoke softly, as if he was talking to himself. "Looks like these two were attacked by smaller carnivores about the head and face. The bears probably took the limbs. The torsos look mostly intact. Two males, most likely, given the size."

"You'll still be able to use dental records, maybe. But DNA will be your best ID under these circumstances," Kim replied.

He swiped a big palm over his face. "Yeah. And enough evidence for DNA samples is about all we'll get out of there tonight anyway. The blizzard is getting worse. And those bodies will need to be air lifted. No other way to move them out of those trees. We certainly can't hand-carry them out. The snow's way too deep for that."

"Right." Over the noisy diesel, Kim could barely hear the snow machines in the distance through the open window. Her nose wrinkled involuntarily when she caught a whiff of something else as it wafted inside the SUV on the wind through the open back window.

She recognized the scent immediately.

Nothing else smelled quite like it.

Wild animals stank. The stench was as far from warm, cuddly images conjured up by a Disney movie as it was possible to get.

As a child, Kim camped in northern Michigan with her family. She recognized the scent instinctively, probably a survival mechanism from ancient times when advance warning of a predator might have kept puny humans alive.

"Do you smell that?" she asked.

"What?" Smithers asked, preoccupied with the images on the screen. His agents were collecting samples from one of the two black lumps.

The two Laconia cops stood near the second body. There were no fresh bear tracks showing on the video feeds. Detective Amos reported on the radio, "Under all that snow, we'll probably find more body parts in the spring. Bears are not tidy eaters."

"Copy that," Smithers said.

Kim murmured, "What a horrible way to die." A shiver of revulsion coursed through her.

Smithers replied, "You're not kidding. Let's hope they were already dead when the bears found them, and not simply wounded."

They watched the screens for a few more seconds before noxious odors churned Kim's stomach. She said, "Smell that?"

CHAPTER TWENTY-TWO

Saturday, February 26
6:40 p.m.
Laconia, New Hampshire

SMITHERS TOOK A QUICK glance around the truck. He sniffed a few times, comically. "You know young white women smell things old black men can't, right?"

"Yeah, I took that training, too. And I'm only half white, but I'm definitely younger than you," she teased back before she frowned. "You seriously don't smell that? When I first noticed it, the odor was faint. But it's getting stronger."

"Actually, my sense of smell was damaged years ago. I can't smell much of anything. Which is a blessing around decomposing corpses in my line of work." He shrugged and shook his head. "What do you think it is?"

"Something large. Could be deer or moose or even bear. They all move quickly when they need to." She paused. "Given the bear food supply we know is out there, and a bear's keen sense of smell, it's reasonable to assume the bear the team saw on the drone video earlier is on its way back to its dinner. And that he knows we're here."

"There's a lot of black bears in this area, so it could be a different one, too." Smithers opened the door of the truck and balanced on the floor to raise himself up above the cab to have a look around. Heat poured out while the cold wind blasted through the cabin faster than a speeding bullet. Or at least, it felt like the warmth escaped that fast.

"See anything?" Kim called out.

He raised his voice to be heard. "With the low clouds, it's black as pitch. And the trees provide a solid wall of cover on both sides. I can't see around the SUVs behind and ahead of us."

He maneuvered himself back behind the wheel and closed the door. "But there's no animals out there that I can see. Or smell. Sorry."

Kim glanced at the screen again. The two FBI agents had finished collecting samples from the first body. They were moving toward the second victim.

Smithers spoke into the radio. "Everything okay out there, Amos?"

When she keyed the radio to reply, Kim heard the wind howling. Amos shouted, "Good so far. Hold communications. Can't hear you."

"Copy that," Smithers replied. He laid the radio on the dashboard of the truck.

The two FBI agents stored the first batch of samples on the snowmobiles and moved to the second body with collection equipment.

"A black bear might not approach the truck. The noise and the lights should warn him off, and they generally avoid humans," Kim said.

"But black bears will attack people for food and the number of bear attacks has been steadily increasing around the country. They've been known to attack houses when people are home inside, too. We can't assume he'll give up," Smithers said.

She inhaled again, deeply this time. "There's definitely a large animal coming this way. The odor was even stronger when you opened the door."

Smithers said, "Okay. The safest thing is to assume it's the same bear my team saw earlier today."

"Right. Call them on the radio. Let them know the bear might be approaching. They might not smell him with those helmets on, either," Kim replied.

Smithers tried to call Amos again, but she didn't acknowledge. On the video feeds, they could see her and the team at the site but couldn't communicate with them.

Kim located a long-range focusing LED flashlight, opened the door, and stood up like Smithers had done, using the extra height to look around outside.

The flashlight illuminated more than twenty-two hundred feet ahead in the spot beam mode, which she tried first.

The diesel was stopped on a curve in the two-track. Like Smithers said, the bureau's SUVs parked behind and in front, blocked the light.

She switched to the flood beam mode. The flashlight provided a consistent circle of illumination seven feet in diameter at a distance up to six feet, which didn't help much. The blizzard conditions all but eliminated the light's effectiveness in both modes, even if she'd been tall enough to see around the big truck.

All of which meant she couldn't see the approaching bear, but she could smell him. A wall of stink too thick to ignore.

She ducked back into the cab.

"He's got to be close and headed directly toward the team. The stench is so thick out there I could hardly breathe without gagging. We need to stop him before he attacks them," Kim said. She located her service weapon, which should fire normally under the weather conditions because it had been kept warm inside.

Smithers grabbed the rifle. "Tranq darts are fine under the right circumstances. But not against a hungry black bear defending its carrion."

Kim climbed down to the cold ground, flashlight in one hand and her service weapon held ready in the other.

Smithers stepped out on the other side of the truck with the rifle.

Kim directed the flashlight into the dense trees on the west side of the vehicles.

The team was located about a mile east of the truck.

The bear could be approaching from any direction, but if he was headed toward the two bodies in the clearing, he'd most likely be traveling from west to east. He'd cross the two-track somewhere near where she was standing.

She sharpened her concentration, straining to hear him in the night. Even if he roared out from a distance, she might miss him because of the truck's big diesel engine noise right near her.

The only advance warning she'd had so far was his scent. He was upwind from her and she was downwind from him, which gave her a slim advantage.

She hoped.

Smithers closed the door to the truck and moved north, rifle at the ready.

Kim walked a few feet south toward the SUV behind the truck, her back to Smithers. Made a wide arc with the flashlight.

Inhaled again. The animal's stink seemed to diminish. Maybe.

She turned toward Smithers. She saw him up ahead, standing in the diesel's headlights beam. He peered into the darkness along the two-track. He paused a few seconds and then turned to walk back.

Everything happened so damn fast after that.

The animal came out of nowhere.

A big black shadow at first. Longer than Kim's full height. Heavier than her by more than a hundred pounds.

She opened her mouth to warn Smithers.

Which was when she heard the huffing noise. The noise was like nothing she'd ever heard before. Instantly, she understood.

Smithers must have heard it, too, because he started to pivot on his right foot and raise the rifle, in one smooth, practiced motion.

Before he could turn around to get off a shot, the bear charged forward, landing on Smithers with his full weight.

The bear knocked Smithers to the ground and the rifle discharged into the air. The noise startled the bear and he huffed louder as he mauled Smithers about the torso through his heavy coat.

The two wrestled on the ground. Kim's superior marksmanship was a moot point. The blinding snow and poor lighting combined so that she could barely distinguish the bear from the man in the darkness.

The last thing she wanted to do was miss the bear and hit Smithers. But if she didn't shoot soon, the bear would do serious damage to them both.

She waited for what felt like an eternity.

Finally the bear lifted up on his hind legs and she had a clear shot.

"Get out of the way!" she warned Smithers.

Smithers struggled to roll aside, putting as much distance between him and the bear as the moment permitted.

She aimed her Glock and emptied the full magazine into the bear's body.

She was sure the bullets landed somewhere in all that fur. But visibility was so bad that she couldn't see entry points or exit wounds.

Fifteen rounds seemed to make no difference to the bear for a full second that lasted forever.

Smithers crabbed further away, out of the cone of weak light, into the blackness. She heard him scrambling to his feet. He stood off to the side, breathing heavily.

Her mind raced to locate another weapon.

Smithers had dropped the rifle in the snow somewhere.

The others were in the truck.

She'd never reach either in time to make a difference.

She looked around frantically for anything she could use to defeat the bear that was more than twice her size and mad as hell.

Which was when she caught a break.

The bullets had done their job.

The bear's bloody body simply collapsed onto the snow.

The noise of gunshots reached her ears from the direction of the clearing in the woods where the team was working on the bodies.

She could think of only one reason they'd be firing out there tonight. They must have seen another bear. If it came running this way, she had no weapon available to defend them.

"Smithers!" Kim called over the noise. She shined her flashlight in the direction she'd last seen him.

He was upright but bent over, holding his torso, not moving. She struggled toward him through the deep snow. "Get back in the truck!"

She directed her flashlight around, but didn't immediately locate the rifle.

She met Smithers ten feet away and he leaned on her the rest of the way back. She'd have made a joke about the petite woman supporting the huge man, had the situation not been so unpredictably frightening.

They scrambled into the cab of the truck, closed the doors, and collapsed against the seatbacks, breathing hard.

"Smithers, are you okay?"

"I think so." He pulled the shredded gloves off and unzipped his torn coat to examine his body. "No bleeding anywhere. But I'll have some bruises and be plenty sore tomorrow."

"You can breathe normally? No sharp pains?" Ribs were easy to break and could puncture a lung or other internal organs. He could have internal bleeding and not recognize it immediately.

He continued patting himself down, checking for pain points. "I'm good. I've been in worse fights over the years, Otto. Relax, will you?"

Kim was about to give him a snappy rejoinder when she heard gunshots from the direction of the clearing.

She adjusted the video feed screens and watched as Amos fired the rifle again. Kim's eyes were drawn to a second black bear, even larger than the dead one lying outside the truck.

The bear rushed Amos and knocked her to the ground with a mighty roar. His powerful jaws clamped down on Amos's body, tearing her flesh through the yellow jumpsuit.

Deputy Gonzalez took aim and fired, hitting the bear's thick skull with enough force to rip the bones apart.

This one died quickly.

Gonzalez and the two agents shoved the dead bear off Amos. They lifted her onto one of the snowmobiles and fired up the machines to return to the two-track.

Detective Amos needed medical care as quickly as they could get her to the hospital.

DNA collection from the bears would have to wait.

CHAPTER TWENTY-THREE

Saturday, February 26
7:15 p.m.
Laconia, New Hampshire

GONZALEZ AND THE TWO FBI agents from Smithers's team got Amos into the SUV and then stayed behind to load up the snowmobiles on the trailer hitched to the big truck.

Smithers was in no shape to drive, so Kim got behind the wheel of the SUV. She could barely touch the accelerator and the brake pedals. She'd pulled the seat all the way up and raised it as high as it would go, but she still felt like a child in a booster seat at a high-topped bar table.

Kim drove the SUV slowly and carefully back to Laconia with Detective Amos laid out on the back seat, moaning. The blizzard had deterred most people from braving the roads.

Amos had been unconscious the whole way, which was probably better than being awake to feel every jab of pain along the road. The ride had been harrowing and several times, Kim worried they might slide off the road into a ditch and not make it back tonight.

Kim finally pulled up in front of the emergency room. She jumped out to get the paramedics and then stood aside as Amos was wheeled into the hospital on a stretcher.

The paramedics had insisted Smithers come in for tests the moment they'd seen his clothing and guessed he'd been mauled, too. He'd objected, but the doctor came out and escorted him inside.

Kim parked, collected her laptop from the SUV, and followed them. She spotted Jim Shaw, the Laconia P.D. chief of detectives, in the waiting room. She poured two cups of hot, black coffee and offered one to him.

"Deputy Gonzalez called me from the road, but the connection was bad due to the weather. I didn't get many details," he said, his voice as tired as the look on his face. "You want to catch me up on what happened out there?"

Kim quickly recited the facts without embellishment. "No way for all six of us to get out to the victims, so Agent Smithers and I stayed back. Detective Amos led the team through the forest to the clearing. Amos and three others—two agents and Gonzalez."

The images of what happened out there were still fresh in her mind. She paused to sip the coffee and inhale some composure. "They were attacked by a black bear. Probably about four hundred pounds, based on what I could see on the video feeds. Could have been larger. Amos got off a couple of good shots, but the bear didn't go down. He attacked her and mauled her before Gonzalez killed him. Gonzalez is the hero in this. Without his quick thinking, Amos would be in a lot worse shape."

"I see," Shaw said wearily, kneading the tension from the

back of his neck with one hand. "First thing Amos will want to know is did they collect good evidence samples from the victims?"

"I think so." Kim nodded. "First, they confirmed what they'd seen earlier on the drone footage was actually two human bodies. No way to tell how long they'd been out there. They were decomposed, but they'd been mauled and frozen and thawed."

Shaw let out a long stream of breath. "Bears would have to be really hungry to go for food that old. Any ID on the vics? Wallets or dog tags or anything?"

"Dog tags?"

"We have a lot of military types out here in the summer months and during hunting seasons in the fall, too," Shaw explained.

Kim shook her head. "No dog tags. DNA and dental records will be all the medical examiners will have to work with. The agents took photos, but the faces are gone. No fingerprints or anything, either."

"Nothing they could tell about the bodies at all?" Shaw drained his coffee and rolled the empty paper cup between both palms.

"They were probably males, guessing from the size. Tattered synthetic black clothing suggested they weren't hunters. At least they weren't worried about being shot accidentally by other hunters. If they'd been worried about that, they'd have worn orange or another visible color," Kim said.

"Meaning they didn't die during hunting season when every hunter out there is probably drunk and could have killed them without even realizing it," Shaw replied with a wry, sad grin.

Kim nodded. "You have any missing persons reports for two adult males, gone from twelve to twenty-four months or so?"

Shaw replied, "Not that I recall off the top of my head. But now that we know what we're looking for, we'll check it out, for sure."

Kim nodded. She poured herself another cup of coffee and opened her laptop to write her reports and upload them to her secure server. Paying her insurance premium, she called it. Like all insurance, she hoped she'd never need anything she included in those reports. But with Gaspar retired and only the Boss and Finlay knowing what she was working on, it felt safer to have a written record somewhere. Just in case.

When she finished, Smithers and Amos were still inside the bowels of the hospital somewhere. She wandered over to the visitors desk and asked about Old Man Reacher. As Myrna had guessed would happen, Reacher had been treated and released. Probably back home now in front of his cozy fire eating whatever the neighborhood meals-on-wheels brought him for dinner tonight. He was a tough old bird. They both were.

The Boss's cell phone vibrated in her pocket on her way back to her seat in the waiting room. She took a detour to an empty office and closed the door for privacy.

"Otto," she said when she answered, as if anyone else ever picked up this particular phone, or that he didn't know precisely whom he was calling.

"Reacher's not there," The Boss said without greeting. It wasn't a question. Because he already knew. Either he'd been watching her or he'd used other resources, or both.

"Some are. Some aren't," she replied. Long gone were the days when she'd responded yes, sir, and no, sir, to him. He didn't like it. She didn't care. He had no leverage to change her behavior and no desire to change his own. The relationship was what it was.

"Meaning?"

"Meaning at least two Reachers are still here in Laconia. Margaret and the old man."

"Right," he replied. He wasn't interested in them. "Sounds like Jake Reacher is headed toward San Diego. Looking for his uncle."

Which answered at least one question. The Boss had been listening in on her conversations. Otherwise, he wouldn't know what Mr. Reacher had told her.

"Maybe," she replied.

"Commercial jets will get you there faster. Can you get to Boston Logan tonight?"

"Absolutely not." Fly tonight? He had to be out of his mind. She hated flying under the best of circumstances. Which was not what she was enjoying at the moment. No way in hell would she get in a plane tonight, even if she could make it to Boston. Not for a million dollars. "We've got whiteout conditions here. I'll be lucky to find a bite to eat and get back to my hotel."

"Tomorrow then. Call if you need transport. Instructions in the usual place," he said before he hung up.

"I'm perfectly fine. Thanks for asking," she said sarcastically into the dead air, resisting the urge to throw the phone in the trash can. As it was, she scowled and dropped the offensive plastic rectangle into her pocket.

She returned to the waiting room. Detective Shaw was still there, still waiting, still worried.

"Amos will be in surgery for a while and Smithers isn't out of the exam rooms yet, either." He paused. "Buy you dinner while we wait? Hospital food isn't terrible here."

She figured he wanted nothing more than to pass the time, but the adrenaline that had been coursing through her since she'd first smelled the bear was gone and she suddenly realized how exhausted she was. A good night's sleep was all she wanted at the moment.

He must have sensed her resistance because he sweetened the offer. "While we eat, you can ask me whatever questions you like. How's that?"

"Sure. Sounds like a plan." She wanted to talk to Smithers again before she left town in the morning and he was still back there somewhere. She'd wait for him anyway. Which meant she didn't have anything better to do at the moment and she actually was hungry. She tossed the strap of her laptop case over her shoulder and walked along with Shaw.

The hospital was small but surprisingly new and well equipped. The corridors were wide and clean and well lit and mostly unoccupied. Given the blizzard, only seriously ill patients or those with true emergencies were likely to show up tonight.

Shaw led the way around a few corners and through a couple of doors until they reached the cafeteria. They split up to order hot food. Her hamburger took a little longer to cook than dishing up his hot beef stew. By the time she'd collected her food, he'd found a table by the window. She joined him there.

"We have a front row seat on the blizzard, and we don't have to freeze to death to get it," he joked.

"That's just swell, isn't it?" She offloaded the contents of her tray onto the table and sat across from him. After a couple of minutes, she said, "What didn't you tell me about Jack Reacher?"

He cocked his head. "Why do you want to know?"

"I'm completing a background check on him for the FBI's Special Personnel Task Force. He's being considered for a classified assignment," she said by rote. It was a question she'd answered dozens of times by now. And it was only a sliver of the truth.

"What kind of classified assignment?"

"I don't know. They didn't tell me. My clearance isn't high enough." She took a big bite of the hamburger to fend off any need to answer further questions. He took the hint.

In the short silence, Kim swallowed her mouthful of burger and asked, "Was Amos telling me the truth? She didn't have a sexual relationship with Reacher when he was here?"

Shaw blushed from his collar to his receding hairline. He cleared his throat. "Uh, well, not that I've asked her. But you do know Brenda's married, right? Husband's a good guy, too. Newlyweds. Your guy Reacher the kind of officer who'd move in on another guy's wife?"

Kim thought about it briefly and then shook her head. She thought Reacher made his own rules in every arena. If he wanted another guy's wife, he'd probably find a way to justify the affair. But each one of the women that Kim knew about had been single when she'd hooked up with Reacher.

She replied truthfully, "I've seen no evidence that Reacher's done so before."

Shaw nodded. "So I'd say that's a hard no to any sort of affair between Reacher and Amos, then. Next question."

"What kind of trouble did Reacher get into while he was here?"

"No complaints were filed as far as I know," Shaw replied using the same dodge he'd offered before while spooning up his beef stew with a biscuit.

He didn't quite lie. But he hadn't told the whole truth, either. He'd finessed the question. Probably for the same reason others she'd asked in police departments in other small towns had sidestepped the Reacher questions. Every time, Reacher had been involved in questionable behaviors. Sometimes, he'd have ended up in jail or worse if he'd been arrested and prosecuted.

No cop wants to get himself into a position where he'd need to take the fifth amendment in response to questions on a criminal witness stand. He certainly didn't want to find himself out of work or behind bars.

But Shaw knew a lot more about Reacher than he was telling. Too bad Gaspar wasn't here so she could place a bet on it.

She narrowed her eyes. "What did Reacher do that no one filed a complaint about?"

"We're a small department. We don't have the manpower to follow every visitor to be sure they're not provoked into fistfights with offensive offspring of prominent citizens," he replied with a shrug as he sopped up the last of the beef stew. "Especially if no complaint is filed, there's no witnesses who will testify, and we can't prove it ever happened."

Kim nodded. "So how do you handle that kind of situation?"

"How would we handle it, if we found out about it, you mean?" Shaw asked, raising his eyebrows. "We'd tell the visitor to leave town before the situation had a chance to escalate, probably."

"I see." Kim cocked her head. "These hypothetical visitors usually take that advice, do they?"

"One hundred percent of the time," he replied. "We don't want any trouble. We avoid it when we can."

"What if they don't leave? Then what?"

"Dunno. Rarely happens." He shrugged again. Then he raised his head and pointed his gaze behind Kim. "Agent Smithers is on his way over. He's walking a bit carefully, but he looks okay."

She turned to see for herself as he approached the table. "What did the doctors say?"

"Battered, not dead," Smithers's deep bass mimicked super spy James Bond's martini ordered shaken, not stirred. He pulled out a chair, turned it around and sat with his legs wide and his arms resting on the back. "I could eat a horse, though. That burger any good?"

Shaw stood and patted Smithers' shoulder. "No wait staff here, I'm afraid. Let me get you a burger. I'll be right back."

Smithers watched Shaw walk away before he asked, "What's up with him?"

"He's worried about Amos," Kim replied. "What did the docs say about your injuries?"

"I got lucky. Nothing broken. No stitches or anything like that. I'll be bruised and sore for a couple of weeks." He paused. "They're doing blood cultures and such, in case the bear had any communicable diseases I need to worry about. Results will take a few days. But the docs signed off. I'm going to San Diego."

She raised her eyebrows. "Guess I'm flying out of Boston tomorrow. Mid-morning."

"I'll get us transportation to Logan," he said just as Shaw delivered his dinner. He asked, "How's Amos? She gonna be okay?"

"She just came out of surgery. She's got a long recovery ahead, but she's going to be fine," Shaw said, as if the weight of the universe had fallen from his shoulders. He looked at both of his dinner companions and said, "Tell me what you know about the motel fire."

Kim shook his hand. "Thanks for dinner, Shaw. Smithers can catch you up on the fire. I need to get back."

CHAPTER TWENTY-FOUR

Saturday, February 26
5:45 p.m.
Manchester, New Hampshire

THE DRIVE TO MANCHESTER was uneventful. Owen, an experienced driver, was behind the wheel. Even as the blizzard conditions increased, he maneuvered the SUV surely and without mishap, following Trevor's directions.

They pulled into a budget chain hotel that advertised free Wi-Fi and free breakfast. Which meant no restaurant and no bar. The last thing Trevor wanted tonight was a bunch of drunks hanging around, poking into his business. Owen found a place to park away from the front entrance to avoid prying eyes.

"Get two rooms. We'll wait here." Trevor said. He handed Owen a new credit card and a counterfeit Tennessee driver's license with a false name and Owen's photo. After tonight, the false identification and the card would be destroyed.

Owen left the SUV and walked into the hotel. Oscar sat quietly in the back. Trevor located a burner phone and fired it up.

The phone's screen showed a special icon. His investigator had forwarded an encrypted file to a covert email address on an encrypted satellite server. Trevor retrieved the file using a single-use mixed-character password.

The investigator, known to Trevor only as Sam, had located the corporate owner of the destroyed motel. Or at least, he had located the officers and directors who were responsible for the offshore corporation's activities.

Sam reported that digging up the information had taken quite a while, partly because the corporation had been dissolved for failure to file annual reports and pay appropriate fees and taxes. Which meant the corporation was inactive and its assets had been seized by the offshore bank that held them.

Trevor scanned Sam's list of names and did not recognize them. If Trevor's partner had done business with these guys in the past, Trevor knew nothing about those activities. The uncertainties continued to mount, increasing the pressure to find Casper Lange as soon as possible.

Trevor read the list of names again, and this time scanned the brief biographical data included on the summary page. One name stood out because the man's birthplace was listed as Laconia, New Hampshire.

Mark Reacher.

There was nothing unusual about the name and Trevor was certain he'd never heard it before.

But the connection to Laconia was a lead he couldn't ignore. People often returned to their places of origin. They came for a variety of reasons. Sometimes, the reason was nothing more than simple curiosity about their heritage.

Trevor had wondered why anyone would own that run-down motel in the middle of nowhere. As a business location, that one was worse than most. Casual tourists would never find the place. Customer acquisition costs had to be through the roof on a destination like that.

In short, the venture was doomed to fail. No experienced businessman would have chosen to place a startup there. Something that tied one of the corporation's officers to Laconia might have been enough to explain why Trevor's partner had gone there instead of some other place.

Sam's full report included short dossiers and photos for each of the corporation's officers and directors. Trevor flipped to the relevant section. Mark Reacher had left Laconia at least ten years before, when he'd graduated from high school. His parents died in a car crash five years later.

Reacher's only brother, David Reacher, was also recently deceased. Cancer. Trevor shook his head and spoke aloud in the empty room, "These Reachers seem to have short lifespans, don't they?"

In Trevor's experience, law-abiding people with low-risk jobs and lifestyles residing in first world countries with access to health care lived to reasonable ages. But some people were simply prone to bad luck and trouble. The Reachers might be like that.

The report listed three surviving Reachers in the area who might have been related to Mark. One was an old man. The other two were Mark's sister-in-law and nephew.

The report listed last known addresses for all three, along with photos and short background reports on each.

Trevor might have assigned another investigator to approach the three remaining Reachers in Laconia, but it would be faster and probably more productive to do the work himself. Time was short. If he didn't find Lange soon, his problems would become insurmountable.

Trevor added the remaining Reachers to the list of things he planned to handle tomorrow.

Owen returned to the SUV with key cards for the two rooms he'd booked.

Oscar piped up from the back seat, "Any chance we can get a bite to eat before we pack it in for the night?"

"Yeah, sure. We'll eat, then make a couple of stops before we come back here," Trevor replied as he gave Owen new driving directions. "We need to get an early start in the morning. We'll head out just before dawn."

Owen rolled the SUV out of the parking lot and turned right, as instructed.

CHAPTER TWENTY-FIVE

Saturday, February 26
8:15 p.m.
Cincinnati, Ohio

JAKE STRETCHED THE KINKS out of his neck and shoulders, realizing how tired he was from sitting behind the wheel so long. The weather had improved, and many flat surfaces were no longer covered with snow. He flipped the satellite radio off to enjoy some silence.

He hadn't seen Julia or any other hitchhikers from the time he left Syracuse until he noticed the sign announcing Cincinnati city center only fifty miles ahead.

Along the way, he'd stopped for breakfast, to buy gas, and take a couple of toilet breaks. He was more than a bit surprised to find he'd left five states behind already. The Jeep was covering more miles at a faster clip than he'd expected.

Drive time so far had been slightly under fifteen hours. Not quite half the distance to California. If he kept going now, he'd cross the Ohio River into Kentucky.

As he'd covered the miles toward Cincinnati, he'd noticed more highway signs for local businesses. Temperatures had been steadily warming along the roads south from Buffalo, but fifty degrees was too cold to hang out on anybody's rooftop bar, no matter how inviting it looked on the billboards.

He'd seen a sign for a lager house on the Ohio side of the river with a big cozy fireplace and some greasy bar food to go with the beer. Both of which sounded good. He'd almost decided to stop there when he saw the billboard for a sports bar he'd heard about from his fraternity brothers. It was a slightly seedy place in an even seedier part of town, but they said the burgers were the best in town.

Burgers, big, cheap, and good, were Jake's favorite food, especially when he was famished and paying his own way.

The billboard was one of those electronic ones that changed its display every minute or two. The next place it advertised was a hotel and casino, not far from the burger place.

The casino helped him decide. He'd stay the night in Ohio. He'd have a couple of burgers, a couple of beers, and maybe play a little poker. Tomorrow, he'd drive on to the Corvette museum in Bowling Green, Kentucky.

Food. Poker. Bed. Perfect.

He punched the name of the casino into his GPS and followed the directions, keeping a lookout for a cheap hotel nearby. He didn't have money to burn yet. Not until after the poker game.

Jake had developed a strong poker face and he had a talent for counting cards. Nothing like as good as those MIT guys who ripped off Vegas. But he was good enough to win some extra walking around money every weekend while he was at Dartmouth. Some of his winnings were financing this trip. But he'd need more money to get all the way to California.

The exit for the Last Chance Casino was well marked and the GPS routed him to the parking lot. He drove on to the brew pub, two blocks away. A low rent hotel with a flashing vacancy sign was half a block down the street.

Like a lot of casinos he'd been to, the area around this one wasn't that great. Derelict buildings complete with homeless junkies of various kinds were bookended at the street corners by liquor stores and convenience stores sporting heavy iron bars on the windows.

He figured the hotel would fill up later, so he stopped and rented a room, which he didn't bother to preview. No need to. He wasn't moving to any of the better places no matter what the room was like.

Bed was solved. Food next. Then poker.

He left his Jeep in the parking lot and walked to the sports bar. He turned his collar up and pulled his gloves on, leaving his arms and hands free. Junkies and thugs looking for an easy mark wouldn't be foolish enough to assault him. Which didn't mean he'd give them any extra incentives, like walking around with his hands in his pockets.

The sports bar's parking lot was full. Locals wandered in and out at a steady clip. Jake stood in a short line for a couple of minutes before he reached the entrance and followed the crowd inside.

The noise was deafening. Bodies three deep were pushed together at the bar and people were leaning against the walls. The tables were all full. Three waitresses were walking around taking orders, collecting cash, and delivering beer in pint glasses and long-necked bottles.

Jake noticed an opening against the north wall and slid in behind the man who vacated it. One of the waitresses came by and leaned close enough to hear his answer when she shouted, "What'll you have?"

She was slender but sturdy. Dressed in jeans, sneakers, and a blue striped shirt, she was plain but pretty enough for any bar rat in the place. Jake guessed she was about five-six. Her chestnut brown hair was pulled back into a ponytail with a bright blue streak running its full length.

He asked for a pint of stout and a table. He gave her a twenty dollar bill for the beer, which covered a nice tip and his reservation when a table opened up. The ploy worked. When she came back with his beer, she gestured toward the center of the crowded room to a two-top vacated moments before.

He ordered two burgers and fries and another stout before she could rush away. Then he savored the first beer while he studied the crowd and waited for his food.

The bar's patrons were mostly sports fans. He could tell because they were cheering the Cincinnati Reds against the Pittsburgh Pirates while their attention was glued to blaring television screens mounted at the ceiling's corners.

Jake liked baseball at least as well as the next guy, but he had no interest in watching a mediocre game replayed from last season. Only a serious Reds fan would do that, even if the game had been a record breaking blowout. Pirate fans wouldn't be interested since their team lost. And cheering for the Pirates here could be enough to start a nasty fight, which he didn't have the time for.

About a dozen of the patrons were men of a certain age with short haircuts who carried themselves distinctively. Posture perfectly straight. Fully occupying the space around them with extreme confidence. Casual clothes were carefully chosen to help them blend, and failed.

Everything about them screamed *off-duty military*.

No question in Jake's mind. He knew a lot about military men. He recognized the signs.

The waitress brought his food and his second beer. One of the loudmouth drunks grabbed her forearm and swung her around.

"Where's my beer, Lucy?" he shouted in her face. The guy was tall and lanky, wiry and almost frail. He looked like he didn't eat much. Any man in the place could have doubled him over with a solid gut punch.

Jake stood up and laid a heavy hand on the drunk's shoulder.

The guy shrugged from Jake's grip and gave him a heavy scowl. "Piss off, pal. I'm talkin' to my girl."

He tugged the waitress's arm and she winced. Jake put his big paw on the guy's shoulder again, gripped it hard enough to leave bruises, and leaned close to be heard.

"It only takes the right pressure in the right place for me to snap your collarbone, dude. One quick strike will do the job. Ever had that happen? Let me tell you, it hurts like a sonofabitch. Takes a while to heal, too." Jake gave the guy's collarbone a harder squeeze to make his point.

The guy's eyes went wild. He dropped the waitress's arm and stepped away from Jake as if he'd seen a rabid animal. Perhaps he had. Jake continued to glare at him until he backed away and blended into the crowd.

Lucy rubbed her sore arm. "I don't want any trouble. I've got a kid. I need the money. All it takes is the right spark in here and we'll have a brawl. Cops will shut us down."

"No problem." He gave her a fifty to cover his bill.

"Thanks," she said, but her voice was drowned out by the cheers when the Reds hit another grand slam. Not too surprising since the Reds hitters delivered plenty of grand slams last season but still managed to have one of the worst records in baseball.

When the cheers died down, Lucy had moved to take drink orders from guys standing along the wall again. The scrawny guy was long gone or hiding out in the men's room or something.

Jake finished his burgers, drained his second beer, and left the pub during the next round of ear-splitting cheers by the Reds fans. He pushed his way past people clogging the doorway to get inside. When he crossed the threshold, the relative silence of Saturday evening traffic was a palpable thing.

Outside, a couple of drunks were arguing over an empty parking space. Two others had slipped and landed on the snow, unable or unwilling to get back up again. The combination of soldiers, beer, and sports was likely to generate conflict every time. He'd engaged in it himself enough to know. Some damage might be done. The cops could show up. Maybe a couple of Muhammad Ali wannabes would end up with stitches and black eyes. But mostly, the soldiers were blowing off steam before they headed back to the base.

Darkness had fallen while Jake was inside the bar. Most of the dingy streetlights were operational, casting cones of yellow bright enough to locate the sidewalks.

Jake dodged the drunks and ambled toward the casino in search of a good poker game. Meaning a game he could win with stakes high enough to make the win worthwhile.

CHAPTER TWENTY-SIX

Saturday, February 26
5:35 p.m.
Siesta Beach, California

PATTY SANDSTROM LOOKED LEFT and right along the
beach as she finished with her new windsurfing student and they
returned the equipment to the racks behind the shop. The student
seemed to have natural ability for the sport and had scheduled
another lesson next week. She'd be a source of revenue for a few
weeks, at least. But Patty's attention had been distracted by this
morning's visitor.

Knowing he was watching, she'd felt oddly both more and
less secure while she'd left Shorty in charge of the shop for the
past two hours.

She needn't have worried.

The shop was busy. Saturday mornings when the waves
were perfect were always their busiest times. She could see that
Shorty had had his hands full with rentals and even a few sales,
which was a good thing. The shop had been profitable for a

while now, but they weren't so flush that they could afford to take a weekend off.

Patty stripped, rinsed the salt water off her body in the outdoor shower, and toweled dry. She rubbed the towel over her sun-bleached, pixie short hair and moved it into place with her fingers. Living on the beach had given her skin a bronzed tan so she never bothered with makeup. She slid a sundress over her head and her feet into flipflops and she was as presentable as any situation required these days. The whole process consumed less than seven minutes.

She walked into the shop during a temporary lull. Shorty was straightening the display of sunscreens, adding more stock from a box she'd stowed under the counter in the back.

He was dressed in one of the specialized T-shirts they sold, boardshorts, and flipflops. He looked less like a potato farmer from Canada and more like a California surfer every day, which made her smile. She'd always hoped to marry a surfer and live on the beach. Some days, she'd pinch herself to be sure she wasn't dreaming in her sleep back in cold, snowy New Brunswick.

Patty glanced around to be sure they were alone. The rest of the store seemed okay to her experienced eye. If anything dangerous was going to happen here, it hadn't happened yet. She breathed a little easier.

"Hey, Shorty," she called out over the Beach Boys music they played while the shop was open to set the upbeat, California mood. The Beach Boys were touring again so the music seemed as fresh as ever to Patty, Shorty, and their customers.

Patty turned the old-fashioned sign in the window from "Open" to "Closed" and locked the door.

"It's our busiest day of the week, Patty. We can't close up

now. What's going on?" Shorty asked while he kept his attention focused on restocking the sunscreen.

Patty walked closer to Shorty and lowered her voice. "I need to tell you something. It's important. I don't want to be interrupted or overheard."

Shorty frowned. "Can't it wait until tonight? After sundown, we'll have nothing but time on our hands."

"Tonight could be too late." Patty put the urgency she felt into her voice. She strode to the staircase and started up to the apartment.

Shorty followed behind her, but Patty could tell he wasn't happy about it.

At the top of the stairs, she opened the door to the flat. After Shorty stepped inside, she closed the door and locked it. Shorty frowned but asked no further questions about her strange behavior.

She led him into the small kitchen and sat down at the table. Shorty leaned against the sink, ankles crossed. "Okay, Patty. We need to get the shop open. You know we make almost half our weekly revenue on Saturdays. Let's get this done. What's up?"

Patty took a deep breath to steady her nerves. "You know that guy you told me about? The one who approached you on the beach last night?"

"Yeah. What about him?"

"He came here this morning."

Shorty nodded. "I told him to come over and sign up for a couple of lessons. I mentioned that to you, didn't I?"

"Yeah, well, I was pretty sure I knew who he was when you told me about him. But when he came in the shop today..." she paused for another breath, "...it was definitely him. No question at all."

Shorty shrugged. "I don't get your point. He was definitely who?"

"The guy who helped me get you out of the woods that night. Back in Laconia," she said quietly.

"I don't remember a guy." Shorty's eyes widened. For the first time, he seemed uneasy. "You didn't tell me anything about a guy helping you."

They never talked about what had happened that night. Shorty had passed out on the way to the hospital because of the pain. And after he reached the emergency room, they pumped him full of pain killers and anesthesia for the surgery.

Patty wanted to put the whole experience behind them and Shorty didn't remember much of it, anyway.

"By the time you were well enough to talk about it, I thought we'd never see him again. We had a lot of other things to talk about," Patty replied. Which was mostly true. She didn't say that the big man she'd met that night in the dark woods had scared her. She didn't want to talk about him, or even think about him, or anything else that happened that night. She never expected she'd need to.

"Okay. How did he find us?" Shorty cocked his head and crossed his arms defensively over his chest.

"I asked him that. He said there aren't that many windsurfing shops in Siesta Beach."

"How did he know we were in Siesta Beach? We didn't tell anyone we were coming here. Hell, we didn't know ourselves until long after I got out of the hospital. We were planning to go to Florida, remember?" Shorty said, like he'd finally picked up on her tense vibe.

"Yeah, and that's what I told him when he asked me that night. Today, when I asked him how he knew we were here, he said he'd been to Florida and we weren't there. Then he said, 'Finding people is a talent of mine.'" Patty replied. "Then he asked how you were doing. He said you looked good. He said he didn't see any scars."

"Since he just met me last night, that seems like a dumb question, doesn't it? He could see for himself that I'm fine. Hell, I was coming off the waves when he walked up," Shorty replied.

Patty shook her head. "Maybe. I don't know."

"What else did he want?"

"He wanted to know about the big duffel bag. He asked if anyone had come around looking for it. Or for the money."

Shorty's eyes widened again. "So he knows about the money, then?"

"Yeah, he knows. He helped me get it into the Mercedes that night."

"What did you tell him?"

"To be honest about it, I was freaked out. We didn't think anybody would come looking for the money. He didn't think so either, back then. Something's changed. I don't know what and he said he just had a feeling in his lizard brain," Patty replied, biting her lip, breathing heavier.

Shorty's eyebrows popped up. "His what? What the hell is his lizard brain?"

Patty shook her head and shrugged. "He meant his instincts, I guess. I asked him if someone was coming."

Shorty pushed himself away from the counter and plopped into the other dining chair. He lowered his head in both hands. Now his breathing was uneven, too. "What did he say?"

"He said not to worry. He'll keep an eye on us. He'd be back to check on us from time to time. Told me not to worry about it."

"That's it? He just comes in here and drops a load like that on you and then leaves?"

"Not quite." Patty took another deep breath. "Actually, he kind of disappeared, almost. He walked out of the shop when my back was turned and when I looked for him less than a minute later, he was nowhere."

"Nowhere?" Shorty lifted his head and met her gaze with a bit of his natural optimism. "Do you think that could be it? Did you maybe, I don't know, just hallucinate him or something? You were tired. You didn't sleep well. You said you had nightmares about the guy last night after I saw him on the beach. Maybe your subconscious was playing tricks on you. Maybe he wasn't really here at all."

Patty's eyes teared up. She blinked a few times to clear them. Hard to be a potato farmer in New Brunswick without irrational exuberance, and Shorty possessed a boatload of it. It was one of the things she loved best about him. He wanted to believe she'd made the whole thing up. She'd love to believe that, too.

But she hadn't conjured the guy out of thin air. Not the first time, back in Laconia. And not this time, either. Reacher was here. Last night on the beach and this morning in the shop. For sure. He looked exactly as she remembered. Big, heavy, hard as nails.

And if Reacher could find them, the only question was how long it would be before the others showed up.

CHAPTER TWENTY-SEVEN

Sunday, February 27
12:15 a.m.
Cincinnati, Ohio

THE RUN-DOWN LAST Chance Casino had no clocks anywhere. The longer gamblers stayed active at the slots and the tables, the more money the casino expected to make. The last thing they wanted to do was to remind patrons of the passing time.

But it was Saturday night, the busiest night of the week for the neighborhood. Which meant the working-class crowd could stay as long as they liked because when the night rolled over into Sunday morning, most of them didn't need to get up for work the next day. They drank and gambled and smoked and every hour the crowd size increased and the noise level rose until hearing anything distinctly became impossible.

A waiter stopped by with a tray of drinks, compliments of the house. Jake accepted two glasses of water and gulped both. He'd been on a strong winning streak and consumed by the game. His eyes burned from the smoke, despite the constant but ancient air filtration, and his neck and shoulders complained about his posture the past few hours at the poker table.

The other chairs had been occupied by rotating locals who normally played against each other. Tonight, there was a new guy at the table and they lost their paychecks, one by one. Jake didn't win every hand, but he'd won more than most. He'd turned his stake into a cool thousand bucks, which would be plenty to cover the next leg of his journey.

When the last game ended with a busted flush, he folded his hand with the rogue Jack of spades on the bottom and glanced at his phone to check the time.

He saw he'd received two voice messages from his mother, calls he'd ignored earlier. It was too late to call her back now. She'd have gone to bed hours ago. Which was what he needed to do, too. It was almost two o'clock. Time to pack it in and get some sleep.

Jake cashed out and stuffed his winnings into his front pocket before he made his way from the back through the crowded casino. The place was overflowing. People with nowhere else to go. Some were perched on stools, feeding nickels and quarters into slot machines. Others were gathered near a stage where a couple of near-naked women sang karaoke to old rock tunes while the drunken crowd cheered.

Thirty feet past the karaoke stage, he found a clear path toward the exit for the short walk to his hotel. When he broke through the crowd and pushed the glass doors open, he walked into the late night air and took a couple of lungfuls. He was sure his clothes stunk to high heaven. Maybe the hotel had a laundry he could use before he left for Kentucky in a few hours.

Jake took a quick look around. The casino was surrounded by a flat parking lot, which was filled to capacity. The lot was enclosed by chain link fencing, allowing only one way in and one way out. He counted at least four closed circuit cameras posted along the fence and aimed at the parking lot.

The extra showing of security probably made casino customers feel their vehicles and their winnings wouldn't be stolen or something. Maybe they stayed inside and spent more money because of it. Or maybe the casino's owners were trying to keep a lid on illegal activities in the parking lot. Jake shrugged, lowered his head, and kept moving toward the exit.

The snow had melted, except for a few dirty piles pushed to the sides by a plow when the snow was fresh. A few guys were gathered here and there, leaning against their pickup trucks and drinking beer from brown long-necked bottles.

Two youngish blondes, tired and worn, wandered from group to group. Probably hookers from the look of their clothes and makeup, Jake figured. He didn't have much experience with hookers, but he knew one when he saw one and he wasn't interested. He kept walking.

Ten yards away and directly in the path between Jake and the exit, a group of four caught his eye. Three men and a woman standing in a pool of yellow light from a fixture on a pole. A skinny guy and two pals who might have been welders. All four looked familiar. At first, he thought he'd seen them inside the casino. Maybe one of the men had played a few hands at Jake's poker table and lost.

The skinny guy on the left of the woman looked up just as Jake was moving close. A scowl darkened his features. Jake remembered where he'd seen the guy before. The woman, too. Hard to forget that hair. It was Lucy, the waitress who'd served him great burgers and beer at the sports bar earlier. And the scrawny dude who'd grabbed her.

Skinny dude's two pals looked like welders. Big. Beefy. Spoiling for a fight.

Jake didn't want any trouble. All he wanted was to find his hotel room and crash for what was left of the night. The only way he could reach the exit was to plow straight through the group and come out on the other side.

He kept walking.

As he came closer, Lucy turned into the light and looked directly toward Jake. Which was when he saw her battered face. She had a vivid red imprint of an open hand on the left side of her face. Her right eye was swollen shut. She was crying.

"Keep on moving, boy," the skinny dude said as he draped his arm around her shoulders, casually demonstrating that she was his property. The two big welders chuckled.

Jake's whole body warmed with anger. He felt it coursing through his veins like a taser shot. His fists opened and closed at his sides without his volition. He fairly burned to teach the skinny dude and his posse a lesson they'd never forget.

But there were cameras everywhere. The casino might even be hard-wired to the local police station. The cops would be called. Everyone would be arrested. The skinny dude and the two welders would get sent to the hospital. Jake had no desire to spend time in jail because of those creeps.

The situation the night before with Julia was still fresh in his mind, too. He'd handled Carl in the parking lot of the brew pub and she'd been angry with him about it. Left the next morning without so much as waking him up to say goodbye. He didn't understand her reaction, but he didn't want to make that mistake again, either.

Not only that, Lucy had flat-out told him back in the sports bar that she didn't want him to make trouble with this guy. But

that was when she was at work. And it was also before Skinny
Dude hit her. At least one and probably two hard blows, judging
from the welt and her eye. What kind of low-life hits a woman
like that? No excuse was good enough to justify it in Jake's
mind.

A dozen more strides and he'd be past them. He could walk
away and never look back. He'd be gone in the morning,
anyway. Lucy could fight her own battles. She'd made that clear
back in the sports bar, too.

He almost made it out of the lot.

He was six feet past the knot of miscreants when he heard
footfalls behind him. More than one person. Heavier steps than
Lucy's or the skinny dude's. Which meant the welders. They'd
come after him.

Both were heavy with belly fat. Shorter and older than Jake.
Big chests, short arms, not much reach at all. Before they could
get close enough to jump him from behind, Jake took one more
step to set up his weight properly on his front foot and then he
turned, sharp and fast.

The surprise stopped their forward momentum and left them
standing still right in front of Jake, just for half a moment. Both
of them wielded baseball bats. They were prepared to swing for
the bleachers using Jake's head for the ball. The blows would
have hurt him badly, just as the welders intended, if the bats had
connected.

The welders were focused on their plans, on their swings.
But they were standing too close together. The angle was wrong.
They couldn't properly address Jake's head now. But they'd
already started. Momentum carried them forward and the bats,
when they connected, barely glanced off Jake's big torso.

As each bat swung through its arc and the batter's shoulders followed through, the welders twisted away from Jake and were slightly off balance. It was the break he needed.

Before the first welder could set up for a second strike, Jake stepped in and smashed his right heel into the welder's right kneecap. The second welder's eyes rounded and he thought better of his actions. He tried to make adjustments too late. Jake switched legs and smashed his left heel into the second welder's left kneecap. Both welders screamed, dropped their bats, and fell to one side holding their ruined knees.

Jake kicked the bats to the side before he looked up. Lucy was standing with her hands covering her mouth, a horrified expression on her battered face. Skinny Dude blanched a shade of white normally reserved for corpses.

Jake took a couple of steps forward but before he could get there, Skinny Dude did the only sensible thing. He turned and ran.

Jake approached Lucy in long strides. He was barely breathing heavy. He reached out to touch her and she backed away. "Are you okay?"

Something like delayed shock had set in. She'd stopped crying. Her eyes were wide and her mouth was set into a little "o". She clasped her hands together and nodded her head. Which meant she still had some level of comprehension.

He said, "Call an ambulance for these two. They're going to need surgery on those knees. As soon as the adrenaline wears off, they'll need painkillers."

She nodded again.

The welders were writhing around, panting and whimpering on the filthy parking lot. Skinny Dude was long gone. No one else seemed interested in the fight. They'd have been okay regardless of who won. They had no stake in the outcome. Or maybe they thought these guys had it coming.

"I've got to go," Jake said. "But tell that creep if he hits you again, I'll be back."

Lucy nodded a third time.

Jake asked, "You got a cell phone?"

Lucy nodded.

"Call an ambulance," he said again before he turned and threaded through the vehicles toward the hotel. He found his Jeep in the parking lot, jumped into the driver's seat, and started the engine. He pulled out onto the roadway and turned toward the interstate.

He'd driven a mile when he heard the sirens approaching the casino. He drove in the opposite direction, made it to the entrance ramp, and headed southwest. With any luck, he'd be out of the state of Ohio before the cops came looking for him.

Better yet, maybe he'd just keep driving straight through to California. Putting as much distance as possible between himself and the Ohio police seemed like the best plan.

Twenty-nine hours of drive time to San Diego. With a few hours' sleep, he could be there Monday afternoon.

CHAPTER TWENTY-EIGHT

Sunday, February 27
6:15 a.m.
Manchester, New Hampshire

THE SKY WAS FULL of dark clouds blocking the rising sun, but the snow had stopped during the night. Trevor watched out the window of his hotel room while Owen got the truck running and Oscar cleaned off the snow.

He'd made a few phone calls yesterday as they left the farmhouse to acquire a new rig. On the way back to the hotel from dinner, they'd dropped off the SUV to be cleaned of all forensic evidence and dumped somewhere far from Manchester, New Hampshire.

At the same time, they'd moved their equipment into a waiting vehicle.

The new rig was stolen from another state and dropped at the location for Trevor's convenience. This one was a used four-door, four-wheel drive diesel pickup truck with a full back seat. It had sufficient towing capacity to haul a heavy-duty trailer

loaded with a powerful snowmobile. It was white, to blend in
with the snow as much as possible.

Owen drove along the back roads toward the destroyed
motel. Trevor's plan was to arrive at the site just after sunrise.
Owen's intel from the local cops said that the FBI had left the
scene. But Trevor never relied on intel unless he controlled its
source. Safer to assume the FBI agents planned to return. They'd
been showing up around nine o'clock every day, Owen had said.

Trevor planned to get in and get out before they came back
to work. He figured he'd need an hour or less at the scene.

Travel speed was slow along the backroads over the fresh
snowfall, even though Trevor's small caravan encountered no
other vehicles. The trip from Manchester ate about ten extra
minutes of travel time, according to the clock on the truck's
dashboard.

When the narrow two-track that led to the motel came into
view, Owen slowed and drove thirty feet past it. When he
stopped, Trevor stepped outside and sent the drone up for a
better view of the area. The drone flew high over the two-track
and captured video of the clearing. Nothing but trees and snow
for miles around. Even the burned remains of the motel had been
buried by the blizzard. Just as Trevor expected.

When he flew the drone closer to the GPS coordinates for
the two bodies he'd seen yesterday, he saw three big lumps in
the snow. He'd expected two. He rechecked the coordinates to be
sure he'd found the right location. He had.

Three lumps. What did it mean? Had there been three
yesterday and, because of the distance or the angle or the lighting
or something else, he'd missed the third one? He shook his head.
Possible, but not likely.

He brought the drone back and returned to the cab and

climbed aboard. "Looks like there's three bodies out there instead of two. We need photos and DNA from all three."

If the extra body bothered Owen, he didn't show it. He simply said, "Copy that."

Trevor replied, "Okay, let's go."

Owen reversed the truck and backed the trailer around the corner. The big engine pushed the weight easily.

There were no visible tracks to help with navigation beyond the snow piles on either side. Which confirmed that neither the FBI nor anyone else had driven into the motel grounds since the snow stopped a couple of hours ago.

Owen watched the rearview and sideview mirrors and used the big truck to push the trailer along the two-track.

Last night, Trevor had studied the drone videos he'd shot at the farmhouse and identified the point in the two-track closest to the bear's feeding grounds. Owen reached the spot less than a mile from the main road and Trevor said, "Stop here."

They wouldn't risk radio communications with each other from this point forward because they could be intercepted from a distance and, eventually, unencrypted. The less said, the better.

To save time, all three men had dressed in their white snow suits before they left the hotel. All three were armed. Owen and Oscar jumped out of the truck, unloaded the big sled, and hopped aboard while Trevor set up the drone.

Trevor checked his watch and flashed five open fingers four times, to signal twenty minutes of total time to get out there, get the photos and DNA, and get back. Owen and Oscar checked their watches and each flashed a thumbs-up.

Owen climbed aboard and Oscar sat behind him. Owen fired up the big machine and sped out toward the small clearing.

Trevor launched the drone and kept it low above the trees to watch as the operation unfolded.

The snowmobile's engine could be clearly heard in the snow-blanketed woods, even as it moved farther away from the noisy truck. The sun was higher above the horizon now, providing extra daylight despite the clouds. The drone's camera had a clear view of the brothers' slow progress through the dense but naked trees.

In a short time, maybe about six minutes, they approached the clearing. They had fourteen minutes to do the job and get back. Which meant eight minutes at the scene. No more and no less.

Owen pulled the snowmobile to a stop near the first lump, which was about twenty feet away from the other two. He climbed off the machine and shut it down. Both brothers struggled through the heavy snow to reach what, with the aid of Owen's body size for perspective, appeared to be much larger than the drone images suggested.

Oscar used his arms to sweep the snow from the body while Owen took quick closeup photos. Even with the zoom lens, the drone's view was not good enough to identify the body, but given its size, it could have been a human.

The two brothers goose-stepped through the heavy snow to the other two lumps, which were smaller than the first, and spaced about six feet apart. Owen cleaned one lump and shot photos while Oscar did the other. Trevor glanced at his watch. When he looked at the drone's video feed again, Owen and Oscar had mounted the snowmobile for the return trip.

When the snowmobile cleared the woods, Trevor retrieved the drone and packed it away. Owen and Oscar loaded up the snowmobile and climbed into the truck. Owen pulled out of the two-track and stopped at the intersection with the county road.

"Back to Manchester. We need to send out the DNA samples," Trevor said when Owen shot a questioning glance across the front seat. Owen turned right, as instructed. "Were you able to identify the bodies back there?"

"Unfortunately not." Owen shook his head. "There were two humans, for sure. Both male, is my best guess based on the size and shape of the torsos. They've been there a while. Quite a bit of decomposition on both. Animals large and small had been feasting on them, too. The faces weren't recognizable. We patted them down for ID, just in case, but didn't find any."

"Any identifying marks?" Trevor was thinking about Casper Lange's tattoos. Trevor wasn't sure how many tattoos Lange had, but he'd seen two, one on his right bicep and one on his left forearm.

"We didn't strip the bodies, but the arms and legs had been torn off or gnawed to the bones. There was nothing left to identify," Owen said. "We took photos of the dentition. Which isn't perfect for identification purposes, but it's something. A forensic dentist with Lange's dental records in hand might be able to make a reasonable guess. One of them had several missing teeth. The other one's mouth looked like a toothpaste model. For an adult male, that's unusual."

Trevor nodded. Lange had perfect teeth. Never had a cavity. It was something he'd casually mentioned once when Trevor's dentist sent him for a root canal.

"Did you find anything else?" Trevor asked.

"Like what?"

"Weapons, backpacks, duffel bags, jewelry, cell phones, anything at all?"

Owen shook his head. "There's so much snow out there, it would be hard to see anything more than say twelve feet away, even if we'd had more time and equipment to look for stuff. But in the immediate vicinity of the bodies, I'd say no. There's nothing else out there."

Trevor nodded, wondering what happened to the duffel Lange had taken from his safe. If he'd left it in that motel, it had probably been burned to ashes. "What about the third body?"

Owen shrugged. "A black bear. Maybe the one you saw yesterday, because it was laying on top of the old snow and under the new snow. But the bad news is that it was shot. Several times."

"Which means someone found the bodies and killed the bear within the past twelve hours," Trevor nodded slowly, thinking aloud.

"Looks that way," Owen replied. "I'll call my source at the local cop shop. See what they know about it."

"Do that. But regardless, someone was out there with the bodies and shot the bear since yesterday afternoon. That complicates the situation," Trevor ran a palm over his face.

Time had grown shorter in an instant.

They'd drop off the truck and pick up another vehicle. Send out the DNA and photos to his experts. He'd have results by tonight. Tomorrow at the latest.

And then two quick stops to make in Laconia before they left town.

CHAPTER TWENTY-NINE

Sunday, February 27
6:05 a.m.
Boston, Massachusetts

KIM HAD BEEN TOO exhausted to review Gaspar's files thoroughly last night. She'd returned to the Laconia Inn from the hospital without stopping anywhere along the way. After a long, hot bath to chase the frost from her bones, she'd fallen into an exhausted sleep until the same room service waiter brought her a way-too-early-breakfast.

Hours ago, she'd rushed to pack up and meet Smithers downstairs where an FBI vehicle waited to transport them to Boston's Logan International Airport. Kim disliked air travel of all types, and Logan was one of her least favorite airports. It was always crazy busy. And the runways were configured way too close to the Atlantic Ocean to suit her comfort level. She had no desire to take an icy bath in the dark with hundreds of panicked passengers.

Even with the Boss greasing the wheels of the security systems, traffic, weather, and crowds meant a mad dash to make the flight on time. Which did nothing to calm her churning stomach. She'd already popped too many antacids this morning, so she sucked it up in the back of the big SUV and tried to focus her attention elsewhere.

Gaspar had sent a text saying he'd uploaded a few more files. She'd downloaded those on the way. She'd have several hours to kill on the long jet flight to San Diego. She could digest everything and come up with a strategic plan. Keeping her mind occupied was one of the best ways to survive cross-country flights since she never, ever slept on planes.

Before they'd reached the monitored airspace around the airport, she'd called Gaspar on a new burner to check in while Smithers was talking to his team on an encrypted phone in the front seat.

"Good morning, Suzy Wong," Gaspar said wearily, like he'd never been to bed at all. Which he probably hadn't. "Take my advice and never have a kid. Nothing worse than a sick baby keeping you awake all night."

Kim grinned because she knew he didn't mean it. Gaspar loved his family like crazy. Five kids and a great wife. Taking care of them was his reason for living and the reason he'd left the FBI, too. More money, better hours on the outside. Or at least, that's what he'd planned. Sounded like the reality was a lot different from the dream.

"Thanks for the files. I'll read them on the plane. Any word on young Jake's whereabouts?" she asked.

Gaspar said, "Yeah. He's got a cell phone that pings off cell towers along the route regularly. With that and his GPS, I can see his progress. Looks like he's making a beeline toward San Diego. He's about six hours from Tulsa at the moment, give or take. You'll beat him to San Diego, if that's where he's going."

"What's after Tulsa?"

"The route he's got in his GPS says the next big city is Albuquerque, but I'll keep tracking him in case he makes a change."

She tapped her fingers on the console. "Anybody in the vehicle with him?"

"Like his Uncle Jack, you mean?"

"It's possible, isn't it?" she challenged. "A normal guy, learning he had a nephew, might be inclined to connect with the kid, don't you think? Could have been the real reason Jack was in Laconia originally, too."

Gaspar chuckled. "Maybe. But we're not talking about a normal guy. Have you seen any evidence of any kind that says Jack Reacher has normal feelings about anything?"

"I hate it when you're right, Chico," she said and she lost the connection as the driver sped along, effectively terminating the argument.

Gaspar wasn't wrong, though. Jack Reacher was the farthest thing from sentimental. He was a vigilante and he knew when he was breaking the law. He'd been a military cop in the army for thirteen years. He'd been well trained in the lawful way to do things. But he chose to administer his own brand of justice instead. Which partially explained why he'd been living off the grid all these years.

Gaspar always said Jack Reacher's choices would send him to prison for a good long time one day, just like his choices got him pushed out of the army.

The civilian criminal justice system would not judge Reacher a hero, for sure. Not by a long stretch.

On the other hand, beneficiaries of Reacher's brand of justice were more than grateful for it. Kim knew because she'd benefitted herself. Reacher had saved her life at least once. He'd done it for reasons of his own, but that didn't make her any less pleased about being alive.

So maybe sentimental feelings were not what drove Reacher, but he still might want to meet his only brother's son.

Which meant that if Kim kept an eye on young Jake, she might find his uncle, too.

Crazier things had happened.

The conversation with Gaspar nagged her as they reached the airport and followed the crowds through security and all the way to the departure gate. She worried that Jake could change his mind. Or Jack Reacher might connect with him before he reached California. Or a thousand other things could happen while Kim was held captive on a jet to San Diego.

Standing in the security line, she pulled out a new burner and used it to look for flights to Tulsa. She could be there before Jake arrived. She bought the ticket, still unsure about whether to take the chance that she might miss him altogether if she tried to intercept.

But hell, the whole hunt for Reacher assignment was a crap shoot anyway. What did she have to lose? She could take a chance on Tulsa and, if she failed, have a second chance to find Jake in San Diego later. He was driving across the country, which meant she could fly to get ahead of him at any point. Not her first choice. But she could.

While Smithers was on the phone on the drive to the airport, he had done some behind the scenes work and managed to get his ticket upgraded to first class. Now, he was seated across the aisle from her while they waited for the remaining passengers to board the flight to San Diego.

The more she thought about it, the more it made sense to

intercept Jake as early as possible. She could be with him when he connected with his uncle. At the very least, she could learn things that would help her find Jack Reacher. Maybe.

The plane's doors would close in the next few minutes. She had to make a decision.

Kim looked across the aisle at Smithers briefly before she stood to collect her bags.

"Where are you going?" Smithers asked.

"Tulsa," she replied.

"Why?"

"Intercept Jake, if all goes well," she said.

"You can't wait until he reaches San Diego?"

She shook her head. "Easier to find him before he gets lost in the crowd. Want to come along?"

He thought about it for a full second before he shook his head. "I'll meet you there."

She muscled her way through the steady stream of passengers moving through the aisle in the opposite direction and finally reached the bulkhead door. A woman waited to one side as Kim deplaned. She hustled along the jetway to the terminal and located an electronic board listing departures to find her gate.

The flight to Tulsa was five gates away and the gate agents were almost finished boarding passengers. She picked up her pace and hustled over. Gate agents were finalizing the paperwork and ready to close the door when Kim ran up and flashed her electronic boarding pass.

The agent frowned at her but allowed her through. She hurried down the jetway and onto the plane seconds before the flight attendant closed the bulkhead door.

She plopped into seat 1A, the absolute worst seat on any plane. From 1A, she could see everything the flight attendants did at the front of the plane. She could hear their conversations. When something went wrong, Kim would be one of the first passengers to know. She'd have way too much time to worry before the catastrophe happened.

She shook off the realities, stowed her bags in the overhead, and belted herself tightly into the oversized seat moments before the plane began to push back from the gate.

She'd be touching down in Tulsa at noon. Which would give her plenty of time on the flight to prepare to deal with Jake and read through Gaspar's files. She ordered black coffee and opened her laptop.

CHAPTER THIRTY

Sunday, February 27
8:35 a.m.
Laconia, New Hampshire

OWEN PARALLEL PARKED THE stolen silver SUV at the curb in front of Margaret Reacher's house. Lights were on inside against the dreary weather.

"Wait here until I call you," Trevor said as he opened the door and stepped out.

The driveway and sidewalks had not been plowed since the blizzard, which made it easy to see that no one had approached or departed recently. He hustled up to the porch and stomped the snow off his boots before he approached the front door and rang the bell.

He waited a full minute before he raised his finger to the bell again. He heard the chimes inside and waited for footsteps. Another full minute passed before his expectation was rewarded.

Through the glass panel in the door he saw a middle-aged

woman drying her hands on an apron walking toward him. He stepped back.

She turned the dead bolt and pulled the heavy wooden door into the house. She had a smudge of flour on her nose. Margaret Reacher. She looked a little older than the photo he'd received from his source, but it was definitely her.

He smiled. This was a neighborhood where housewives felt comfortable opening doors to strangers.

"Can I help you?" she said, as if he might need something she could provide.

He grabbed the handle on the storm door and pulled it toward him. There were no barriers between them now and he could easily have pushed his way inside. But he wanted her cooperation first. He had just enough time to try to get the answers he came for the easy way.

"Mrs. Reacher?" he asked in the way of door-to-door solicitors everywhere. He extended his hand as if he might be a friend of a friend. "I'm Adam Prince. I knew your husband. May I come in?"

She cocked her head and frowned with uncertainty. The combination of cold air blowing through the open door, his friendly smile, and mentioning her husband seemed to override her natural reticence. She stepped aside and he walked into the living room.

"It's warmer back in the kitchen," she said, after she'd closed the heavy door solidly behind him. "Would you like a cup of coffee?"

"That would be great," he said as he followed her down the narrow hallway toward the kitchen.

Once they were seated at the kitchen table, he folded his hands and leaned forward. In a tone filled with mock sympathy, he said, "I recently heard about David's death. I'm sorry for your loss."

"Thank you," she murmured, lowering her eyes for a moment.

He continued talking in an effort to avoid her tears. "I didn't know David very well. But I worked with his brother, Mark, in Europe."

She nodded but made no reply.

"In fact, it's Mark I'm looking for. I was hoping you might be able to tell me where he is."

She shook her head slowly. Her eyes were glassy, but she wasn't crying. "I would help you if I could, Mr. Prince. I've never actually met Mark and I have no idea where he is."

Trevor ignored her objections. "Mark has something that belongs to me and I need to get it back. I have reason to believe that he left it here when he came for his brother's funeral last month."

Her eyes rounded and she shook her head. "I don't know what Mark told you, but he didn't come for David's funeral. He certainly didn't leave anything here."

Trevor stood and put a bit of steel into his tone. "Then I'm sure you won't mind me having a look around for my property."

Margaret's shoulders squared and her head snapped back to look up into his eyes. "I most certainly do mind. There's nothing here that belongs to you. Please leave my house before I call the police."

"That would be a serious mistake, Mrs. Reacher." Trevor narrowed his gaze and sneered. He reached into his pocket and pulled out a small cellphone. He pressed a single button. "I need your assistance. Both of you."

"Copy that," Owen replied.

Trevor waited.

Margaret wrung her hands and her face became more agitated. She pushed her chair back to stand, preparing to call the police using the cordless phone in a stand on the countertop across the room near the sink.

Trevor swiped a heavy boot behind her ankle and pulled hard, yanking her foot off the floor. The move was swift and sure.

"Oh!" Margaret cried out, as her full weight plopped down hard onto the chair.

Trevor heard the front door open and close as Owen and Oscar came into the house. "Don't get up," he said, pressing down on her shoulder to emphasize the point as he strode past her into the living room.

"Search the house," Trevor instructed Owen.

"What are we looking for?" Owen asked.

"The black and brown leather duffel bag. And anything else that might be useful," Trevor replied.

Owen nodded. He sent Oscar down to the basement as he peeled off to search the other rooms in the house.

Trevor returned to the kitchen. "Where's the kid?"

"What kid?" Margaret replied.

Trevor slapped her twice. A quick slap on one cheek with his open palm and the second a quick backhand on the other cheek. Not too hard. He wasn't interested in sending her to the hospital. He only wanted her to understand he was serious.

Tears sprang to her eyes and rolled to her chin and she reached up to hold both cheeks in her hands. "You mean Jake? H-he's not a kid anymore."

Trevor narrowed his gaze. "Where is he?"

"I-I don't know," she said, sniffling a bit. She reached into her apron pocket for a tissue to dry her tears and blow her nose.

When she'd finished, Trevor slapped her again. Twice more. A little harder this time. His fingers left a vivid red mark on each cheek.

She gasped and tears sprang up, but she didn't cry out this time. She was tougher than she looked.

"Where is Jake, Mrs. Reacher? I'm going to find him whether you tell me or not. Save yourself some grief and tell me while you still can." Trevor heard Owen opening and closing drawers and closets in the bedrooms. Oscar's activities in the basement were quieter.

"He left on a driving trip. I haven't talked to him since he left. I don't know where he is," she said.

Trevor's patience snapped. He grabbed her wrist and twisted her arm back and up. "I could snap your arm, Mrs. Reacher. Right now."

He gave her arm a little jerk to emphasize his point. She wailed with pain.

"Where is your son going?"

Her breath came and went in short gasps of pain. "California."

"Where in California?"

"San Diego, I think. He wasn't sure when he left here."

"Where's your cell phone?" Trevor asked, giving her arm another jerk.

She nodded her head toward the end of the counter. His eyes scanned in that direction. He saw keys, gloves, a handbag. He dropped her arm. She gasped as the pain stopped and used her other hand to rub the spot briskly.

Trevor opened her bag and dumped the contents on the counter. He swiped through the pens and tissues and old receipts and linty breath mints until he located the old flip-style phone. He flipped it open.

No missed calls, no messages. He pushed the button for recent calls. Nothing from the kid.

Briefly, he considered taking the phone, but he didn't. Tracking her calls seemed like a more productive use.

He scrolled through the contact list until he found Jake Reacher's number and committed it to memory. He called one of his burners from her phone to be sure he had the correct number for her. He'd dump the burner somewhere here in town.

Then he dropped her phone into the pile of crap he'd emptied out of her purse just as Oscar came up from the basement empty handed.

"Check the garage and meet us out front," Trevor ordered. Oscar nodded and left through the back door. Trevor watched him trudge to the detached garage, around to the side entrance, and go inside.

Mrs. Reacher was still sniveling and rubbing her sore arm when he turned his attention back to her. Owen stepped into the kitchen and shook his head. Trevor tilted his head toward the front of the house and Owen left.

Trevor waited until he heard the front door close. He saw Oscar leave the garage and plow through the snow toward the street.

Trevor pulled his gun from his pocket and held it where she could see it. He tilted his head as if he might be thinking about what to do next.

"Can I trust you, Mrs. Reacher?"

She nodded her head vigorously. "I've never met Mark Reacher. I swear I don't know him at all. If he ever calls me, I won't say anything to him."

Trevor nodded, still holding the gun. "What about your son? Can I trust you not to tell Jake? It seems like you've been calling him a lot. He'll call back eventually. Be easier for me if you never answered the phone."

"Don't kill me. Please," Mrs. Reacher begged, crying quietly now. "I won't tell anyone you were here. I won't call the police. You haven't really done anything and they wouldn't try to find you, anyway."

"I can easily come back here and finish what I started," Trevor mused as if he was thinking and she couldn't hear him.

"That won't be necessary. I promise," she said, barely coherent now as she continued to cry and beg.

He let her babble on for a bit before he adjusted his grip on the gun. He swung and hit her on the temple with the butt of his handgun. A satisfyingly hard whack that reverberated up his arm.

She stopped talking immediately. She fell sideways off the chair and landed on the kitchen floor.

He looked down at her for a few moments. She didn't move. She didn't speak. Her sobs had stopped.

She was probably unconscious and not dead. He could check her pulse to be sure. But he didn't.

He shrugged and returned his gun to his pocket. He walked through the back door and out to the garage. Inside, he found a relatively new sedan. He stooped to attach the tracking device and returned to the kitchen.

He locked the back door, checked to be sure the stove and oven were not on, and flipped the lights off in the kitchen.

He reversed his path from the kitchen through the hallway to the front room. Along the way, he grabbed one of the framed photos of Jake and his parents off the wall. He turned the lights off. When he reached the front door, he set the lock to snap into place, and closed the door behind him.

He found a fresh burner cell phone in his pocket and placed a call to a number he'd memorized long ago. "Yeah, I need a twenty-four hour trap on three phone numbers." He rattled off Margaret Reacher's home and cell numbers, and finished with Jake Reacher's cell phone.

"Anything else?"

"Not at the moment." He disconnected the call. He walked to the SUV and climbed inside. "The cash isn't here."

Owen replied, "If Lange is dead, the money could have burned up in the fire. Otherwise, I'm guessing the kid took it with him. We need to find the kid."

Trevor nodded. "There's one more place to look first."

He supplied driving directions.

CHAPTER THIRTY-ONE

Sunday, February 27
9:35 a.m.
Laconia, New Hampshire

TREVOR WAITED IN FRONT of the three-story brick townhome until a neighbor collected the old lady for church. She would be gone a couple of hours, which was more time than he needed. He worked his way around to the back, unlocked the door, and slipped inside.

The house was oppressively warm and humid inside. Old people were always cold, he remembered.

He found the old man in a large room that doubled as a study and a bedroom close to the front entrance. Trevor knocked once lightly and entered the room without waiting for an invitation.

The room was even warmer and more humid than the rest of the house. A gas fire burned in the fireplace. The old man had nodded off. His chin rested on his chest and he snored gently.

Since he was sleeping, Trevor was free to search the room. There was only one closet large enough to hold the black and tan duffel containing his money, and it wasn't there. Trevor hurried through the rest of the house. He searched each closet, under the beds, every space large enough to conceal the duffel. No luck.

He had no time to exhaust every nook and cranny in the place. If the duffel was here, the only way to find it quickly was to wake up the old man and make him talk.

Trevor hurried back to the old man's room. He was still asleep, snoring softly. Trevor strode swiftly across the carpet to the wing chair by the fire. He grabbed the old man's shoulder and gave him a hard shake.

His eyelids popped open. Trevor placed one hand on each chair arm and leaned over him. He opened his mouth to scream but no sound emerged. He flailed his head back and forth, attempting to avoid Trevor's vicious stare.

"Where is my money, old man?" Trevor demanded.

His mouth opened and closed. The sounds he made were not words. He emitted a series of grunts growing louder with each effort to communicate.

Trevor's patience exploded. He grabbed the old man's bony shoulders and shook him violently. The man's body seemed boneless, like a rag doll.

"Mark Reacher left my money here. I want it back. Tell me where it is and I will leave you in peace," Trevor said, leaving little doubt what he would do if the old man refused.

He shook his head back and forth, wildly now. The grunts and guttural sounds became louder but still impossible to comprehend. Spittle drained from the corner of his lips.

Understanding dawned.

The old man couldn't talk. He might not understand a word, either.

Trevor took a few deep breaths to slow his thundering pulse.

He stepped back from the chair, giving the old man a chance to calm down. Which was when Trevor noticed a writing pad and pencil on the table next to the chair.

Trevor handed the pencil to the old man.

He could barely grasp the fat black pencil in his right hand, holding it in his fist like a young child.

Trevor laid the pad on his lap. He looked up at Trevor with pleading eyes.

"You understand me?"

The old man nodded to signal that he could hear and understand.

"Where is my money?" Trevor demanded again.

The old man shook his head and lifted his shoulders.

"You don't know? Is that it?" Trevor said, his rage barely contained. "I don't believe you. Where is Mark Reacher?"

As before, the old man shook his head and lifted his shoulders.

It was too preposterous to accept. Of course, the old man had to know more than he was letting on. There was no other reasonable answer.

Mark Reacher owned that motel. The last place Trevor's partner went to before he disappeared. He was probably dead. Mark Reacher had probably killed him. Most likely for the money. Nothing else made any sense.

And this old guy had to know about it. If he didn't have the money, he knew where it was. Or where Mark Reacher was. He had to know *something* useful.

Yet here he was, claiming that he didn't know. That he couldn't even talk.

Well maybe he couldn't talk. What kind of life was that? Who would want to live like that?

But this guy obviously did.

Maybe Trevor had gone about this the wrong way. He took a step back. Took a few breaths. Changed his approach.

"Okay. The money's not here. You don't know where Mark Reacher is. What *do* you know that would help me get my money back and give me a reason to leave you alive when I walk out of here?"

The old man gripped the pencil in his fist and moved it to the pad. He moved his entire hand to write two words. *Don't Know.*

Trevor read the words. "That's a lie."

The old man's head wagged vigorously, his face reddening like a balloon that might pop at any minute.

"Jake Reacher. He's what, Mark's nephew? Did he take my money?"

The old man scrunched up his face and opened his mouth and bellowed a howl that might have been the word no. Or it might have been almost anything else.

He repeated the howl as he tried to stand. He was too feeble. Too weak. He managed to put space between himself and the chair. Then he fell to the floor, writhing and howling until Trevor could listen no more.

Trevor took long strides over to the bed and grabbed a pillow. He brought it back to the rug in front of the fireplace and used it to smother the old man until everything stopped. The howling, the writhing, the breathing. Even his heartbeat. It all stopped.

The old man's glassy eyes looked straight up. All life had left him.

Trevor waited a few minutes to be sure the old man was gone. Then he replaced the pillow on the bed, left the room, left the house through the back door, and returned empty-handed to Owen and Oscar waiting in the SUV down the block.

Owen pulled into the roadway. At the first intersection, he asked, "Where to?"

"Boston," Trevor replied as he pressed the redial button on a burner phone. "Talk to me. Where's the kid?"

"We pulled some voicemails from the mother's phone. The kid is headed to San Diego. Took a bit of digging, but we've located him on I-44 northwest of Tulsa."

"Keep me posted," Trevor said before he disconnected the call.

He checked the clock. The kid would arrive in Tulsa about the same time Trevor arrived in Boston.

The Gulfstream was fast, but he couldn't reach Tulsa before Jake arrived. It would take the kid another nine hours to drive to Albuquerque. Along the way, he'd pass several airports with runways long enough to land the Gulfstream.

Trevor considered executive airports between Amarillo and Albuquerque until he settled on Tucumcari, New Mexico, as the best location. He spent the rest of the drive scheduling a reservation and organizing ground transportation.

When Owen pulled into the parking lot at the executive airport, he parked close to the building and outside the range of surveillance cameras. All three men turned up their collars and donned hats and gloves. They pulled their travel bags from the vehicle and turned toward the entrance.

Before they reached the glass doors, a fourth man approached the silver SUV and slipped behind the wheel. He drove the vehicle off the lot. The SUV, its remaining contents, and all forensic evidence would disappear like the other vehicles had, long before the Gulfstream reached Tucumcari.

CHAPTER THIRTY-TWO

Sunday, February 27
1:25 p.m.
Tulsa, Oklahoma

JAKE PULLED OFF INTERSTATE 44 at a truck stop just on
the other side of Tulsa, Oklahoma. He filled the Jeep's gas tank,
scrubbed the bugs off the windshield with a long-handled
squeegee, checked the tire pressure, the oil, and topped off the
window washer fluid reservoir. All good.

He waved at a couple of friendly long-haul truckers talking
in the parking lot where the big rigs rumbled. He was about an
hour from Oklahoma City where he'd pick up Interstate 40 west.
The weather was clear. He'd left the snow behind and there was
no rain anywhere in the forecast. The GPS said the route was
free of construction zones and, at the moment anyway, not
snarled in traffic.

Sundays were good days to travel, he'd discovered. No
rush hour traffic and few trucks on the road. He'd made good
time all the way from Cincinnati so far, but he was still

twenty hours of drive time from San Diego.

Could he stay awake that much longer?

He'd pulled all-nighters in college plenty of times, and he'd probably do plenty more when he entered law school. He had friends in med school who talked about thirty-six hour rotations, and he was at least as tough as they were. He could do this. He was sure of it.

He could go 248 miles on a full tank of gas. Which would get him well past Oklahoma City. He shouldn't need to stop again.

He moved to a parking space on the side of the building. He dug a clean pair of jeans and a Hard Rock Casino T-shirt out of his black leather duffel bag and rolled them into a big beach towel. He grabbed his toiletry kit and went inside for a quick shower and shave.

Afterward, he felt like a new man. Tired, but energized, too. He'd been running on caffeine, sugar, and an intense desire not to go to jail since he'd left Cincinnati. All three were powerful fuels. He felt wired and ready for anything, but he would have preferred to have a traveling companion at this point. Someone to keep him from falling asleep at the wheel, or maybe even drive while he slept.

Back in the parking lot, he called his mother again. He'd tried calling her several times earlier in the day, but he kept getting her voicemail on both her home phone and her cell phone. She'd probably gone to church this morning, as she usually did, and left her cell phone in the car during church. She hated it when cell phones disrupted the worship service.

He left another message telling her where he was and asking her to return his call after church. He signed off with, "Love you, mom," as he always did.

At the fast food joint inside the truck stop, he refilled his thermos with hot, black coffee, and bought a big bag of road food. He added a six-pack of water and a Powerball lotto ticket to his bill. He was feeling lucky and the jackpot was a billion dollars.

"What would you do with a billion dollars?"

He grinned, thinking about what he might do with the money as he turned toward the voice. Immediately, he felt underdressed.

A tiny Asian woman, cute as anything, stood behind him in the line. She looked about eighteen. No more than five feet. No more than a hundred pounds. Maybe less. She was dressed in jeans, boots, and a white T-shirt under a brown leather flight jacket. Her hair was drawn back into a low ponytail. A pair of aviator Ray-Bans sat atop her head. Gold earrings were secured to her tiny earlobes.

Four guys wearing army fatigues stood behind her. Clean-shaven. Military haircuts. Perfect posture and confidence. Last names on the tape above their breast pockets. All four seemed interested in the Asian woman, which was understandable. In a word, she was hot. Too hot for all of them, Jake included.

"What would I do with a billion dollars? I'd buy you dinner for starters," Jake replied, emboldened by the ancient alpha male's need to best his competition. The four army guys widened their grins and nodded like they were right there, next in line when she shot him down.

She seemed to size up the situation in a quick glance. Friendly male competition, Jake's relative inexperience, and decided to have a little fun.

With a pointed look at the tables off to the left side of the store, she said, "How about we start with coffee and conversation and we'll see where it goes?"

"Sure." Jake swallowed hard. His cheeks flushed. He glanced at the army guys and joked, "Sorry, fellas. Better luck next time."

They nodded, clapped him on the arm. One said, "Way to go, buddy."

Jake paid for the coffee and carried it to her table. He offered her the coffee and took the seat across from her. He said, "Thanks for doing that. It was nice of you. Made my day."

"You ever think about joining the army yourself? You're every bit as good as those guys, I'd bet," she said.

"I did think about it a few times, actually. I was in Junior R.O.T.C. in high school and I thought I wanted to go to West Point. Make a whole career out of it, you know?"

"What happened?"

He took a deep breath. "My parents weren't cool with it. They thought I might get shot and maimed or killed or something."

"That's an understandable fear that parents have, don't you think?"

"Yeah. I'm an only child and they were worried. I thought they were going to consent, mostly because West Point would have been free tuition. They're teachers. They didn't have a lot of money to pay for school."

"Sounds like a reasonable solution. West Point's a great school."

"Then Dartmouth accepted me. I played football in high school and I was good enough for college." He shrugged. "I was a kid. I loved playing football. My parents were over the moon about Dartmouth because my dad went there. So we made it work."

"I see," she said.

He took another deep breath, blew it out on his coffee, and took a gulp. Then he grinned. "So that's the reason I'm not standing over there with those guys in fatigues. Kinda cool that you chose me anyway."

She smiled at him and changed the subject. "Out of curiosity, what would you really do with a billion dollars?"

He shrugged. "I don't honestly know. That's more money than I expect to see in my lifetime. But help my mom first, for sure. Then probably travel the world, I guess. Meet new people. Stay a while in other places and soak up the culture."

"Is that what you're doing now? Traveling the country?"

"Yeah, sort of. I'm headed to California. San Diego. Looking for a guy." He paused to drink the coffee. "What about you? You don't look like you live here in Oklahoma."

"No? Lots of good farms in Oklahoma still. I'm a farm girl at heart. I come from a long line of farmers," she replied with a smile. "But you're right. I don't live here. I'm on my way to San Diego, too, as it happens."

He widened his eyes. "Why?"

"Same reason you are, Jake," she said evenly.

"How'd you know my name?"

She pulled out her badge wallet and showed it to him. "FBI Special Agent Kim Otto."

"So you were waiting for me? How'd you know I'd come here?" He wiped his sweaty palms on his jeans. Was the FBI chasing him down because of that business in Cincinnati? Surely not. But what else could it possibly be?

"I was in Laconia for the past couple of days. I met your mother. And Old Man Reacher. That's how I knew you were driving toward San Diego," she explained like she was talking him off the ceiling or something. "We pinged your cell phone and your GPS to find your exact location. You'd marked this place on your GPS the last time you stopped for gas, probably because you could get a shower and takeout food and quickly get back on the road, am I right?"

"Okay. Makes sense, even if it's a bit unnerving to think about you watching me like that," Jake said, nodding. "But why go to all that trouble? You could have just called me on the phone. Asked to meet up."

"How about if I tell you all about it in the Jeep when we get on the road? Save some time. We've got a long way to drive," she replied.

"You want to ride with me? All the way to San Diego?" he asked, not sure what to make of the request. Would it be better or worse to have an FBI agent in the car with him for the next two days?

Which was when he noticed that she had travel bags with her. She stood, waiting. He collected his road food. "Okay. Well, my Jeep's parked in the side lot."

"Yeah. I know," she replied with a smile. "Lead the way."

She followed him outside and stowed her bags in the back of the Jeep. They settled into the cabin with fresh coffee and his foot-long sandwich and headed toward the I-44 West entrance ramp.

A couple of miles later, Jake had finished his food while thinking about the situation and he wanted some answers. He glanced across to her. She was staring out the windows like she was looking for something in particular. She was wearing aviator style sunglasses, making it impossible to see her eyes.

He cleared his throat to get her attention. "What did you mean when you said you were going to San Diego for the same reason I am?"

"You want to find Jack Reacher and so do I. Pretty simple."

He took a minute to think that through. "My mother tell you that?"

"No. Old Man Reacher did."

"So you know why I want to find him, then?"

"Because you think he's your uncle," she said.

He frowned and kept his eyes on the road. The conversation was becoming more surreal by the moment. It was strange to talk about the situation openly when his parents had kept it secret all these years. He wasn't sure how he felt about any of it yet.

"Did you know Joe Reacher?" he asked.

She shook her head. "No. I don't know Jack, either. But I know a lot about them both."

"Why? Is this a manhunt? Are they bank robbers or something?" His frown deepened and his voice was laced with concern.

She was quiet for a long time and he thought she might not answer. But she finally did. What she said went off on a tangent.

"Both Joe and Jack Reacher were army officers once. West Point grads. Did you know that?"

Jake shook his head. "I don't know anything about them except that Joe was my biological father and he was killed in the line of duty."

"They were both honorably discharged from the army. Joe took a job with the Treasury Department. He was killed while investigating a case," she paused for a breath. "Joe's brother, Jack Reacher, was a military policeman. He served for thirteen years, most of them honorably according to the records."

"Sounds like things went sideways somewhere along the line," Jake replied slowly, struggling to put the pieces together to form a picture that made sense.

She said, "Maybe. Jack left the army early at the request of his bosses and under a cloud. If he hadn't agreed to go voluntarily, he might have ended up in prison."

Jake grimaced. "Yeah, I know how that works."

She said nothing, but he could read between the lines. She knew more about him than she was telling. He didn't really want to hear her repeat it all. Hell, he tried to forget his wild child days as much as possible.

"Why are you looking for Jack Reacher now?" He yawned. Man, he was tired. He'd been sleepy before he ate that big sandwich and now he really wanted a nap. On the other side of Oklahoma City, he might stop for a while.

"Simple background check. He's being considered for a special classified assignment. We need to know if he's still fit for the job," she replied.

"Still? What do you mean?" He widened his eyes and glanced across the console to look at her again.

"It's been fifteen years since he left the army. We don't know where he is."

Incredulously, he asked, "What? Didn't you tell me you could find anyone? That's how you knew where to find me?"

"Unfortunately, he's not driving around in a tech-equipped vehicle like you are. He's not living a normal life, either. He's been off the grid all these years." She cleared her throat.

Jake raised his eyebrows and stared at her. "Off the grid? You mean like a prepper survivalist or something?"

"He could be. We just don't know."

"What *do* you know?"

She cocked her head. "No IRS files, nothing from the banks, no debts or loans, no titles to houses or cars or boats or trailers, no arrest record, no convictions major or minor, no rental agreements on file anywhere, no land line or cell phone, ever, no ISP data and he's not in prison. He's not in witness protection or undercover for any of the other government agencies. He's not a hospital or institutional inpatient anywhere."

"Could he be living outside the country? An expat someplace?" Jake asked.

She shook her head. "We don't think so. He has a bank account and an ATM card. Both get used now and then from inside the U.S."

He sped up and moved out to pass a slow moving panel van traveling in the right lane. "So why do you think he's in San Diego? You can't find anything on the guy. You've probably looked other places before now and haven't found him."

She stretched her shoulders and rotated her neck, as if she was cramped up or something. "Tell you the truth, Jake, I don't know whether he's in San Diego or not. But I'm hoping we can draw him out. Once he knows you exist and you're in town, maybe he'll find us."

He looked at her again. "How likely is that?"

She sighed. "Not very. But you're the best lead I have right now. You're the only bet I can make."

They traveled another few miles in silence before Jake asked another question. "So you really do think that Joe Reacher was my biological father, then?"

As soon as the words left his mouth, he realized how skeptical he remained. When Jake was ten, his mother had the DNA tests done. But they'd had no samples from Joe Reacher to match. All the results really proved was that David Reacher was not his biological father. Which was bad enough, from Jake's perspective and from Dad's, too.

But Joe Reacher's paternity had never been conclusively proved. He'd trusted his mother's word. A woman who had lied to him about his father for his entire life. And how reliable was that?

"Do we think Joe was your biological father? Actually, we do. But we're working on DNA to prove it," she replied.

He raised his eyebrows and widened his eyes. "Why do you think Joe Reacher was my sperm donor?"

She took a deep breath and exhaled slowly through her nose. The sound was like something a delicate puppy might make. "Because of the way your mother reacted when I asked her about your father. And because you look exactly like both of the Reacher brothers. Jack and Joe."

CHAPTER THIRTY-THREE

Sunday, February 27
6:30 p.m.
Tulsa, Oklahoma

KIM HAD TAKEN HER turn behind the wheel an hour east of
Amarillo. They had picked up Interstate 40 in Oklahoma City
and they'd stopped once for gas and to change drivers. Soon
after, Jake had reclined his seat and gone to sleep.

He slept deeply, like an exhausted six-year-old. He'd been
driving for way too many hours. His eyes were bloodshot and his
eyelids drooped closed several times before she told him to pull
over and let her drive for a while. He hadn't argued.

Before he dropped into oblivion, Jake had asked, "What will
happen to Jack Reacher once you find him?"

She'd shrugged. "I honestly don't know. I don't know
anything about the job he's being considered for, or whether
he'll be willing or able to do it."

"So there's really a job? You're not just saying that? You're
not planning to arrest him? Send him to prison?" Jake had asked

with a wide yawn. He'd closed his eyes and a few seconds later, she'd heard him snoring.

Which meant she hadn't been required to answer the question.

The interstate along this stretch was straight, flat, and hypnotic. Traffic had been steady but moving along well in both directions. With Jake sleeping like every metaphor for an innate object she could think of, she took the chance to call Gaspar using one of the new burners she'd bought back at the Tulsa truck stop where she'd waited to intercept Jake.

"I've been listening," Gaspar said when he answered. "And if I can, others can."

"Right," she replied, brief and cryptic. No reason to add to the sound track and not much she could do about hackers while driving down the expressway at eighty miles an hour. The Boss monitored everything she did or said, all the time, unless she actively avoided him, which wasn't always successful. And it was impossible to avoid anyone with the right equipment hacking into the Jeep's systems or Jake's phone.

All of which meant it was safe to assume she was the subject of constant surveillance. She limited her conversations accordingly.

The burners she used and discarded provided a slim chance that phone conversations could stay private for a few brief minutes. Reasonably competent hackers could hear anything she said inside the Jeep, but couldn't hear what was said by the people she called until they isolated the burner's frequency and tapped into the call. She kept the conversations brief to minimize the risks.

Gaspar said, "There's a navy blue Escalade, couple years old, on your ass. Been following you for the past ten miles. It's hanging back, moving with the traffic, trying to avoid detection. But it's there."

She checked the rearview. The land was flat here, which made driving easier but reduced her visibility range behind the Jeep. She could see two or three vehicles behind her in the right lane. In the left lane, a tractor-trailer blocked her view. She didn't see a navy Escalade.

"Who is it?"

"Dunno. Vehicle's stolen. Still checking the occupants. Not FBI. Not cops of any kind, if I had to guess."

"Why do you say that?"

"A single big thug in the front seat, for one thing," he replied. "Cops travel in pairs."

She nodded. "Right."

"He's not talking much. But don't get your hopes up. It's probably not Reacher coming for the kid."

"How do you know?"

"Guy's big enough and ugly enough. But someone is feeding him directions through the SUV's speaker system. Reacher usually works alone," Gaspar said.

She paused to let the data sink in. "Any idea what he wants?"

"Not precisely. But whatever it is, they think it's in the Jeep you're driving." He paused for a long sigh. "Could be Jake. Could be something Jake's transporting. Did you inspect the vehicle before you jumped in with the kid?"

She scowled. Mostly because she didn't like him scolding her. But also because he had a valid point. Jake could be running drugs or guns or some other contraband in the Jeep. She hadn't checked the cargo. She should have.

"Just the one vehicle?"

"Only one identified so far. But muscle usually travels in packs."

"Right."

"You've got plenty of gas. As long as you keep moving, stay ahead of him, you should be okay until we come up with a plan," Gaspar said.

"We?"

"Yeah. Sorry. Had to call in some help on this one. When this goes south, you'll thank me for batting cleanup," Gaspar said before he signed off.

Kim disconnected the call on her end, too. Then she took the burner phone apart, yanked out the electronic insides and tossed pieces out the window in three groups as she sped along the highway.

Jake slept through everything.

The Boss's cell phone vibrated five minutes later. She answered, "Otto."

"The Jeep's the target. It'll get ugly. Do what you need to do. I'll handle the fallout," he said.

"Copy that," she said as she returned both hands to the steering wheel.

"Learn anything useful from the kid?"

"No."

"I've got eyes on you. Keep in touch," he said before he hung up.

CHAPTER THIRTY-FOUR

Sunday, February 27
7:30 p.m.
Tulsa, Oklahoma

A STEADY LINE OF traffic had materialized in the left lane as the big rig pulled closer and she could see behind it. She held the Jeep steady in the right lane and searched vehicles in the rearview until she found the navy blue Escalade with a big dude behind the wheel, hanging in the big rig's shadow.

She could see him clearly, which meant the Escalade was coming up behind her in the left lane way too fast.

She pushed the accelerator closer to the floor. The Jeep's speed jumped to close the gap between the Jeep and the full-sized sedan ahead that was traveling at the speed limit. From this angle, she saw that several vehicles were traveling close in front of the eighteen-wheeler. Kim couldn't move into the left lane ahead of the big rig.

The Escalade was eating the pavement behind her at a faster clip. He'd catch up soon.

She reached across the console and gave Jake a hard push. He barely moved. The kid was a tank and he was dead to the world.

She grabbed a water bottle from the cup holder and twisted off the cap. She doused his face with water while shouting. "Wake up, Jake!"

He turned his head toward her and opened his eyes. "What the hell?"

"Get up. Put your seat back in the locked position. Make sure your seatbelt is snug."

"Why?"

"Just do it, okay?" She accelerated again.

The sedan ahead of her was still moving at the speed limit. The Jeep was blocked in on all sides. She had no choice but to slow down or ram the sedan hard enough to start a chain reaction collision, which she and Jake were unlikely to survive.

The ribbon of expressway curved to the right up ahead leading to a long bridge over farmland with a shallow creek running through it. No doubt the Escalade planned to hit the left front side of the Jeep and push it over the low guard rail on the bridge. At these travel speeds, a fifty-foot drop followed by a likely rollover might be survivable. Maybe.

Her mind whipped through all available options. Which didn't take long because her choices were few.

There was an exit on the other side of the bridge. If she could exit the expressway, she'd have a chance. But first she had to reach the exit unscathed.

She reduced the pressure on the accelerator and pushed the button to turn on the emergency flashers. The Jeep slowed as much as possible, given the traffic coming up behind her.

The Escalade was two car lengths back, still hanging behind the eighteen-wheeler, but moving closer by the second. At these speeds, he'd only need to give the Jeep a solid glancing blow on the left side near the front to send the Jeep flying off the bridge. If he timed it right, the Escalade would barely suffer any damage and could simply drive away with the traffic.

Timing was critical.

If the Escalade moved too soon, the Jeep would still go over the guard rail on the right side of the interstate, but the fall would be survivable.

If he bashed the Jeep from any other angle, the crash could easily kill them all, and take out a few civilians, too. Whatever it was that the driver wanted, she figured he didn't plan to commit suicide in the process.

Her best chance was to keep the Escalade behind her until she could exit. She slowed the Jeep to keep pace alongside the big rig.

The exit was less than three minutes ahead.

Traffic in the right lane was traveling slower than traffic in the left lane. The eighteen-wheeler inched ahead with every passing second. The sedan in front of her kept a steady speed, which meant Kim was losing her shield against the Escalade and there was not a damn thing she could do about it.

Jake was upright and paying attention. "What can I do to help?"

She shook her head. "Keep your eye on that navy Escalade at seven o'clock."

He twisted his head and shoulders to locate the vehicle. "Who is that guy?"

She shrugged.

"He's at eight o'clock now."

"He's moving faster than we are by about twenty seconds a minute."

He stared at her. "You just calculated that in your head?"

"I'm good with numbers."

"Who is that guy? Why is he after us? Some kind of road rage thing? What'd you do? Cut him off?"

Kim shrugged, every ounce of attention focused on her driving.

She reached up and pulled the alligator clamp from the seatbelt at the retractor and tossed the clamp to the floor. This was one time when she wanted the seatbelt to be tight across her body.

The big rig was going to pass her. The Escalade would be at the best angle to hit the Jeep before she reached the exit. She inched the Jeep forward, tailgating the sedan in front of her in an effort to block the Escalade from entering her lane.

She looked ahead along the right shoulder of the road. Nothing had changed. It was still narrower than she needed it to be. Driving the remaining distance along the shoulder was not feasible.

The sturdy steel guardrail ran along the outside edge of the shoulder. She'd seen guardrail collisions before and she knew the statistics. Passengers in vehicles rarely survived them.

The sedan immediately ahead of Kim was a subcompact. There were two more sedans ahead of that one. Then a crossover SUV. All were driving the speed limit. One at a time, the vehicles in the left lane ahead of the truck were moving over into the right lane, allowing the eighteen-wheeler to pass.

The exit ramp was not quite a mile away. She'd be there in fifty seconds. Plenty of time for the big rig to pass and the Escalade to shove the Jeep over the edge.

The rear wheels on the eighteen-wheeler were parallel to the Jeep's front seats. The Escalade was too close behind. If the driver barely tapped his brakes, the Escalade would slide up under the trailer and decapitate him. But she couldn't count on that.

Kim could see inside the Escalade clearly using her left sideview mirror. The driver's head and shoulders were in plain view. She was certain she'd never seen him before.

Thirty seconds to the exit ramp. The eighteen-wheeler was slowly pulling ahead. The Escalade followed closely. He could shove the rear left quarter of the Jeep, but the physics were wrong. The Jeep would spin left, away from the guardrail. He stuck to his plan.

The Escalade moved inexorably forward. Kim held her speed.

The exit was twenty seconds ahead on the right. At the last possible moment, she'd need to slow slightly to bear right and down the cloverleaf to the county road below. The Escalade wouldn't be able to move over. He'd be forced to stay on the interstate until the next exit. By the time he circled back, she'd be gone.

She cast a meaningful glance toward Jake and tilted her head toward the right. If she'd warned him aloud, listeners would hear and be forewarned. He nodded and grabbed the sturdy handle in the roof above the passenger door to brace himself for impact. She tightened her grip on the steering wheel.

The exit loomed ahead. The sedan in front of her was half a car length ahead. The sedan behind her was half a car length back. The Escalade wouldn't fit in the open space.

If he tried to follow the Jeep down the exit ramp, he'd hit the second sedan and push it over the guardrail instead of the Jeep.

She tapped her brakes to warn the sedan at the same moment she swerved to the right, out of the flow of traffic and onto the ramp.

The Escalade was too far advanced to see the brief flash of her brake lights. He didn't anticipate her actions.

Half a moment after she swerved out of the travel lane, the Escalade moved sharply right and then left again, in an attempt to slam the Jeep's front left quarter with the Escalade's right rear quarter. He wanted a glancing blow. Hard enough to lift and push the Jeep, but not so hard that it severely damaged the Escalade or simply pushed the Jeep sideways. And the blow needed to be fast.

His timing was off.

The impact glanced off the Jeep behind the driver's door instead. The Jeep bounced and Kim struggled to hold it on the road. Miraculously, the vehicle kept moving in the right direction, but she was fighting the steering wheel to keep the Jeep on the road.

"Whoa!" Jake yelled at the moment of impact.

The Escalade outweighed the Jeep by more than a thousand pounds. But the extra distance between them along with the change in angle of impact made a big difference. The Jeep was badly damaged, but it limped along and Kim fought to hold the vehicle on the ramp as she slowed and steered around the cloverleaf.

At the bottom of the ramp, she moved the Jeep off to the side of the road. She glanced up at the interstate and saw the Escalade sailing past. She was breathing heavily and her heart pounded wildly in her chest.

She turned the engine off and jumped out. She ran around to the passenger side of the vehicle and pulled her bags out.

Jake looked like he'd survived the worst thrill ride of his life. He opened the passenger door, stepped outside.

She said, "Grab your stuff and follow me, Jake. I smell gas.

The impact may have ruptured the tank. One spark and this thing could explode."

"You think he'll come back?" Jake asked.

"Yes. It'll take him a while to reach the next exit and swing back. We've got some breathing room, but not a lot. Come on."

She walked quickly to put as much distance between them and the Jeep as possible. Jake walked ahead at a faster clip. When they were half a mile away, standing in the road that ran through the middle of an empty field, The Boss's cell phone vibrated in her pocket.

"Otto," she said when she answered.

"Nice work."

She said nothing.

"Helo will be there in ten. Bring the kid."

"What about the damn Escalade? Who was trying to run us off the road?"

"Working on it," he replied before he hung up.

Jake had waited for her to catch up. When she did, he said, "I guess my Jeep is totaled."

"Yeah." She heard the helo in the distance. She scanned the sky to find the bird heading toward them at one o'clock.

"Now what? Hitchhike? Wait for a bus?" Jake said.

She cocked her head and looked up at him. Hitchhiking or riding a bus was exactly what Jack Reacher would do. As Gaspar would say, the apple doesn't fall far from the tree.

CHAPTER THIRTY-FIVE

Sunday, February 27
11:30 p.m.
Siesta Beach, California

KIM NEEDED SLEEP, BUT before that, she left the hotel and went down to the beach. The salty ocean air made her sneeze. On the north side of the beach was a long public fishing pier that extended into the Pacific. Wood rails rested on either side of the concrete walkway supported by concrete pillars. The sign at the entrance said the T-shaped structure was 1,873 feet long. The platform at the end extended 320 feet south and 198 feet north. The Sunset Café, open twenty-four hours, perched at the end of the pier.

She walked toward the café. It was three hours later on the East Coast, where she'd last seen Finlay. He traveled the globe and she had no idea where he actually was at the moment. Using a new disposable phone, she dialed the private number she'd memorized when he first gave it to her.

On the tenth ring, he picked up. "How can I help you, Agent Otto?"

"I'm in San Diego."

"So I heard."

"I think Reacher's here."

"I think so, too."

She concealed her surprise. Finlay never admitted that he knew Reacher's whereabouts, whether he did or not. "Tell me why you think so."

"He's been seen in the vicinity. You're walking on the Siesta Beach Pier. He's been hanging around that exact spot, off and on."

Kim paused to let her tired brain absorb the data.

Finlay replied, "He's not there for the kid."

"How do you know that?"

"Because he's been there since before the kid left home," Finlay paused to let the information sink in. "And because he doesn't know the kid exists. Not yet, anyway. So if you are keeping the kid around in an effort to lure Reacher out, you don't have the right bait."

"Jake's the right bait. Reacher hasn't seen him yet. It'll be like looking in a mirror when he was twenty-two. He'll be curious. Anybody would be," she replied. "But if he doesn't know about Jake yet, why is he here?"

"My guess? Something to do with that Canadian couple, probably. The guy that owned the Honda. The one Smithers found up in Laconia. If I were looking for Reacher, I'd start with them," Finlay said before he hung up.

Finlay's comments were more than mere suggestions. Maybe he knew Reacher had been in touch with the Canadian couple. She was on the right track. Good to know.

She destroyed the phone and casually tossed most of it into the trash as she walked by. She dropped a few essential electronic pieces into the ocean for good measure.

She turned to look back at the community of Siesta Beach resting to the east, across the sand from the Pacific.

Siesta Beach was a funky, eclectic place. The main street was dominated by small retail businesses. Mostly antique shops, tattoo and piercing shops, bars, bike and surf shops. Plenty of head shops, too, selling cannabis paraphernalia mostly. Siesta Beach was almost like San Francisco's Haight-Ashbury of the 1970s had been frozen in time and relocated to the oceanside.

The Canadian couple Finlay mentioned owned the windsurfing shop on the south side of the boardwalk. Patty Sundstrom and Shorty Fleck lived upstairs. She could see the bungalow now from her vantage point.

Perhaps Reacher had watched them from here, too. The pier was a place for people to stand and gaze. He wouldn't seem unusual in any way. No one would give him a second glance.

But why would Reacher watch them? The connection between them was nothing more than a guess based on timing, location, and her gut.

The sand between the pier and the boardwalk was cold and windy and cast in shadows. It was not easy to see anything clearly from this distance. The windsurfing shop was closed and all the windows were dark. Would Reacher have been able to see the couple in daylight or when the lights were on inside? Impossible to say.

She stuffed her hands into her pockets, leaned against the siderail, and glanced around.

The pier was not crowded tonight, probably because of the coming storm. The ocean was already promising big waves tomorrow. High tide and strong winds were catnip to surfers. Storms lured them to ride the swells in droves, even when the storms were fierce and the waves treacherous. The beach would be busy in the morning.

A few other hardy souls had ventured out to admire the roar of the ocean and the growing waves. The café was busier, but not full. A couple stood close together near the end of the pier on the left. Two men were smoking on the other side. She saw the glow from a couple of cigars and caught a whiff of tobacco. A few people strolled in pairs along the concrete in both directions.

When she turned to look back at Siesta Beach again, she caught his silhouette out of the corner of her eye. A lone man lurking in the shadows of the café. She couldn't see his face, but he was the right size and shape to be Reacher.

Had Finlay been suggesting that Reacher was standing on the pier watching her? Right here, right now?

Her breath caught until she consciously reminded herself to breathe. Her pulse pounded in her ears.

All the times she'd imagined the moment she'd confront Reacher, none of them involved a pier that protruded into the Pacific in the dead of night with the cold wind whipping up the ocean's spray.

She pushed off the side rail and walked toward him. He didn't move.

She'd covered about half the distance between them when he stepped out of the shadows and her heart almost stopped. Raw power and confidence radiated off him in waves.

Hands the size of turkeys. Broad shoulders. Six foot five inches tall and the way the moonlight glinted off his fair hair made him seem almost anointed or something.

The light hit his face. And she recognized him.

Jake Reacher.

He looked so much like Reacher. The differences were imperceptible in the darkness. But the differences were there.

Slowly, her internal threat level backed off the red zone. Her heartbeat slowed to its steady rhythm and she began to breathe normally again. She stopped thinking about how to reach for her gun without tipping him off, should the need arise.

She stepped into the cone of yellow light from the overhead streetlight and waited as Jake came closer, until he recognized her, too.

He approached saying, "I couldn't sleep. Too much excitement today. Too geeked up about tomorrow, I guess. How about you?"

"Same," she said, although she suspected he was lying, just like she was. He'd come out here to find Jack Reacher. Had he succeeded? They walked along together toward the hotel.

"What do you think will happen tomorrow?" he asked. "Will that couple Smithers found tell us whatever they know about Jack?"

"I don't know. But don't get your hopes up." She sighed. "I've interviewed a lot of witnesses with ties to Jack Reacher. Most of them won't talk about him at all. And the ones who do rarely have anything good to say about the guy."

Jake hung his head and scuffed his sneakers along the pavement. "You said he was a military cop. He received a bunch of medals in the army. Some of them were pretty impressive, too. He's one of the good guys. Right?"

They walked a few yards in silence. When they stepped off the pier onto the sand, Kim felt the cold through the soles of her boots.

What should she tell the kid? She didn't want to lie. Was he one of the good guys? Was Jack Reacher friend or enemy?

Impossible to say. Alternative arguments bounced around her head like a tennis ball at Wimbledon.

Reacher was an enigma. A force to be reckoned with. A bundle of contradictions.

He deserved respect. He had been a decorated army officer. A war hero. A solid military cop for thirteen years.

He was also a brutal man. He'd killed off the battlefield, sometimes in self-defense or defense of others, and sometimes not.

He'd appointed himself judge, jury, and executioner. He didn't seem to care whether the law would view his actions as justified. His opinion was the only one that mattered.

The truth was that her feelings about Jack Reacher were just as conflicted as the facts.

She was a cop and every cop on the planet would say he belonged in prison for some of the things he'd done. Many of the witnesses Kim had interviewed during this assignment probably belonged in prison with him. It was her job to arrest criminals.

But there was more to Reacher's story. She knew it as well as she'd ever known anything.

There were valid reasons why good people wouldn't turn on Reacher. Of that, she was absolutely certain, because hers was one of those lives he'd saved. Gaspar, too. More than once.

Until she figured out why the Boss wanted Reacher and what he intended to do with him once she found him, Reacher's status would stay the same. Missing.

But she wasn't going to tell Jake any of that. All he wanted was to meet his uncle because he'd never met his father. Afterward, he'd go back east, go to law school, and become the kind of model citizen Jack Reacher hadn't been in a long, long time.

In the end, after wrestling with herself for a while, she shrugged and replied, "Come on. We've got a big day tomorrow. I need some sleep."

CHAPTER THIRTY-SIX

Monday, February 28
6:30 a.m.
Siesta Beach, California

PATTY SLEPT FITFULLY AND awakened early, as she had
every night since Reacher showed up in Siesta Beach. She
heard the storm's building intensity outside. Waves crashed
harder and more frequently against the sand and the roar was
unmistakable.

The shop opened every morning at seven-thirty, so she gave
up trying to sleep. Shorty was still snoring softly and she didn't
want to wake him. The poor guy needed rest even more than she
did. She padded quietly to the kitchen to brew coffee and make a
slice of peanut butter-slathered toast before she showered,
dressed, and went downstairs.

She unlocked the front door and flipped the sign to "open."
She carried her hot coffee back to the counter and lifted the lid
on the laptop to check the shop's finances, like she did every
Monday.

They were doing okay. Sometimes, she was tempted to spend some of the money they kept in the black duffel at the storage place, but she never did. The money seemed dirty because of the way they got it. She and Shorty weren't used to luxurious living anyway. Never had been. As long as they could make it on what they earned in the shop, she was satisfied.

She heard the bell ring when the front door opened. She finished with the financial reports and closed the laptop before she looked up. By that time, the customer had already reached the checkout desk.

"I'm interested in a windsurfing lesson today," he said, although he looked more like a bouncer in a biker bar than a windsurfer. A big man with brown eyes, broad shoulders, and long arms. Dressed in jeans, a plaid shirt and cowboy boots. He'd shaved his head like a lot of guys did, but it made him look dangerous.

"A storm's coming in and it's already rough out there. How about we schedule you later in the week when things calm down?" she replied as she opened the laptop and pulled up the scheduling program. "I can put you down for Thursday. Would that work?"

"No. I'm leaving town tonight. It needs to be today." He pulled a wad of bills from his front pocket and peeled off a few. He laid them on the counter. "I'll pay extra for the inconvenience."

She frowned and chewed on her cuticle. She'd never lost a student in the surf, and she didn't want this guy to be the first. She probably couldn't save him if he got in trouble out there.

Before she had a chance to reply, he said firmly, "Look, I'm not a novice. I've had some experience. If we go now, before the weather gets worse, we should be okay."

"If you already know how to windsurf, why do you want a lesson? I can rent the equipment to you."

"No." He shook his head. "I said I had some experience, not that I was an expert."

She saw that he wasn't going to take no for an answer and the last thing she wanted was trouble.

The guy said. "Let's go before the storm blocks us. I really want to get out there. I saw some guys on the waves and it looks awesome."

Somehow he didn't look like a guy who would say the waves look awesome. Her internal radar was already elevated and his choice of words made things worse.

"Let me call my partner to watch the shop while we're gone."

"Just leave him a note. Let's get going," he demanded.

"We'll need to get your equipment together first."

"I've got mine down there already. We can both use it. Come on." He paused, like he knew he was pushing too hard, and softened his approach. "Don't worry so much. This is going to be fun. I've never had a chance to ride waves like these before. If we get out there and you want to come back, we'll do that. But let's at least give it a shot. Okay?"

She thought things through for a moment. They'd be using his equipment so hers wouldn't be damaged. She could leave him out there on his own if the waves were too dangerous. So what was the worst that could happen? He'd stiff her for the lesson fees? She was willing to risk that much. She shrugged.

"Okay. Let's do this," she said as she headed for the door.

CHAPTER THIRTY-SEVEN

Monday, February 28
8:30 a.m.
Siesta Beach, California

FROM HER HOTEL ROOM, Kim drank coffee and looked through the windows toward the Pacific to watch the raging storm while she listened to her voice messages.

News reports warned against going into the ocean today, citing the dangerous wind conditions and powerful rip tides, but as she'd expected, surfers were already out there. She watched a few surfers riding the waves toward the beach. She saw quite a few more wipe out trying.

Huge waves crashed across the pier where she'd stood last night. Some looked to be twenty feet high from this distance. If she'd been standing there now, she'd have been swept out to sea. She shivered to think about being sucked away in the rip currents.

Farther from the shore, fog was rolling in. She could only see about twenty feet along the pier. The café at the end was totally obscured by weather.

Smithers had left her a long voicemail. He'd interviewed Shorty Fleck about the Honda yesterday while Kim was with Jake. Fleck told Smithers the Honda broke down on their way to New York City and they'd abandoned it when they couldn't get it started again. Fleck gave him dates, times, and places to corroborate. Smithers was checking the story out, but said it sounded plausible and consistent with the other evidence at the scene of the motel fire. He was headed back to Boston. He'd keep her in the loop as more forensic evidence was analyzed.

She hadn't told Smithers she was no longer interested in the identity of the bodies. She felt sure in her bones that Reacher wasn't one of them. The rest of that case was in Smithers's capable hands and, thankfully, not on her plate.

Gaspar had left a long report on her secure server, which she'd downloaded last night. He'd located Joe Reacher's autopsy samples and pulled a couple of strings to get expedited testing. Results were pending.

Kim had considered Gaspar her secret weapon because he thought like Reacher. Was Jake her ace in the hole? Would Reacher try to approach the kid? Could she simply sit back and wait?

Kim met Jake in the lobby of the hotel for the short walk to the windsurfing shop. She wanted to interview Patty and Shorty herself. They may have abandoned the Honda, like Shorty told Smithers, but there was more to that story and Reacher was involved. She'd bet on it.

Besides, Jake wanted to satisfy his own curiosity. So they grabbed umbrellas from the hotel's stand and walked outside.

Kim led the way and Jake followed. Gusting wind battered and lifted the umbrellas, but Kim held on. A strong gust inverted Jake's umbrella as they were walking across the first side street.

He stuffed it in the trash can on the next corner and hunched into his jacket while the cold rain pelted him.

Kim lost her umbrella the same way at the next corner. Within moments, they were both drenched.

At the third traffic light, they crossed to the beach side of the street, walking straight into the fierce wind. The windsurfing shop was another half block south. There were lights on inside the bungalow and an old-fashioned "Open" sign hung on the front door.

Jake followed Kim along the sidewalk and toward the entrance. When they reached the shop, he opened the door and she stepped inside first. He pulled the door against the wind to close it.

Shorty Fleck was alone in the store. Kim recognized him from the photos, although his appearance was not exactly the same. Brown hair had been bleached by the sun. Bronzed skin he'd acquired living on the beach. But it was him. Same brown eyes. Same build. Same age. Same name.

Kim glanced around the place. It looked like she'd imagined a windsurfing shop should look, which is to say it was filled with all sorts of beach sports paraphernalia. A video played on a loop above a display for windsurfing gloves. The sport looked more than dangerous to Kim, but she'd never tried it. Today would not be the day she took her first lesson.

She didn't see Patty Sundstrom anywhere. Perhaps she was asleep upstairs. Shorty had barely looked up when the bell over the door rang to announce that a customer had entered. He fidgeted like a caged tiger, pacing from one side of the small shop to the other.

When he stopped short of the outside wall, Kim noticed a large black duffel bag trimmed in brown leather rested at his

278 | Diane Capri

feet, looking decidedly out of place amid the sunscreen, beach towels, and assorted beachwear.

"Are you Shorty Fleck?" Kim called out.

He looked toward her, perhaps startled to hear her voice inside the store. "I'm sorry. We're closed."

"Are you sure? The door was unlocked and the Open sign is showing," Jake said.

"Is it? I must've forgotten to lock up. Sorry. We're closed," Shorty said again. "If you know what you want, I can handle it quickly for you. I'm expecting a phone call. I'll need to leave right away when the call comes in."

Shorty seemed particularly agitated. His breathing was ragged and he was perspiring heavily. He kept glancing toward the duffel bag as if it might have sprouted legs and walked away on its own. Whatever was inside, he watched it like a hawk watched a field mouse.

Jake stuffed his hands in the pockets of his jeans and said, "Just wanted to talk to you, man. About my uncle. Jack Reacher. Has he been around here lately?"

Shorty stopped pacing. He leaned forward and looked harder at Jake. His face turned ashen, like he'd seen a ghost. Had the situation been less tense, Kim would have laughed. She understood the feeling. Totally.

"Jack Reacher is your uncle?" Shorty asked, eyes wide and wild. "He never mentioned a nephew."

"You've talked to him recently, then?" Jake replied.

"Yeah. Couple of days ago."

"Where is he now?"

"Dunno." Shorty shrugged and tilted his head toward the Pacific. "He was interested in windsurfing. Maybe he's down there. Waves are crazy today."

"Jake, lock the front door and put the closed sign in the window, please," Kim said. She pulled out her badge wallet and showed Shorty her ID. "I'm FBI Special Agent Kim Otto."

Shorty's eyes widened and he took a step back. "I told Agent Smithers everything I know about the Honda when he was here yesterday."

Kim frowned. "What's really going on here?"

Shorty shook his head. "What do you mean?"

"Where's Patty Sundstrom?" Kim asked.

His breath whooshed through his lips like she'd punched him in the gut. His knees buckled and he staggered back. He slid down and landed on his ass on the floor behind the cash register. Half a moment later, he scrambled to stand.

"What's in that duffel bag, Shorty?" Kim asked. "Open it."

He shook his head fast. "Can't do that. Sorry."

"Why not?"

Which was when tears sprang to his eyes. His voice broke when he explained. "B-Because he'll k-kill Patty if we open it. He said b-bring it and d-don't look inside. Not even once."

"But you'd already looked inside, hadn't you?" Jake said.

Shorty nodded. "It's cash. I don't know how much. Maybe a million dollars. We never counted it. Never used any of it, either."

"Why not?" Jake asked incredulously, as if the idea of having access to a million dollars and not spending it was beyond his comprehension.

Shorty shrugged.

"Someone has kidnapped Patty? Holding her for ransom?" Kim asked.

Shorty nodded miserably.

She'd have called Smithers for backup, but he was already in the air headed to Boston. Gaspar had no forces at his disposal ready to assist her immediately. Which left Finlay or the Boss. She'd have preferred Finlay, but the Boss was more likely to have local resources at the ready.

After a brief hesitation, she fished the Boss's cell phone from her pocket and dialed.

"What's his name?" Kim asked while she waited for the Boss to pick up the call.

Shorty shook his head.

"This place doesn't look flush with cash. How did he know you and Patty could pay a ransom?" Jake asked.

Shorty squared his shoulders. "Because he says the money in the duffel belongs to him. Says we stole it. He wants it back. Or else."

"So you talked to him. Did you see him? Can you tell me what he looks like?" Kim asked.

"I heard the front door slam on my way downstairs. Patty was walking down toward the water with a bald guy and I saw her meet up with the others. One of them grabbed her arm. Big guy. Not as big as Reacher or," he nodded toward Jake, "him. But bigger than me. There were three of them. One was about the same size as the first. The third guy was average-sized. None of them were dressed in boardshorts or wet suits or anything. They didn't have any equipment."

"So you're saying they weren't windsurfers and they lured Patty down there to kidnap her?"

"Yeah. They must've. When one of them grabbed her like that, I ran down there. Tried to stop them. But when I got there, they all had guns." He paused and wiped his running nose with his sleeve.

"And then what happened?" Jake asked. Kim shot him a glare.

Shorty said, "The two big guys must be brothers. They

looked kinda like twins, but the one that grabbed Patty had a long brown ponytail. Both big. Broad shoulders. Long arms. The average-sized guy was calling the shots. Trevor, I think they called him. He told the ponytail guy to take Patty over to the pier café and wait for his call. He grabbed Patty tighter and dragged her off. Trevor and the bald one came back here with me."

"What did they want?" Jake asked.

"They said they'd let Patty go if I gave them the duffel. I said they could have it, just don't hurt Patty. But it wasn't here. I'd told them I'd have to go get it. Trevor told the bald guy to come with me. We went to the storage place and I got the duffel. We came back here to wait for the call."

"*We*? You mean the bald man is here with you?" Kim's pulse pounded in her ears. She reached for her gun and dropped the phone into her pocket, leaving the connection open.

Shorty nodded miserably. He lifted his eyes and his chin toward the upstairs apartment.

Jake asked, "The leader said he'd call to set up the exchange, right?"

Shorty nodded.

"How long have you been waiting?"

He shrugged. "An hour. Maybe a little less."

"You've heard nothing at all from Patty?" Kim asked.

Shorty shook his head. "They won't hurt her before we give them the duffel, will they?"

Jake glanced toward Kim and held her gaze for a long moment. She shook her head. They'd likely kill Patty and Shorty as soon as they got what they wanted. Jake nodded as if he understood.

Which was when Kim heard the toilet flush. Heavy footfalls crossed the room overhead and a door squeaked open.

CHAPTER THIRTY-EIGHT

Monday, February 28
9:30 a.m.
Siesta Beach, California

THE HEAVY FOOTFALLS BEGAN to descend. A man's voice called out, "Shorty!"

Shorty didn't respond. Whether he was too scared or what, it was the right move.

She noticed movement in her periphery. Jake dashed to the duffel, grabbed it, and ran out the front door. What was he thinking? Probably that keeping the duffel away from the kidnappers as long as possible was a better plan. He was probably right.

She couldn't go after him now. One hundred percent of her attention was focused on dealing with the thug speeding down the stairs.

When Jake rushed outside, the wind caught the door and slammed it all the way open, banging hard against the outside wall. Rain pelted into the bungalow. Thunder and lightning added to the soundtrack.

She gestured Shorty to hide behind the counter opposite the staircase, and she flattened her back against the wall beneath the stairs.

The door's banging caused the footfalls upstairs to come faster.

He was directly above and behind Kim's location on the wall.

If she stepped into view, he'd have a close and easy target.

He yelled over the storm's cacophony as he descended rapidly. "What's going on, Shorty? Shorty! He'll be calling any minute. It's almost time to make the swap. If we're even five minutes late, you know what will happen to Patty."

Kim took a chance, turtled her head out, and looked up the stair treads. She saw a big left foot clad in a cowboy boot descending, followed swiftly by the right foot, then left again. His weight shifted from one to the other as he picked up speed. Each footfall landed heavily. Rapidly.

He outweighed her by a hundred and twenty pounds, at least. And he was armed. Her options were limited.

As long as he was up the stairs and she was at the bottom, he had the advantage. If she could strike a hard blow to his leg at the right time, downward momentum would cause him to fall forward.

But her leverage was wrong. She couldn't get enough speed or heft behind the blow to topple him. She had no choice. She was forced to wait.

It didn't take long.

He reached the bottom of the stairs and noticed the front door flapping open. He didn't bother looking around the shop. He must have guessed Shorty took the black duffel and escaped with it. He hit the ground running.

Dashing toward the exit, he held a gun in his right hand, shoving merchandise out of his path like a running back headed to the end zone.

Kim stepped from the shadows and yelled. "FBI! Stop!"

In a split second, he pivoted on his left foot and turned to face her. He fired twice.

Both shots went wide.

Kim fired back and ducked low behind the counter.

He shot two more rounds.

This time, his aim was better.

The bullets landed mere inches from her torso.

He half-turned toward the door, presenting a broad target.

Kim aimed at the center of his back and fired four times.

All four shots landed exactly where she'd placed them.

He fell forward and landed face down. His heavy body jarred the floor of the old bungalow. Kim felt the shock run through her boots and up through her torso.

Quickly, she approached him. She kicked his gun aside and kept hers trained on the target as she felt his jugular for a pulse.

Dead.

The weight of his body had landed with enough force to smash his nose and both cheekbones.

Blood pooled around him as gravity drained his system.

Kim glanced over her shoulder. Shorty hadn't moved. He was still standing stock still at the end of the counter in the back of the room. His eyes were wide as golf balls, and his face was even whiter.

The front door banged open on its hinges. The wind howled and rain pelted through the open doorway. Jake was out there somewhere with the duffel. He had a good head on his shoulders. All she could do at the moment was hope that he'd use it.

She yelled to be heard over the noise of the storm. "Shorty! Close the door!"

Shorty moved to do the job while she fished the Boss's phone from her pocket. "You heard?"

"Yeah. Cleanup on the way. Guy you killed is Owen Brady. Has a brother, Oscar. Fraternal twins. You've seen one, you've seen them both. Hired muscle."

"He looks like the guy driving the Escalade who tried to run me off the road yesterday."

"Could have been either one. The two are a team. Always together. Arrest records say Owen's the smart one. Oscar's a little dim, which means his reactions are more…predictable."

"Predictably violent, you mean." She let the intel sink in for a few moments. "Who do they work for?"

"Desmond Trevor. Billionaire involved in several shady businesses in South Africa. He's accused of tax evasion and set to testify next week in Belgium."

She cocked her head. "He's a billionaire and he's kidnapped Patty Sundstrom for the contents of a duffel bag full of cash that can't be more than a million bucks? That makes no sense."

"It's not the amount of cash that he's worried about. It's what's stored with that particular cash inside the duffel."

"It's not a bomb, right?"

"A flash drive. Hidden in the lining somewhere," he replied.

She nodded. "What's on the drive that's so damn essential?"

"Video of a double homicide. If it falls into the wrong hands, Trevor and his business partner will be lucky to spend the rest of their lives in prison," he said as casually as if he was discussing the weather. "Which means your boy Jake just became Trevor's number one target."

"You've got eyes on the beach out there. Have you found Patty Sundstrom?"

"The storm's a monster. Too much cloud cover. Satellites can't penetrate to see people on the ground. Your best option is to wait for Trevor to call Owen and have Shorty talk to him. Shorty tells Trevor that he's got the duffel. Put a tracker in it and give it to him."

Easier said than done, since she didn't have the duffel and had no idea where Jake was holding it. Trevor would find all of that out quickly. And Shorty wasn't calm enough to talk to the guy even if she'd had possession of the duffel.

She scowled. "You aren't sending any backup."

"You know I can't do that."

"I know you *won't* do it. Big difference," she said. "You think Reacher's out there. You expect me to find him and then you swoop in to pick him up. You don't plan to rescue these civilians at all. You're using them to bait Reacher."

"You have a fanciful imagination, Otto." He sighed, but he didn't deny her accusation. "Do your job. I'll handle the rest."

When he hung up, she noticed the relative quiet. The storm raged outside, but inside the bungalow, the only extra noise was Shorty's feet hitting the floor, rhythmically pacing, as if he was thinking hard and needed the movement to assist.

She patted the dead guy's pockets until she found his cell phone and wallet. The wallet contained some cash, a couple of credit cards, and a New York driver's license issued in the name of Owen Brady.

She scrolled through the call log on the phone. Two numbers appeared repeatedly as both incoming and outgoing calls. She could've asked Gaspar or Finlay to trace them, but logically they had to belong to Trevor and Oscar. Question was, which was which.

She looked at Shorty. "Let's go out to the café. Jake's probably headed that way. If Patty's there, we can make the trade. If she isn't, at least we'll have Jake and the duffel back. Do you have any rain gear?"

Shorty stopped pacing and nodded. He found two bright yellow waterproof ponchos, handed one to her and donned the other. She pulled the hood up and tightened it around her face.

She returned her pistol to its holster and slid Owen's cell phone into the poncho's pocket. "Lock up behind us. We don't need a potential customer coming in here and finding a dead man on your floor."

"Okay," Shorty replied. He picked up Owen's gun and slipped it into his pocket.

"Can you shoot?" Otto asked.

"I guess we'll find out," he replied before he pulled a key off a hook near the door before he turned the knob and opened it. The wind nearly blew the doorknob out of his hand, but he held on.

She crossed the threshold and waited in the driving rain while he locked up. Together, they started out across the sand to the pier.

CHAPTER THIRTY-NINE

Monday, February 28
10:55 p.m.
Siesta Beach, California

WHEN JAKE GRABBED THE black duffel and ran out of the windsurfing shop with it, he'd expected the thug running down the stairs to follow him. He'd planned to lead him away from Shorty and Kim, give them a chance to rescue Patty from the other thug. Then they'd search and destroy their leader.

But the thug didn't give chase immediately, and Jake had hoofed fifty yards inland on the town's main street before he concluded the guy hadn't taken the bait.

He turned and ran back toward the shop. From the boardwalk, he saw Kim and Shorty moving toward the pier to rescue Patty. Which meant Kim had neutralized the thug.

He revised his plan on the fly.

The duffel was awkward and heavy and slowed him down. He looked around for a place to stash it.

He found several big, empty, plastic trash barrels clustered in an alley behind a T-shirt shop. The barrels were only half-full. Which meant there were probably a couple of days left to fill them before the pickup service. He muscled three barrels together deep into the alley away from curious passersby, should there be any. He dumped the trash from one barrel into the dumpster and stuck the duffel inside. He put a plastic bag of trash on top of it and replaced the plastic lid.

He stood back to examine his work. The rain had drenched what might otherwise have been obvious dry pavement under the barrels. He used his shoes to splash some dirty water from a pothole over the rest of the dry pavement. He stood back to admire his camouflage job. He nodded, satisfied that no casual pedestrian would notice the barrel containing the duffel before he came back.

He stuffed his hands in his pockets and tucked his head down against the rain as he entered the sidewalk on the main street. He'd covered a couple of blocks toward the windsurfing shop when an average looking guy walking toward him, head down, suddenly slipped on the wet pavement and lunged forward.

Jake put his hands up to help him, but not fast enough. The man fell onto Jake before he could regain his balance.

Jake felt something hard jab his left side under his ribs. The pain sliced sideways before the man righted himself and stepped back. Jake slapped his right hand over the wound and felt the warm, sticky blood leaking out to soak his shirt.

He staggered to one side, prepared to swing a strong right hook to knock the bastard on his ass.

Until he saw the gun in the man's hand. A long silencer was screwed onto the end. In the raging storm, silenced gunshots wouldn't be noticed.

"Get in the car, Mr. Reacher," the man said. He gestured toward a black sedan parked at the curb, engine running, back passenger door open.

Jake felt the widening pool of blood on his torso. He glanced up and down the sidewalk. Few pedestrians were outside in the storm. Shops were open, but customers weren't walking in or out. Given the disparity in their sizes, the guy couldn't drag him into the vehicle. But he could sure as hell shoot him on the sidewalk and drive away.

"If I'd wanted you dead, you'd be dead already," the man said.

Jake replied, "So you're the guy who wants the black duffel bag. You want me to take you to it."

"That's right. Get in the car," he practically growled.

The vein on the man's right temple pulsed visibly. All the while, they were both battered and drenched by the storm.

Which meant his gun hand and the gun itself was wet. It would still fire and hit the target at close range.

But his grip might be more than a little slippery.

Jake could overpower him and knock the gun loose before it did too much damage. Without the gun, the man was no match for Jake. But then he'd need to stash the guy somewhere. Better to get him to his storage place first.

He pretended to think about it for a couple of seconds. The man was impatient and maybe more than a little nervous. He *really* wanted that duffel.

Jake made him wait a bit longer before he grinned and said, "I'll get blood all over your upholstery."

"No problem. It's a rental," the man replied.

CHAPTER FORTY

Monday, February 28
10:45 a.m.
Siesta Beach, California

KIM FORGED AHEAD PUSHING against the wind, cold rain pelting her body. The beach was deserted. She didn't see Jake anywhere. If Trevor saw him with the duffel, he would be in trouble. But Jake could take care of himself. Patty couldn't. First things first.

Shorty caught up with her and plowed past. The entrance to the pier was barely visible in the distance through the storm. The café at the end was lost in the clouds. Waves crashed against the pier, dumping gallons of water across the concrete walkway and sweeping everything in its path into the ocean.

The combination of higher than average tide, and stronger than normal winds attracted the foolhardy. Surfers brave or dumb enough to ride the waves whooped as the water moved them ever faster.

When Kim reached the pier's entrance, Shorty was waiting.

The pier was closed. A decorative gate crossed the entrance. Shorty showed her how to squeeze through the bars to the other side.

When they were both on the pier, he shouted to be heard over the deafening noise of the storm. "You can swim, right? If you get swept away, caught in a rip current, you know what to do?"

"Yeah. Stay afloat. Let the tide bring me back," she shouted in reply. "You still have the weapon?"

He nodded his head and raised both fists in response.

"Follow me!" he yelled. He turned and started along the right side of the pier holding the broad wood railing, moving toward the café.

She would have objected, but saved her breath. He couldn't hear her now anyway. She grabbed the slippery top rail on the right side of the slick concrete pier with both hands and trudged carefully behind him.

The distance between them widened with every step until she couldn't see him at all as they became engulfed in the foggy storm.

The wind came in strong gusts. The waves were somewhat more rhythmic. The first big crash of salty water landed to her left and receded, washing across the pier and splashing off on the right side in the exact spot Kim had occupied moments before. Almost continuous waves followed the first one, landing ahead and behind and beside her as she made her way slowly forward.

The café emerged from the mist. She could see it vaguely at the end of the pier, but the T-shaped pier extensions were still shrouded. An entire army patrol could have been posted on either side of the café, cloaked by invisibility.

She assumed Jake had headed to the café with the duffel, but she didn't see him anywhere. She didn't see Patty Sundstrom,

Oscar Brady, or Desmond Trevor, either. She didn't see anyone at all.

As she moved along the pier, farther away from the beach and into the ocean, the waves picked up speed and strength, repeatedly battering the pier ahead and behind.

Eventually, between the waves crashing over and through the wood rails, Kim drew closer to the café and saw more clearly. The lights were on inside. A few people were seated with food and drinks, seeming to enjoy the front row seats to view Mother Nature's fury.

The shadowy corner behind the café where she'd seen Jake last night was empty. He wasn't there. Where did the kid go with that duffel?

The big waves were coming faster now. She had less time between them to steady herself. She put her head down and trudged forward through the wind and rain, knowing the next wave could land ahead, behind, or on top of her. The only dry spot along the entire pier was inside the café.

After another few steps, she thought she heard shouting up ahead. She lifted her face and stared into the storm, straining to hear voices over the deafening noise.

Two big waves washed across the pier in rapid succession. She leaned against the side rail and held on as tightly as possible.

The first wave battered her against the side rail.

The second shoved her hard toward the beach.

The third one knocked Kim off her feet.

She slammed onto the concrete. The impact knocked the wind from her lungs.

She heard what could have been a gunshot or thunder. It was impossible to distinguish the sounds.

She gasped for air and swallowed salt water. She struggled to hang onto the wide wooden railing as the wave receded, taking a chunk of the opposite rail along with it.

She retched the ocean water from her body and climbed to her feet.

CHAPTER FORTY-ONE

Monday, February 28
11:05 a.m.
Siesta Beach, California

PATTY SUNDSTROM'S VIEW OF the café door was blocked by Oscar's broad torso and her rapidly swelling right eye. Keeping her eye open was difficult. She'd have a hell of a shiner tomorrow, assuming she lived that long.

But she wouldn't go down without a fight. She'd resisted as he'd tried to drag her along the beach and then along the pier. She didn't get away, but she was a big girl and she was much stronger than he'd expected. He'd had to struggle to get her all the way to the café and he'd suffered along the way.

She'd kicked him solidly in his sensitive regions a couple of times before he'd wacked her in the face. She'd practically torn his ear off with her teeth while he was bent over holding his balls, too. More blood was trickling down the side of his neck than pooling in her eye socket, which was just fine with her. Too bad he still had another ear. But she wasn't done yet.

The storm had been building in strength since Oscar pulled her away from Shorty. The wind howled louder as it passed over the café. They'd lost their opportunity to leave a while ago. If she was going to take him down and escape, the battle would be fought here. But the only weapons she had were the cheap flatware and her wits.

When they first arrived at the café, she'd tried engaging Oscar in conversation, but he wasn't the least bit chatty. Which meant he'd told her nothing. At this point, his plan seemed to be to wait out the storm unless one of the other toads ordered him to do something else.

Which was fine with her. As long as they were inside the café with a few other customers as witnesses, Oscar wasn't likely to kill her. She'd still have a chance to get away. Or kill him first, if it came to that.

She'd never killed anyone in cold blood before. Could she do it? She'd had the chance once. Turned out she hadn't needed to execute the guy, because Reacher had been there to do it for her.

She'd half expected Reacher to show up long before now and solve her problems again. He'd told her he was watching them. What was the point of watching if that's all he did?

But maybe he was helping Shorty. Which was fine with her. She could take care of herself. Shorty was less ferocious. He needed the help. Reacher had made the right choice.

The longer Oscar held her here, the more she expected to learn how cold-blooded she actually was. She'd had time to think about the situation. She figured their plan was pretty simple. After Shorty handed over the duffel, Owen would kill him. Oscar would kill her. The three amigos would fly off into the sunrise. Or something like that.

Keeping the duffel away from these goons was the best chance they had. Shorty would understand that, too. He wouldn't give it up unless he was forced to.

Oscar had put his phone on the table to be sure he heard it when his brother called. For more than an hour, it had lain silent. Oscar wasn't the least bit fidgety. He sat there like a mannequin, stone still.

The café door opened and the howling wind blasted into the room before the door closed again. Oscar didn't bother to turn his head. Patty couldn't see the door, but she wondered who would be crazy enough to come out there in such weather.

She didn't have to wait long to find out.

Shorty came into her periphery as he approached from the side. He was holding a gun. Several of the customers gasped and screamed and moved aside, as if Shorty might shoot them. Which, of course, he wouldn't do.

He stopped advancing ten feet away, pointed the gun at Oscar and said, "Let her go."

Like a thick-necked hippopotamus, Oscar turned his head toward Shorty and blinked slowly.

"Let her go, or I'll shoot you. I promise," Shorty said.

While Oscar's head was turned, Patty grabbed a fork in her right fist and stabbed Oscar's hand with it. She shoved the fork straight down into the web between his thumb and first finger. The tines punctured his tough skin and stuck into the wooden table beneath. Blood trickled from all four punctures.

He lifted his left arm and backhanded her hard enough to bounce her head off the wall behind her. Then he pulled the fork out and threw it on the floor.

She fell off her chair, seeing stars, ears ringing. Her head began to throb.

Oscar shoved his chair back and it clattered to the floor.

Shorty pulled the trigger. The gun's blast added to the storm's noise. Customers screamed and scattered to hide under the tables.

The bullet struck Oscar's torso, below his ribs and above his pelvic bone, traveling deep into his flesh. If the bullet exited on the other side of his thick body, Patty couldn't see where. Blood rapidly soaked through his shirt. Oscar howled louder than the storm and then charged toward Shorty.

Shorty tossed the gun toward Patty. He turned and ran outside, with Oscar in hot pursuit.

The café door banged open and slammed shut in a matter of moments.

When Patty closed her eyes, she saw flashing lights. Her ears were ringing and her head throbbed from the two hard blows, one when Oscar hit her and the other when she hit the wall. Her teeth felt a little loose on that side, too.

But she couldn't wait until she could see straight. If Oscar caught up with Shorty, he'd kill him.

Patty scrambled to find the gun and push herself off the floor. She staggered to the door and pushed it open using the full weight of her body. She was already unsteady on her feet and the gusting wind shoved her backward.

She was drenched in seconds by the cold rain and ocean spray. She used the building to stay upright as she moved, sliding her back along the wall. When the wall ended, the wind's full force pushed against her body while the rain pounded harder.

She struggled to see clearly through her left eye. The right one had swollen completely shut.

Fog and mist covered the pier, limiting her visibility to about thirty feet ahead between the big waves that crashed over the wide plank rails.

She couldn't see Shorty or Oscar or much of anything else. She struggled to hold onto the gun and keep her balance. She turned her back to the railing along the pier and kept moving toward the beach.

Up ahead, she heard noises that might have been Shorty and Oscar fighting. She moved as quickly as she dared. Oscar's broad back came into view. He had Shorty up against the opposite rail and stood over him, landing blow after blow. The railing was already damaged from the repeated pounding of the waves and a big chunk of it was missing. The rest would have been weakened by the surf's constant battering.

"Shorty!" she screamed as loudly as she could. If he heard her, he didn't answer. And Oscar, as usual, held his focus.

Patty held the gun as steadily as she could manage and squeezed the trigger. The shot landed somewhere on Oscar's body, but she didn't have time to assess the damage. A wall of water headed straight for the spot where Shorty was leaning against the broken wood.

The huge freak wave crashed down, completely covering Shorty and Oscar and everything ten feet on either side of them. A second big wave followed almost instantly. And a third.

The third wave crashed through the damaged guard rail and demolished the side of the pier.

When it receded, the ocean had taken Shorty and Oscar along with it.

Patty screamed, "Shorty! Shorty!"

The next round of waves were less punishing. She left the guard rail and fell onto her hands and knees. She crawled along the slippery concrete toward the big, gaping hole in the other side of the pier.

Before she got there, a tiny Asian woman ran to her, wrapped her arms around Patty's waist, and pulled her back.

"Come on! Come this way!" she yelled, pulling Patty along a narrow section of wet concrete, away from the destroyed section of pier, toward the beach.

"Shorty! He fell into the water! We can't leave him!" Patty shouted, even as she knew there was no way the two women could find him now.

CHAPTER FORTY-TWO

Monday, February 28
11:45 a.m.
Siesta Beach, California

KIM MANAGED TO GET Patty back to the beach, fighting the storm all the way. They'd been battered by waves and pelted by rain. But they made it.

When they reached the end of the pier, the gates were closed and locked. Cell signals were weak on the pier but closer to shore Kim was able to call 9-1-1.

Patty was emotionally and physically wrecked. But she held herself together long enough to tell Kim what had happened inside the café. Until she reached the part in her story where Shorty and Oscar were swept out to sea. She stopped there, unable to revisit the harrowing experience. It was too fresh. Too raw.

But Kim didn't need to hear about it. Because the storm was unrelenting, she didn't see Shorty and Oscar captured by the ocean. But she had witnessed the damage to the pier firsthand.

She'd been on the beachside of the three big waves that took out that section. She'd narrowly escaped being swept away along with them.

First responders arrived to open the gate and help carry Patty the last few feet to the beach. Paramedics loaded her into the ambulance and took her to the hospital.

Rescue teams were on the way to evacuate the café. Kim reported Shorty and Oscar missing and was assured teams were on the way to find them, too. They'd keep looking as long as they could, they said. But Kim had the impression they had little hope of finding Shorty alive.

She found her personal cell phone and called Gaspar. The Boss and Finlay and anybody else who wanted to listen to the call could have at it. She didn't care.

When Gaspar picked up, she said, "I've lost Jake. Ping his cell phone. I'll wait."

Gaspar sighed. "Probably wouldn't get me anywhere to remind you that I no longer work for the FBI, right?"

She waited.

Gaspar clicked keys on a keyboard. After a couple of seconds, he said, "Looks like he was about six blocks from where you're standing. He's entered a moving vehicle traveling along the main street."

"Moving in what direction?" she asked.

"Toward the windsurfing shop. Maybe five minutes out," Gaspar replied. "Before you ask, I can't get eyes on him. There's still too much cloud cover. Your Boss has access to satellites that could see through, maybe."

"Anyone else been near the shop since I left it?" she asked.

"Can't say. Can't see it. No surveillance cameras in or around the place I can tap into, before you ask," he replied.

"I'll head back there. Thanks." She disconnected, dropped her phone into her pocket, and located her gun. She quickened her pace along the wet, hard-packed sand. The wind was at her back now, pushing her along.

The gray midday weather cloaked the windsurfing shop in foggy semi-darkness. There were no lights on inside. A black sedan pulled up to the curb.

Jake got out of the back seat and walked toward the shop.

A smaller man she didn't recognize exited from the driver's seat. He held his right arm bent at the elbow. She couldn't see whether he held a gun in his hand, but smart money would bet on yes. She was too far away to hear any conversation between them.

Jake reached out to turn the doorknob. He pulled the door open. Once again, the wind caught it and banged it back against the wall.

Shorty had locked the door before they left to find Patty. Someone had unlocked it.

The man waved Jake inside with his weapon and followed him. He pulled the door closed behind them. They flipped a light on.

Kim hustled to the shop. She looked in the window. Owen Brady, the man she'd killed earlier, was gone. The Boss probably found a way to remove him. She didn't see Jake and the guy with the gun. If the place had a back door, she hadn't seen them use it to leave the bungalow. Which meant they'd probably moved upstairs.

She turned the knob on the front door and opened it only wide enough to slip inside. She kept a good grip on the knob until she could latch the door securely again. Then she turned and moved toward the staircase.

On her way past, she briefly examined the area where the dead man had fallen. Most of his blood had been wiped up, but some had been smeared around in the process. The Boss's people would have been more thorough.

She heard footsteps overhead in the apartment. The two men were walking from room to room. Like they were searching for something.

She started up the steps, as quietly as possible. About half way up, something heavy hit the floor. She dashed up the remaining steps and shoved the door to the apartment wide open.

"Don't get up," Jake said, barely breathing hard. A wide gash on his forehead dripped blood down the side of his face like a horror movie.

The smaller man was bleeding, too. His nose was a pulpy mess in the center of his face.

She assessed the situation instantly.

A brass candlestick lamp lay near the sofa.

The smaller man was on the floor. Jake stood over him like a towering colossus.

Jake had punched him hard enough to knock him to the floor, but not before the guy had hit Jake a couple of solid blows to the side of the head with a blunt object.

Neither one of them looked her way. They were too hot-blooded.

Kim saw the next move before Jake did.

The man rolled to his left, pulled his right arm from under his torso, and lifted his gun to point it at Jake.

"Gun!" Kim yelled, a split second before the man squeezed the trigger.

The timing was enough.

Jake fell sideways. The bullet zinged past him, through the sofa, and embedded itself into the bungalow's wall.

Smoothly, the man rolled toward Jake and aimed to fire again.

Kim fired first. Three rounds. Three head shots.

The man's arm fell to the floor almost at the same time his head exploded.

Kim waited until her breathing evened out before she searched the guy's pockets to find his car keys.

"Let's get you to the hospital, Jake. Looks like you need some stitches."

CHAPTER FORTY-THREE

Tuesday, March 1
11:45 a.m.
Siesta Beach, California

THE STORM FINALLY ENDED and sunny California weather had returned. From her hotel room, she saw the ocean's enormous waves had deposited tons of kelp and debris on the beach. Heavy equipment was down there now to handle the cleanup.

The pier was still closed. The morning news reported it would take months to repair the damage done by the storm. The owner of the café had said, "When these gates are closed, our business doesn't exist. The mayor's promised the pier will reopen as soon as possible."

No doubt. Tourism was a big segment of Siesta Beach's economy and the pier was a significant reason tourists came to this particular beach. When repairs were completed, Siesta Beach would resemble all the cheerful chamber of commerce photos she'd seen online before she'd arrived.

In a few months, only those who had lived through it, fought against it, lost because of it, would know the storm's fury had come and gone. Until the next storm. And the one after that.

As it was, Kim was battered and bruised and exhausted. She felt like she could sleep for a solid week. She left the room and let the door slam behind her.

A line of taxis were waiting at the valet stand. "Siesta Beach Hospital, please," she said.

The doorman called one up and opened the door for her. She sank into the back seat. The doorman closed the door for her and told the driver her destination. The taxi rolled easily into traffic.

She had news she wanted to deliver in person. Jake had been admitted yesterday. They'd kept him overnight for tests and observation because of his head injuries and the blood he'd lost through the knife wound.

The taxi dropped her off at the front entrance. "Want me to wait?"

"Thanks. That won't be necessary," she replied. She paid the fare and hopped out, moving quickly to the front entrance.

She spent a few minutes figuring out where Jake was and finally found him in a private room on the fifth floor with a view of the ocean. She knocked lightly on the door.

"Come on in," he called.

He looked like an oversized child for sure lying there dressed in one of those hideous hospital gowns, stitches closing the jagged cut in his forehead. But it was the big grin that capped the illusion of youthful enthusiasm in his case.

"You look pretty happy for a guy who almost died yesterday," she said, grinning back at him because it was impossible not to.

"Nah. That guy was no match for me. I've been in worse

fights. I always win." He saw the look of skepticism on her face. "I do appreciate you helping me out, though. From what I hear, it takes a while to recover from gunshot wounds. And I'll be out of here tomorrow at the latest."

She nodded. She handed him one of her cards. "I stopped by to tell you to keep in touch. There's a private number on the back of that card. If you need my help, call me. But use a disposable phone. I don't want those calls traced."

He looked at the card, front and back. "Thanks."

"One more thing." She paused briefly before she said, "We've confirmed that Joe Reacher was your father. We expedited DNA samples from his autopsy and compared them to yours and your mother."

The grin disappeared and he asked quietly, "No question about it?"

She saw he was conflicted about the news. He'd loved David Reacher as his father for his entire life. Now, both David and Joe Reacher were dead. But she couldn't change the facts and neither could he. "It's a one hundred percent certainty."

He took a few deep breaths before he blinked and raised his eyes to meet hers. Solemnly, he said, "Jack Reacher came to see me last night. He was on his way out of town, he said."

She nodded. She wasn't surprised. He'd been in touch with Patty and Shorty last week, too. The only thing she'd wondered about was why he hadn't helped them when they needed it, since he'd told them he would.

"What did he have to say?"

"He's the one who moved Owen's body."

"Did he tell you why?"

"He thought maybe Shorty or I had been the one who shot him. He said he didn't want to see our lives ruined because of that. Owen had it coming, he said." He grinned again like the Jake she'd first met. "His exact words were 'No reason to ruin your life over a dead asshole like that.'"

She smiled. "Sounds like something he'd say."

Jake nodded. "But doing that, moving Owen, meant he couldn't help me with Trevor. And it made him late getting out to help Patty and Shorty at the pier."

Kim raised her eyebrows. "So he wasn't at the pier at all?"

Jake shrugged. "That's the impression I had, but I guess thinking back on it, he didn't really say."

"Did he say where he was headed?"

Jake shook his head. "Sorry. No."

Kim took a deep breath and made the decision. "You should know that two bodies were found on the beach south of the pier. One was Owen. The other was Oscar. The local authorities say there were two bullets in Oscar's body. Both came from Owen's gun. But that's not what killed Oscar."

Jakes eyes grew wide. "He drowned?"

She shook her head. "His windpipe was crushed. Brutally smashed, in fact. Medical examiner won't know more until they do the autopsy, but he said it looks like Oscar was strangled by huge, powerful hands."

Jake paused to think about it. "You think Jack killed him? How would he even have done that?"

"Do the math." She shrugged, using Gaspar's all-purpose gesture, and laid out the facts. "The two brothers were big and heavy, which means they were hard to move. They were a long way apart when they died, but their bodies were found together on the beach, quite a distance from the pier. Owen was shot and killed in the windsurfing shop, and we know Reacher moved his body because he told you so. Oscar apparently survived two bullet wounds and a pounding by the Pacific Ocean. But what killed him was a crushed windpipe. Probably after he washed ashore."

She waited to let him draw his own conclusions.

Jake was silent a long time. When he spoke again, he said, "How's Patty and Shorty?"

Kim cocked her head. Jake knew more about his uncle now, and she wasn't sure how he would process it. "They're both going to be okay. Shorty was banged up and he swallowed a lot of seawater, but he managed to stay afloat and rode the riptide around until it dumped him back on the beach. They're both in a room on the sixth floor if you want to see for yourself."

Jake nodded. "I'll do that before I leave here."

Kim said, "What are you going to do when you're released?"

"I've been thinking about that. Especially since it's not likely I'll win the lottery with that ticket I bought in Tulsa," he said with a grin. "If I'm going to see the world, I'll need someone else to foot the bill, you know?"

Kim nodded. She had the feeling she knew what he was going to say next before he said it.

"I joined the army before I left Laconia. I have time to change my mind. Undo it, you know? But being a lawyer's not for me. I don't have the patience for it," he said, as if he was practicing the speech he planned to give his mother. "Besides, it's what Reachers do. We're military men. Hell, I might even become a military cop. Who knows?"

"When do you report for duty?"

"I've got a few weeks yet. I'll take some vacation time. Fly back home after the snow melts to see my mom first." He blushed and ducked his head. "She won't like it. I'm not looking forward to telling her."

He extended his hand to shake hers. "Oh, forgot to ask, did you find the duffel?"

"Right where you said it would be. You did a good job, Jake. Use me as a reference when you're ready to move into police work. The good guys could use another one like you," she replied on her way out.

The Boss's phone vibrated on the way down in the elevator. "Otto," she said when she picked up the call.

"Reacher's in the wind again. No reason to hang around there. You're booked on a flight out of John Wayne Airport," he said.

"Copy that," she replied and disconnected the call. She'd be glad to get home. She sent a quick text to John Lawton, inviting him to breakfast in Detroit.

She grabbed a taxi at the hospital's main entrance. She returned to the hotel and asked the taxi to wait while she grabbed her bags and used the video checkout.

On the ride to the airport, she saw she had two voice messages. The first was from Smithers. It was long and involved and most of it was stuff Gaspar had already sussed out and reported to her. Smithers confirmed what Trevor had done to Margaret Reacher and to Old Man Reacher. Margaret was going to be fine.

Smithers said they were starting to get IDs on the bodies they'd recovered at the motel. One was a guy named Casper Lange. Businessman from South Africa, partners with Desmond Trevor, who was also missing. Smithers said he'd kicked that one upstairs to the Boss because of the international implications. Which was just as well. The Boss could handle it anyway he wanted. At least she'd be spared the paperwork on Trevor.

Smithers didn't ask her what had happened with Jake or with Reacher, which saved her the task of ignoring his questions. But she figured he wouldn't be as quick to help her the next time they met, either.

She was satisfied that both Trevor and his partner had already paid the ultimate price for Old Man Reacher's murder, even though Smithers didn't know that.

The second voice message was from Jack Reacher. It was, as always, succinct.

"Thanks for saving the kid, Otto. I guess I'm the closest thing he's got to a father now. I won't forget this. I owe you one."

The other big news is Diane Capri—a friend of mine—wrote a book revisiting the events of KILLING FLOOR in Margrave, Georgia. She imagines an FBI team tasked to trace Reacher's current-day whereabouts. They begin by interviewing people who knew him—starting out with Roscoe and Finlay. Check out this review: "Oh heck yes! I am in love with this book. I'm a huge Jack Reacher fan. If you don't know Jack (pun intended!) then get thee to the bookstore/wherever you buy your fix and pick up one of the many Jack Reacher books by Lee Child. Heck, pick up all of them. In particular, read Killing Floor. Then come back and read Don't Know Jack. This story picks up the other from the point of view of Kim and Gaspar, FBI agents assigned to build a file on Jack Reacher. The problem is, as anyone who knows Reacher can attest, he lives completely off the grid. No cell phone, no house, no car…he's not tied down. A pretty daunting task, then, wouldn't you say?

First lines: "Just the facts. And not many of them, either. Jack Reacher's file was too stale and too thin to be credible. No human could be as invisible as Reacher appeared to be, whether he was currently above the ground or under it. Either the file had been sanitized, or Reacher was the most off-the-grid paranoid Kim Otto had ever heard of." Right away, I'm sensing who Kim Otto is and I'm delighted that I know something she doesn't. You see, I DO know Jack. And I know he's not paranoid. Not really. I know why he lives as he does, and I know what kind of man he is. I loved having that over Kim and Gaspar. If you haven't read any Reacher novels, then this will feel like a good, solid story in its own right. If you have…oh if you have, then you, too, will feel like you have a one-up on the FBI. It's a fun feeling!

"Kim and Gaspar are sent to Margrave by a mysterious boss who reminds me of Charlie, in Charlie's Angels. You never see him…you hear him. He never gives them all the facts. So they are left with a big pile of nothing. They end up embroiled in a murder case that seems connected to Reacher somehow, but they can't see how. Suffice to say the efforts to find the murderer and Reacher, and not lose their own heads in the process, makes for an entertaining read.

"I love the way the author handled the entire story. The pacing is dead on (ok another pun intended), the story is full of twists and turns like a Reacher novel would be, but it's another viewpoint of a Reacher story. It's an outside-in approach to Reacher.

"You might be asking, do they find him? Do they finally meet the infamous Jack Reacher?

"Go…read…now…find out!"

Sounds great, right? Check out "Don't Know Jack," and let me know what you think.

So that's it for now…again, thanks for reading THE AFFAIR, and I hope you'll like A WANTED MAN just as much in September.

Lee Child

ABOUT THE AUTHOR

Diane Capri is an award-winning *New York Times, USA Today,* and worldwide bestselling author. She's a recovering lawyer and snowbird who divides her time between Florida and Michigan. An active member of Mystery Writers of America, Author's Guild, International Thriller Writers, Alliance of Independent Authors, and Sisters in Crime, she loves to hear from readers and is hard at work on her next novel.

Please connect with her online:

http://www.DianeCapri.com

Twitter: http://twitter.com/@DianeCapri

Facebook: http://www.facebook.com/Diane.Capri1

http://www.facebook.com/DianeCapriBooks

Made in the USA
Coppell, TX
24 May 2021